A LOVE STORY

THE CONNECTOR

LIFE IS A ROAD TRIP...

Harper Dale

This book is a work of fiction, the product of the author's imagination. Any resemblance to actual events or places or persons living or dead is entirely coincidental.

Copyright © 2024 by Rupert Bossier

Paperback ISBN-978-1-964011-08-0

Paperback ISBN-978-1-964011-09-7

EBOOK: ASIN: B0DMP19W1D

All rights reserved.

No portion of this book may be reproduced in any form without written permission from the publisher or author except as permitted by U.S. copyright law.

CONTENT WARNING

THIS BOOK CONTAINS CONTENT that may be triggering for some readers, including language, violence, drug abuse, and sexually explicit scenes.

DEDICATION

For my husband and the working men like him who helped build America.

CONTENTS

8 TRACK

Born to be Wild… Steppenwolf

Sundown … Gordon Lightfoot

Heart of Gold … Neil Young

My Maria… B.W. Stephenson

Movin'… Little Feat

Dixie Chicken… Little Feat

Bus Stop… The Hollies

I'm Sorry… Brenda Lee

Purple Haze… Jimi Hendrix

In-A-Gadda-Da-Vida… Iron Butterfly

Bellbottom Blues… Derek & the Dominoes

Brown-Eyed Handsome Man… Waylon Jennings

Now I'm a Believer… The Monkees

Summer Breeze… Seals & Crofts

Bad Moon Rising… Creedence Clearwater Revival

For What It's Worth… Buffalo Springfield

Different Drum … The Stone Poneys

Time in a Bottle … Jim Croce

8 TRACK

Side Two

A Love Song… Loggins & Messina

Stumblin' In… Chris Norman & Suzi Quatro

You'll Accompany Me… Bob Seger

Peaceful, Easy Feeling… The Eagles

Pride and Joy… Steve Ray Vaughan

Longer… Dan Fogelberg

Danny's Song… Kenny Loggins

Air That I Breathe… The Hollies

Fire & Rain… James Taylor

How Am I Supposed to Live Without You… Laura Branigan

Yesterday… The Beatles

I Like Dream' … Kenny Nolan

Tears in Heaven… Eric Clapton

You Ain't Seen Nuthin' Yet… Bachman-Turner Overdrive

Stairway to Heaven… Led Zepplin

CHAPTER ONE

HELLO WALLS

PATSY

June 1974

WE'RE HALFWAY ACROSS TENNESSEE, which feels damn near as wide as Texas, when he says, "I can't drive any longer. I'll find a spot to pull off and get some sleep." B.J. never cries uncle. If he says he's too tired to drive, he doesn't need to.

"I can drive."

He eyes me with suspicion. "Are you sure?"

Why is he surprised? He knows I can drive the van. "Yeah, I had a good nap earlier."

"I don't know..."

"What's the problem? I'm not sleepy." I like to drive.

B.J. shrugs and pulls over on the shoulder of the Interstate, puts the van in park, and squeezes between the two seats to reach the back. "Okay, it's yours."

With the gear shift on the steering column and the console attached to the dash in a little half-moon, we have plenty of room to move from side to side and front to back.

As I slip into the driver's seat, he slips off a boot.

I don't have to look to know he pulled off that first boot with his hands and let it *clunk to* the floor. Now, he's using his free toes to remove the other. One at a time, his heavy work boots thud onto the van floor as I roll down the driver's window and smile at a drawn-out *ahhhhh* from the back.

Him. Thinking about B.J. makes me smile. This ungodly odyssey is because of his big heart. His best friend finished his master's degree from the University of Richmond in some useless knowledge, evidenced by the fact that despite six years of higher education, Al Mancini is as broke as we are. B.J. volunteered to drive cross-country to bring him home.

The scent of pine wafts through the open window, whisking me back to childhood, to my grandparents' home in deep East Texas, surrounded by towering pines, oaks, and sweet gum trees.

Vivid memories accompany the aromatic air: my grandfather on the porch swing holding a slingshot, ready for any blue jay unwise enough to torment his songbirds, a weathered barn, and a Jersey milk cow. Mamaw fussing around her stove, pickling green tomatoes while my brother, sister, and I played in the rich, red earth.

"We stay on the Interstate for another two hundred miles." B.J.'s voice pulls me back to the moment. "But we'll need gas before then. We'll trade out when you stop."

"Okay." I scoot the seat and adjust the mirror, watching him stretch out on his back beside our son. B.J. built that bed with the storage compartment underneath.

"Now, listen." He yawns. "Be careful."

"I'm always careful. I've never had a ticket."

"Don't speed."

"Okay." Geez.

"I've got weed in the walls. We don't want to get pulled over."

Did he say what I thought he said? "What?" I whip my head around. "What did you say?"

"I've got some dope in the walls. Don't get pulled over."

That's what I thought he said. My scalp begins to tingle.

He lined the van walls with wood paneling when he built the bed. And now, he's stashed marijuana behind the paneling? "Why?"

He mumbles sleepily, "Because it sells for twice as much on the East Coast. We can make some money."

A high-pitched, loud ringing noise pierces my ears. Selling a baggie or two in Austin is one thing, but why would he carry illegal drugs across state lines without saying something to me?

It takes a moment to gather my senses. "How much?"

Nothing.

I twist in the seat to see him. "B.J.! How much are we carrying?"

Nada.

I turn on the cabin lights. He lies flat on his back, his left arm over his head, his head rolled to the right, and his mouth already open a bit. He is dead asleep with our baby, Jim Beau, under his left arm. He pushed himself to the limit—so like him.

Okay. We do what we have to do.

My heart pounds as I peek out the window to check for oncoming traffic and put the '72 Ford Econoline van into gear. How much are we carrying? I mean, a few ounces? Or a whole pound?

Jail time goes by weight. Quantity. Whatever they call it.

My heart drums rapidly against my blouse. How can I hear my heart in my ears when I have this ungodly deafening ringing going on?

If we get caught, they'll put both of us in jail. With his mother and father behind bars, the state will take custody of our son.

My baby! My parents! Daddy will kill us both.

My sister is a kindergarten teacher, and her husband is an accountant. My husband is going to be a jailbird, and I'm going to be right there with him. I don't like stripes. Shit!

The farther I drive, the madder I get. Paranoia seeps into my every bone.

Miles later, in the side mirror, red lights are flashing behind us. This can't be happening. They're getting closer. What am I going to do? You can't outrun cops.

I maintain my speed. As the siren gets louder and the lights draw closer, I slow and pull to the shoulder, ready to surrender.

An ambulance zooms by.

I may throw up.

I take a slow, deep, cleansing breath—and get a grip. It was just an ambulance. Calm down.

B.J., how could you do this to us? My gaze shifts to heaven. "Please, God, don't let me lose my son."

I keep an eye on the speedometer. Don't speed, but don't go too slow, either. That's suspicious in itself. Mile after mile, I fear a cop car is waiting behind some tree.

We're in Tenne-fucking-see. I mean, friggin' Boondocks, Tennessee. They will throw two hippies from Austin, Texas, so far back in the slammer we will never see daylight. They'll take our son. Transporting drugs across state lines? I'm pretty sure that's a federal offense.

I roll down the window and yell, "Dammit!"

No one wakes up, so I yell again into the rushing wind, "Damn! Damn! Damn!"

I check the rearview mirror. Maybe I hoped that would wake him up so I could have the fight now, but B.J. is sound asleep. Okay, I guess I've gotten it out of my system. For now.

There's no traffic in either direction after the ambulance and no radio stations after midnight in the middle of Bum-fuck, so I punch in the eight-track tape still in the deck. ...*Carefree highway.* Perfect. I'm driving across eastern Tennessee listening to Gordon Lightfoot with my window down. We're climbing. The summer air is sweet and cool, and I begin to sing along to *Sundown.*

We both love that song. I'm pretty sure Jim Beau was conceived with that song playing in the background.

Chemistry. We have that.

But damn, B.J. Pot in the walls of the van? Really?

I don't care if he smokes pot. B.J. doesn't act any differently when he is or isn't smoking pot. He can smoke a joint and talk to a cop ten minutes later, and the cop will never be the wiser. From my observation, people act better on pot than booze. Alcohol brings out the mean or the goofy. Pot just mellows most people down.

But don't bring it across state lines, doofus.

Me? I might as well take a sleeping pill as to take a hit off a joint. My body can't handle it. Or alcohol, for that matter. It doesn't take much of either to put my lights out, but my husband can, as he likes to say, maintain.

According to the gospel of B.J. Cole, it's some kind of measure of manhood, how well you can maintain. It doesn't bother me that I can't. I'm not trying to be a man.

He rises before the sun and goes to work every day climbing steel. He's an ironworker. I don't care if the winter wind blows sleet or the sun shines so hot it fries a man's bare hands; my husband is up there connecting structural steel beams thirty, forty, sometimes a hundred or more feet in the air.

Yes, he works high. And I don't mean just in altitude. He's admitted, sometimes, they burn one, waiting for the next column to be lifted by the cranes. Now, that I don't like because it doesn't matter if B.J. is a hundred feet in the air or twenty; a fall from those heights will kill him or cripple him for life. His work scares me if I let myself think about it. So, I don't.

He says it's mind over matter. "If I can walk a straight-line shadow on the ground, I can walk a six-inch beam in the air."

There's no point in me arguing. B.J. loves what he does. He's fearless, and I have to admit, that is a turn-on. My husband can do anything—build anything, fix anything.

His knowledge is not useless, and that man still takes my breath.

His touch, oh Lord. Those strong working man hands can be amazingly tender. So sensuous. His lips, his mouth, his tongue on my skin when he wants me—I cannot deny he melts me.

His hair is almost as long as mine, only much lighter and sun-streaked, and when he sweats, it gets wavy. He pulls it back in a ponytail at the nape of his neck, and what's sexy as hell is that his sideburns and the hair at the base of his neck are darker than the rest, black and curly. I don't know. Something about that, especially when he's working, his body is sweaty, and his hair is wavy—oh, my Lord.

Thinking about him, about us, I forget about the pot inside the walls of the van and everything else. I don't know how long it is before I glance at the fuel gauge.

Well, crap. I'm not catching a break. The needle is in the red, and I have no idea how far it is to the next town.

B.J. warned me never to let a vehicle run out of gasoline because restarting the engine would be too hard if it did. So, I slow down, pull over on the side of the Interstate, and turn off the engine and headlights. Hum. Should I have left it running with the headlights on, like he did when we traded out?

No. I'm afraid to waste what little gas is left.

Now, here's a conundrum. Do I turn on the flashers or not? What if a cop comes by, stops to assist the stranded motorist, and somehow snaps on the dope in the walls of the van?

But what if I don't turn them on, and a big truck zooms by, doesn't see us parked on the edge of the Interstate, and swipes us? We'll all be dead.

"B.J.?"

Still nothing but that soft snore. It's his 'I'm exhausted and dead asleep' snore. 'You'll never wake me up,' snore.

I turn around in the seat. With the engine and headlights off, it is pitch black back there. Curtains that cover the back windows are closed for privacy, but a sliver of moonlight streaks across the bed from the gap between them.

"B.J.! Wake up!"

He doesn't stir.

Inch by inch, I feel my way through blackness to the silver beam. My hand finds that familiar shoulder. Sitting beside him, I stroke his face and whisper so I don't wake Jim Beau. "Baby, wake up. I haven't passed a gas station, and I'm afraid to drive any farther."

My eyes are adjusting to the darkness.

He rubs his hand over his face. "What time is it?"

"I don't know." I don't own a watch, and the van doesn't have a clock. "I've been driving two or three hours. I'm afraid to go any farther. We're on empty. I haven't seen an open gas station."

He draws up on his elbow. "I've got a gas can in back. It'll get us to the next town."

Of course, he's prepared.

B.J. swings his feet to the floor. He pulls on his boots, opens the van door, which wakes the baby anyway, and leans back in. "I love you," he says with a beautiful smile that I can see in the dome light of the van. "Thanks for letting me sleep."

Now, why'd he do that?

I know why. Because B.J. Cole knows I'm going to take off his head for hiding weed in the walls of the van, and he's making a pre-emptive move to disarm me.

I check Jim Beau's diaper, which is soggy, soggy, soggy. Playfully, I sing to him as I wash, powder, and change him. Don't ask me why I make up songs and sing to him. I guess because I'm a goofy music-lover mother, and I love that my baby giggles and claps when I sing to him. He is the perfect audience.

Jim Beau reaches out with his chubby little hands, clenching and unclenching his fists. "Ba-ba, Momma." He gets a big smile back and a smooch. I dig in the ice chest, grab a milk bottle, and give it to him with a bear hug.

If only I could brush my hair, wash my face, and stretch my legs. Austin seems so long ago.

B.J. climbs back in the truck, re-adjusts the seat and mirrors, and starts the engine. The music comes on as he glances out the window and pulls back on the Interstate. "We're still listening to Gordon Lightfoot?"

"Yeah. I was afraid if I went digging around for another tape in the box on the floor, I might swerve or something." My snide comes out. "I didn't want to give someone an excuse to pull us over."

Silence.

He infuriates me sometimes. My heart starts throbbing all over again. "Why didn't you tell me?"

Nothing.

"Dammit, B.J.!"

Our gazes meet in his rearview mirror. "That's exactly why I didn't tell you."

Okay, maybe I was a tad shrill. I take it down a notch, asking in my sweetest, most wifely voice, "Did you think about what would happen if we get caught? What will happen to our son?"

His eyes are on the road, his tone calm. Anytime I worry, B.J. blows me off. He never worries about anything. "We're not going to get caught."

"But what if—?"

He holds up his hand, cutting me off. "Babydoll, we've been through this a thousand times. I don't do what-ifs."

"Well, maybe you should."

"Maybe you shouldn't." He glances over his shoulder and aims his thumb at the back of the van. "Get me a couple of Mollies, will you?"

Black Mollies are amphetamine. Pure speed. He took some when we left Austin. I think he took more somewhere around Texarkana or Little Rock and again in Memphis.

"How about you go one day without anything? No pot. No speed. One day." He scowls at me in the rearview mirror as I hold up my index finger. "One day, B.J. No drugs. One day. Nothing."

He growls and shifts his gaze back to the road. A couple of minutes later, he yells over his shoulder to be heard above the music and the wind roaring through his open window. "Why are you on my ass?"

"I don't want you getting hooked on speed," I holler back.

He rolls up his window and turns off the stereo. "I'm not getting hooked on anything, Pat. Mollies just help me stay awake for this long-ass drive."

"So, let's stop somewhere and rest. We don't have a set time when we have to be there."

He glances over his shoulder again with his snide on full display. "I have to be at work on Monday."

Oh, yeah.

"I don't need it, Pat. I bought it for this trip. That's all."

"It's addictive, B.J."

"Not to me."

I swear, he thinks he's Superman. "So, you're impervious? It can't happen to you, right?"

"No, it can't. People who get hooked on anything let themselves get hooked. They have no willpower. I do. Now please, stop pecking my ass. I'm not a damned dopehead. Don't treat me like one."

"Then don't act like one!"

That was that. Not another word passes between us for miles.

He trades Gordon Lightfoot for Neil Young, rolls his window down, and cranks up the stereo. I'm good with "Heart of Gold," but I'm not a big Neil Young fan, and I'm not good with silence. I had my fill of it driving while they slept, so I take a stab at conversation, talking loudly from the back so he can hear me over his blaring music and the wind. "Tennessee's as wide as Texas!"

He snickers as he checks the rearview mirror, not bothering to turn the music down. "Not hardly."

Okay. So, he's really, really mad at me.

I snap back. "Well, it feels like it."

He's the one with dope in the van that could get us in trouble, but he's mad at me. Go figure. I'm the one who has the right to be angry.

I brush Jim Beau's hair with that soft baby brush, dress him in a fresh T-shirt and shorts, and fill his Sippy cup with Cheerios. He is a chunk.

After spreading up the bed, we climb into the passenger seat, and Jim Beau stretches for his father, who grabs him with his big bearpaw.

B.J. draws his son to him, holding him against his chest as he drives. Jim Beau clutches his cup of Cheerios with two little fists as B.J. rubs the baby's soft yellow hair and kisses the top of his head.

With chubby little legs, Jim Beau straddles his Daddy's thigh and munches on his cereal. It is their routine. B.J.'s crazy about our little boy.

I'm fully aware I'm skating onto thin ice, but I'm not through giving him a piece of my mind, and seeing him doting on his son offers the perfect opportunity. "If we get caught carrying illegal drugs across state lines, we could lose him. Do you realize that?"

B.J. shoots me a fiery glance. No answer. He just holds onto our boy and keeps his eyes on the road.

Okay. That didn't go so well. So my timing sucks. The thin ice I skated onto broke, and I'm suffering from a miserably cold shoulder. I let out a demonstrative sigh. "Fine."

Digging in the glove box, I draw out a yellow pencil, twist my hair on top of my head, thread the pencil through to hold it in place, and roll down my window. Traveling seventy miles an hour down the Interstate before daylight, a cool wind blows in my face. I can still smell pines.

Forget him. I'd crawl in the back and go to sleep—but I'm not sleepy.

Another hour or so, and I notice faint light in the sky ahead. It's a little exciting. I never watched a sunrise before. Bit by bit the sun nudges back the night until bright, wide streaks of white light burst from the glowing orange orb. The mountains and tree lines become silhouettes. As the sun keeps climbing, daylight bathes the mountainous landscape and I become absorbed in it.

CHAPTER TWO

HER PROBLEM

B.J.

WHY DID I LET her drive? Why didn't I just say, "No thanks, Babydoll. We need to pull over and rest for a while."

Instead, what the fuck did I do? Give in. Let her have her way—and drive.

Fuck me.

"Daddy?" Jim Beau offers up his cup filled with Cheerios, holding them in my face. "Hungry bite?"

He makes me laugh. "No thanks, buddy. Those are your hungries."

"Hungries!" He coos, plunges his little hand into his plastic cup, and stuffs his mouth with another handful. As many Cheerios spill on me as make it into his mouth. God, he's fun.

Who knew having a kid could be this much fun?

I rub his soft blonde hair and kiss the top of his head. Him, we did right.

Patsy doesn't even notice. She's too busy fuming over there. I am guilty of failure to fully disclose. Busted. And I know my wife. She is itching for a fight.

If I wanted her to know we were hauling weed, I'd have fucking told her. I knew she'd do exactly what she did: throw a hissy fit. We'd still be in Austin.

Patsy doesn't understand. We. Need. Money. No matter how much I work, there's always something. I didn't tell her I borrowed two hundred dollars from Dad last month after Jim Beau had an ear infection that ended us up in the emergency room. Fucking doctors. You pay, or you won't be treated. He had to be treated, whether the rent and electricity were paid or not. The fucking ER charges an arm and a leg. And we have one car. I had to take off work to take them to the doctor.

That. Costs. Money.

Medicine costs money. Tires, diapers, the laundromat, food, electricity, the telephone—everything costs money. I don't say anything to her about the money because I don't want her to take a job. Not while our son is a baby. Her job is raising him, and she's batting a thousand.

My job is to provide for them. And I'm striking out.

Al offered a fix: He has the connections. He buys, I fly. We split.

Yeah, I'm taking the big risk on the road, but the cops aren't going to pull us over if I don't speed. And I haven't. And if they do—I'm not smoking pot. They've got no reason to search. And they won't find anything without one hell of a search. I made sure everything worked before I let them load the stuff in the van. Taillights, blinkers, headlights, tire tread. I took care of it all.

We're good. We're not going to get caught. Why doesn't she trust me?

Because she's afraid.

Patsy has never broken a rule in her life. Hell, she's never had an overdue library book. The only risk she has ever taken was falling in love with me. Marrying me.

I cut my eyes to sneak a peek.

She's staring out the window, the wind in her face. Her long hair is pulled up on top of her head, showing that long, graceful neck. Her little proud chin is up in the air. God, she's beautiful even when she's mad.

Delicate.

Patsy Anne Cole is a living, breathing China doll. And she's mine. A handful—but she is all mine. And I wouldn't have it any other way.

She won't even look at me right now. She's furious, like a little cartoon character with steam coming from her ears. I want to chuckle because I know her. She'll get over it. But right now, that would be like throwing gasoline on a fire.

I know she loves me. But I've wondered if she doesn't pray every night that I'll quit connecting and ride a fucking desk somewhere. Take the safe, boring way through life like her sister's husband and all of her friends' husbands. They probably give her a hard time. About me.

I sneak another peek. Is she sitting over there regretting me?

Fuck. No.

I know she loves me. She wouldn't have me any other way. Patsy knew exactly who I was when she married me.

I don't know. Maybe she does regret it. Maybe she wishes she'd fallen in love with some dickhead lawyer or doctor or engineer. Women. Those guys might provide better, might be safer, but no one can love her more than I do. Nobody ever will.

I pull into the first gas station with lights on. Moths and June bugs swarm the big windows and glass doors of the whitewashed concrete block building. I get out with Jim Beau and head inside while Patsy grabs her bag out of the back, calling after me. "Give me Jim Beau! I'll take him with me!"

No way. She's getting a taste of her own medicine. I don't look back at her. "We're good."

"What are you looking at?"

The hillbilly station attendant is drooling, watching my wife sashay to the restroom. She's doing a little dance, trying to dodge crickets and June bugs. I mean, he's slobbering into his filthy, gnarly beard. "That your woman?"

The way he's leering at Patsy is downright disrespectful.

"She's my wife." I lift Jim Beau in front of his face. "And she's his mother. We'll thank you to keep your eyes to yourself."

The old man shifts his gaze from Patsy to me and shrugs, wiping his hands on his already grimy overalls. "Sorry, bud. We don't see women that look like that around here very often." Those knotted hands look like he just did an oil change, but I know he didn't. The sun is barely up. How long has it been since he bathed? At least wash your hands, man.

I tilt my head toward our green van at the pump. "I need to fill up."

He turns his head and yells. "Charlie! Fill up on pump two!"

"I've got a gas can in the back that I need to refill, too. I'll get it for him. And we'll take some drinks and—"

"Chockie mick!" Jim Beau squeals and points at the cooler. "Chockie, Daddy, chockie!" God, he makes me smile. His blue eyes sparkle as he points at the jug of chocolate milk behind the glass. With Patsy's eyes, this kid will have to fight the girls off with a stick when he gets into school.

"We'll take the chocolate milk, too. Give us a minute to round up some other stuff."

"Yessir. I'll fix you up while Charlie fills your tank. You folks staying around here?"

I'm watching a bent-over man slowly make his way to the pump. Arthritic and bowlegged, the old boy moves like Methuselah.

"Just passing through. On our way to Richmond."

"Richmond." The attendant whistles as he rings up our food on his ancient cash register. "You've got a long way to go, son. And you've already come a long way." He nods at the van. "Noticed the Texas plates."

"Yessir." I hand him a twenty.

"Don't see many folks from Texas around these parts." He glances back toward the corner of the building where Patsy disappeared and twists his neck. "They sure grow 'em pretty down there."

Are you shitting me? "Like I said, man: that's my wife. Understand?"

"No offense meant."

I flash him a scowl, hoping he finally gets my drift, and say, "Some was taken." Our eyes are locked. He is one slow son of a bitch.

Finally, he nods. "Got it. Sorry."

I nod and tell him, "I'll get the gas can so he can fill it. I'll come back in to pay for the fuel when your guy is finished."

CHAPTER THREE

OH, NO. HE DIDN'T!

PATSY

FINALLY, I CAN STRETCH my legs. But I can't walk without stepping on crickets. *Yuk!* They crunch under my feet. And now they're mushed onto the soles of my shoes. Gross. The surrounding woods are filled with a high-pitched chorus of cicadas.

The women's room on the side of the building is unlocked and surprisingly clean. No crickets or bugs are inside.

After locking the door, I clean up and put on fresh clothes. I pull out the pencil holding up my hair, bend at the waist, brush it out upside down, and whip it back over. My self-taught technique of brushing it upside down makes it fluffier.

My straight, dark brown hair hangs to my shoulder blades, and my bangs fall into my brows. Five foot two, eyes of blue, B.J. likes to say when he's not mad at me.

Come to think of it, B.J. is almost never mad at me. He's just tired, and I scolded him for bringing the pot. Which I had every right to do.

And he took all those damned Mollies.

Speed scares me. But then, B.J. says everything scares me. A couple of his friends are messed up on speed. One is in jail because of it. They got into meth, the hard stuff. They snort it or shoot it.

Don't dwell on it. He'd never do that. B.J. would never put a needle in his arm.

I married a wild boy. I knew it when I married him. Momma said you can't marry a man and plan on changing him. I don't want to change him. Just tamp him down a bit. Maybe we don't have to live with a toe over the edge—at least, not all the time.

But, God, I love him.

One last check in the mirror before I head back. I consider slathering on lipstick just to make me feel better, but this isn't a special occasion that warrants lipstick. So, I just dab on the coconut perfume he bought me.

We were in a little shop on Guadalupe, right across from the university, and I mentioned how much I loved it. The next time he got paid, B.J. surprised me by bringing home a bottle.

That's the man I love.

———

When I open the door to the van, father and son are waiting in the driver's seat. Jim Beau always sits in B.J.'s lap or mine.

They're talking about making it a law that kids have to travel in car seats. Now, where would we put a car seat in this van?

Chunking my bag in the back I notice the sack of dirty diapers is gone. Good job, B.J.

I climb into the front to see B.J. also bought ice-cold sodas and chips. Jim Beau proudly displays his bottle of chocolate milk as I settle into my seat. "Chockie mick, Mama!"

He waves his bottle, showing me the treat his father bought for him. Looking at his big smile and the twinkle in those blue eyes, you'd think it was Christmas.

"I see. Daddy got you chockie mick. Yay!" I clap my hands with the baby still proudly showing off his bottle.

"Chockie mick!" Jim Beau plugs it into his mouth and starts sucking on that sweet chocolate milk as his father's eyes take me in.

I like it when B.J. looks at me that way. Seeing B.J. holding and loving our son and ogling me—keeps me smiling. It doesn't get any better than this.

B.J. looks at me through golden brown eyes with little specks of green. I've always thought that dimple in his chin was sexy.

The sun not only bleaches his hair, but it also bronzes his skin. Because of all the climbing, B.J.'s body is rock solid, from his calves to his chest and arms.

He doesn't try to hide what he's thinking. We know each other too well. "Damn, Babydoll." He leans over and his mouth finds mine. His kiss is hungry, one hand holding Jim Beau, the other on the side of my neck. "You look good."

Thank the Lord. He let go of his mad. I'll deal with the dope-in-the-walls issue later.

I kiss him back, and it's a kiss that promises more to come. He never needs much encouragement. B.J. slips his hand under my blouse.

A few years before, we burned our bras, which B.J. celebrated. I close my eyes and sigh as he gently fondles my breast, his tongue taming mine. B.J. knows exactly how to make me ache for him.

Somehow, Jim Beau is still drinking his bottle, oblivious to his parents groping each other.

B.J. mutters through our sloppy kiss. "Do you want to eat breakfast? We can stretch our legs... and other things, if you want."

I chuckle, "Jim Beau's wide awake." I play coy, smiling back encouragingly, and take a long sip of the soda he bought. It's sweet and refreshing. "Baby, I don't think either one of us has much of a chance of getting lucky for a while."

It's perfect. We're perfect again. Then, dammit!

He grabs his drink and tosses something back—a Black Mollie or two or three—washing them down with a long swill of his soda.

My hackles rise along with my volume. "You just had to help yourself, I see."

He cuts his eyes at me. They are full of surprise. His smile fades, and he glowers back. Doesn't answer.

"One day, B.J. One day was all I asked."

Nothing. He clenches his jaw, slams the van into gear, and we get back on the road.

A few minutes later, B.J. points at black and white Holsteins in a pasture that is knee-deep in the greenest grass I have ever seen. "See the cows?"

Jim Beau points out his Daddy's window with his almost empty bottle. "Moo cow, Daddy, moo!"

B.J. laughs and hugs his boy to him. "Yeah, buddy. Moo cow, moo."

I might as well not be here. Ostracized by the boys for making legitimate legal points. Fine.

Once again, I lean back in my seat, turn my head, and watch the world whiz by. The landscape couldn't be more different than it is in our part of Texas. We're off the Interstate, winding up and down two-lane state roads, passing through one tiny town after another.

I dig in our tape box, find a B.W. Stephenson tape, and pop it in.

Not a word passes between us as miles and, eventually, hours pass.

It's a frigging standoff. Who can go the longest without speaking?

Easy answer. He can.

I think we're out of Tennessee and into Kentucky, maybe. Actually, I'm not sure what state we're in when I crane my neck to spy on the speedometer. "You're speeding."

His gaze shifts down. He checks his speed and eases up on the accelerator.

I'm tired of the silent treatment. "Do you know how to get to Al's house?"

"Apartment. Yeah." He clenches and unclenches his jaw as he grips the steering wheel. He better watch out. He'll break a tooth grinding his teeth like that. His eyes are glued straight ahead on the road.

Occasionally, he glances out his window. He looks anywhere but at me.

It's the Mollies. They're making him mad.

Speed does that to people. It makes me grit my teeth. No, I can't smoke dope or hold my alcohol, but I've taken speed a time or three cramming for finals. It's the one drug I could get hooked on if I was the hooking type, but like I said, it made me grind my teeth. That I didn't like.

"Surely, we're getting close." I squirm in my seat, done with the silence. "My butt is numb. We've been on the road forever."

"Got a long way to go."

Another curt response. Still no eye contact.

Fine.

I'm tired of that tape, too, so I dig around in the box. Little Feat. I like Little Feat. So does he. I shove it in. The first song up forces a grin to take over my face, singing about weed, whites, and wine. How appropriate.

Okay. You win.

I crawl in the back, onto the bed. The rocking of the van promises to put me to sleep the same way it does Jim Beau.

B.J. keeps driving with nothing but the music from the eight tracks, and occasionally, he and Jim Beau comment on the countryside. "Cows." "Horsey." "Donkey." "Train."

The last thing I remember ...*I'll be your Dixie Chicken. You'll be my Tennessee lamb....*

Chapter Four

Unbelievable

B.J.

She gives me a hard-on and then bites off my head. Dammit. She might as well have chomped the tip of my goddamned pecker. Why is she being this way?

We're not going to get busted.

She's crossing a line. Un-fucking-believable. I still can't believe she said that. Patsy honestly thinks I'd risk losing my son? We're not going to lose him. No way.

And what's with her harping on me about the Mollies all of a sudden? She's never bitched about me taking a hit of speed before. She didn't bitch about anything until I told her about the weed in the walls. I still can't believe I was that stupid.

She knows me. She knows damned good, and well, I'm not going to let myself get hooked on drugs. Any drugs. I can give up pot tomorrow if I need to. But right now, I need the Mollies to stay awake because I'll be damned if I'll let her drive again.

Not after her little temper tantrum. And not with this kind of load. Normally, this would have blown over by now.

Jim Beau tugs on my T-shirt and points out the window. "Donkey, Daddy."

"How do donkeys go?"

"Hee-haw, Daddy. Hee-haw!" The way he says hee-haw. Too funny. Thank God he's with me. Otherwise, this trip is going to be un-fucking-bearable. I'd never do anything to lose him.

She started this shit. She's the one who has blown everything out of proportion.

I check the rearview mirror. She can lay back there and stew all day for all I care. Hell, she can stew all the way to Richmond and back. I don't give a rat fuck. Just stay off my ass.

And it still fries my ass that she gives me a come-hither kiss and knees me in the nuts. She needs to leave me the fuck alone for a while.

Patsy Ann, you can get happy in the same pants you got mad in. You think you're going to change me? Dream on, Babydoll. Dream fucking on.

CHAPTER FIVE

A BRIDGE TOO FAR

PATSY

WHEN I WAKE UP and crawl back into the front passenger seat, Jim Beau is asleep, still sitting in his father's lap, his little head resting on B.J.'s powerful forearm. He's drooling.

"How long has he been that way?"

"A while." Still no eye contact.

"Let me have him. I'll lay him down. He'll be more comfortable in the back."

I take our sleeping son, who turned a year old last month. His back is soaked with sweat from being pressed to his father for so long.

The van has a heater for winter, but in the summer, open windows are our air conditioner, and as the day progressed, that cool night air warmed. Those two bodies pressed against each other for hours. Both are damp.

B.J. would never complain.

I lay Jim Beau on the bed and surround him with pillows. Pillows are one thing we have plenty of. I run my hand over his precious face. His hair is wet, too, so I strip off everything he has on and change his diaper, hoping he'll sleep more comfortably.

I climb into the passenger seat, and we drive through the mountains in silence, me changing tapes as they play through.

I've been too preoccupied to notice; he hasn't smoked a joint since we left Austin. That's unusual. He can steer the van with his left knee while rolling a joint.

I don't care if he's giving me the silent treatment. I want to know. "Why aren't you smoking?"

A cold glance. A hesitant answer. "If we get pulled over, I don't want to give them an excuse to search."

I should have known that. Okay, I get it. Hence, the speed. One day was all I asked.

His eyes are riveted to the road like I don't exist.

I'm not sure how much longer it is until I give up, exasperated. "You're going to give me the cold shoulder for the rest of the trip?"

Looking straight ahead, he answers, "I don't know." He cuts his eyes at me, and when he does, fire spews from them. "Are you going to rag my ass for the rest of the trip?"

I turn in the seat and jab my finger at him. He hates it when I do that. "I'm going to rag your ass for the rest of your fucking life if you don't straighten up!" Flabbergasted, my hands rise high. "You want to go to prison for drug trafficking? Leave me and Jim Beau out of it!"

His jaw is hard. He narrows his gaze, and his upper lip snarls. "Maybe I'll just leave you out. Period."

I suck in air. His face is so mean it shocks me. He's never looked at me that way.

My mouth falls open. Now, it's me who is speechless. Nothing. I've got nothing. No quick comeback.

B.J. reaches for me. "I didn't mean that. I'm sorry."

I still can't close my mouth.

Neither of us ever said anything like that to the other. I could rag his ass forever because we'd be together forever. That was a given. We don't threaten to leave each other, not B.J. and me. We aren't that kind of couple.

I thought we were forever—for better or worse. All that. I never imagined anything else. But he just said, 'Maybe I'll leave you out. Period.'

Don't let him see you cry.

I turn my head, peering out the window, but I can't see anything out there through the rising tide of tears.

A bit later, B.J. tugs at my shoulder. "Come on, Patsy. You know I didn't mean that."

Shifting my shoulder sharply, I rebuff his touch. My heart is a chunk of lead. I can't look at him. I can barely breathe.

We drive on, and there is more silence, more mountains, and more trees. But honestly, I can't see the countryside. It passes by in a blur, with road noise and wind in the windows. I don't even know what music he's playing.

He turned it down or off.

A torturous time later, B.J. breaks the silence. "I said I'm sorry, Pat."

Yes, his voice is soft, but that doesn't erase what he said, or how he said it, or the look on his face when he said it. It's not something you forget.

He tries again miles later. "I didn't mean what I said. I don't know why... that just came out."

"It wouldn't have come out if you hadn't thought about it." I cover my face with my hands and gulp back tears. I cannot bring myself to look at him. If I do, I might see that horrible snarl I saw earlier, like he hates me. He despises me. "You have. You absolutely have. You've thought about leaving me."

"No, Babydoll, I haven't." He sounds more mad than apologetic.

He was the one who put us in this position, hiding dope in the van and carrying it across state lines, and he just threatened to leave me. I can't get my head around it. B.J. threatened to leave me.

He pulls into a parking lot. As soon as the van stops moving, I jump out, slam the door, and run, stopping when I reach a little grassy area with a shade tree. I refuse to cry.

How can this be happening?

I turn in a circle. Where are we? This isn't one of those tiny towns. There are lots of cars and loud traffic noise. I lean my head against the tree. Despite my best efforts, tears roll down my cheeks. How did we get here? I can't believe it.

Yes, we fuss, but I never doubted B.J.'s love. Not for a second.

He said maybe he'll leave me. Our foundation cracked. My world tilted on its axis.

His hands are on my shoulders, and his muscular body is against my back. His chin is over my head. I stiffen and shift my shoulders, telling him not to touch me, but he ignores my body language.

"I'm sorry." He rubs his thumb on the back of my neck.

I'm not sure if it's B.J.'s gentle touch or his come-to-bed-with-me voice, but everything inside me wants to turn around and let him wrap those powerful arms around me and make this ache go away.

But I can't.

I pull away from his grip, taking a step back from him.

He's frustrated and getting louder. "Dammit, Pat, how many times can I say I'm sorry?"

I want to forgive him. I want to believe him. I also want to scream at him: It's too late! You can't take that back.

So, I'm silent. Just nothing. My heart is empty. It's the first time I understand the meaning of the word heartache. I mean, physically, my chest hurts deep inside. It's like an anvil dropped on my heart.

We have a child. B.J. and Jim Beau are my everything.

"Say something." B.J. squeezes my shoulders. "Talk to me."

Something inside explodes. "You want me to say something?" I feel fire in my cheeks as I whirl around to face him. "Put me and Jim Beau on a bus and send us home."

B.J. recoils as if I slapped him. It takes him a long moment to speak. "What?"

I point at the van. "I don't want to be in our van with that dope. Buy me a bus ticket so I can take the baby home."

The color drains from his tanned face. A second later, it flushes deep red. He looks like he may explode. "You want to leave?" Now he's yelling. "You want to go home? On a fucking bus—without me?" He's crazy livid, and it frightens me. I've never been afraid of B.J.

He turns in a circle, surveying the parking lot. It's a big shopping center with a grocery store. Not far away, a woman is rolling a shopping basket to her car. B.J. cups his hands and hollers, "Hey, lady! Where's the bus station?"

She's petite and old, with permed white hair, and she responds to him by pointing. "Turn right at the second light. You'll see it about a mile down, on the left."

He yells back. "Thanks!"

B.J. turns, glares at me for another second or two, and clenches his jaw so tightly that the tendons in his neck bulge. "You want to go? Let's go." He grabs my upper arm.

I have never seen him act this way.

We walk to the van, his grip firm on my upper arm. He doesn't hurt me, but he's making sure I get into the van and to the bus.

I didn't think he'd do it—send us away on a bus—I was just mad. But I said it, and I'm not taking it back. My heart is dragging on the concrete, but the tears have stopped.

He's going to do it. We are going our separate ways.

B.J. does want to get rid of me.

I'm too empty to cry.

CHAPTER SIX

JUST. GO.

B.J.

"YOU WANT TO LEAVE? You want to go home? On a fucking bus—without me?" My heart's going to rip out of my chest.

She just stares back. Mute.

I can't get my head around it. She wants to leave me? Over this bullshit she's blown out of proportion?

My fucking chest may explode. My heart pounds in my ears. This... this is unreal.

An old lady in the parking lot gives me directions to the bus station.

I grab my wife by her upper arm. My wife. The woman wearing my ring. The one who promised eternity. The one who gave me a son. The one who just threatened to take him away from me. The one who wants to get as far away from me as she can. "You want to go? Let's. Go."

Just. Fucking. Go. We have different definitions of eternity.

Still, she doesn't say a word. Not a goddamned word.

At the bus station, I get out and leave her in the van. Alone.

Right now, I need to cool off. I need to walk away before I say something or do something I'll regret even more than I regret telling her about the weed in the walls.

I want to hit something or kick something—anything. But all I can do is stand in this drag-ass line. I'm behind half a dozen other people, twiddling my thumbs like a fucking fool. Just waiting... to buy her a ticket. So she can leave me.

I can't stifle a snort. The chick in front of me turns around, wondering what I'm laughing about. I shake my head. None of her business. I'm not about to explain the absurdity of the situation. I'm standing in line to buy a ticket so my wife can leave me. And take my son.

What the fuck?

How slow can that clerk be? Geez.

Oh, well. Maybe it'll give me time to cool off.

What's to cool off about? Patsy is leaving. And taking Jim Beau. Away from me.

I want to roar. I want to rip the wheels off the motherfucking bus.

Out of my peripheral vision, I spot a cop. Cutting my eyes left and right, I spot another near the entrance, another outside the restrooms, and the third just trying to wander around inconspicuously.

I've got news, buddy. Cops in uniforms don't blend in. What's going on?

My shoulders tighten. Shit. Are they randomly checking people? Tell me I didn't just walk into some kind of drug sweep. I cut my eyes both ways again. No drug dogs—not inside.

Oh, shit! If they're checking vehicles outside—if they check the van—Patsy's so paranoid, she'll spill her guts. What have I walked into?

Tell me this isn't happening. My heart is racing again.

I stare at the floor. Be calm, man. Just be cool.

Fucking Al. Why did I agree to do this?

Someone yells, "Stop!" and I flinch.

I turn—hell, the whole lobby turns—to watch two uniforms chasing a guy headed for the entrance. He's wearing Army fatigues, trying to run with a duffle bag over his shoulder. Sucker's holding.

Before he reaches the door, someone sideswipes him—maybe a plain-clothes cop. Whoever he is, he makes a flying dive, taking the runner down. Poor guy never saw him coming. They're all on top of him, wrestling, slapping cuffs on him, picking up the duffle bag, checking inside.

What a Bozo. You don't carry a bag of dope through a bus station.

My stomach twists in a knot. They were waiting for him. What if one of the guys who loaded my van was a fucking snitch? Or cop?

Chill out, man. Nobody followed us. They couldn't know we were going to stop here because, hell. I didn't know we were going to stop here.

"Next!"

I startle again. I've been too preoccupied watching the cops to move up in the line. "I need a one-way ticket to Austin," I tell the agent.

"Texas?" she asks.

Lady, I'm not in the mood. "It's the only Austin I know of."

The old girl glares at me and snaps. "I hate to break it to you, cowboy, but there are more than twenty Austins in the United States of America."

Why does everyone think if you live in Texas, you're a cowboy? "Look at me, lady. Do I look like a cowboy? I need a one-way ticket to Austin, Texas. Please."

She checks her manifest. "There's not a direct bus to Austin, Texas." She sneers through Texas. "We have a bus to Nashville leaving in an hour." She flips through some pages. "In Nashville, you have a six-hour layover to catch the next bus to Dallas. And in Dallas, let me see...." More page flipping. "In Dallas... there's a bus to Austin two hours later."

"Six hours sitting in the Nashville bus station and another two-hour wait in Dallas—on top of the drive?"

"That's what I just said." She's a testy old bitch.

I don't want Patsy and Jim Beau sitting around in bus stations for eight hours with pimps and perverts. Hell, the dregs of society hang out in bus stations.

But she wants to go. I don't know. A part of me is still seeing that guy being carted off in cuffs.

"Sir! Do you, or do you not want the tickets?" She points behind me. "I have people waiting."

I check over my shoulder. Yeah, the line is growing. They can wait like I did.

I don't know. I guess if Patsy wants to go through all of that to get away from me. "Fine. How much?"

The agent, who looks a little bit like a bearded turkey, holds up her index finger. "Let me see. Just a second." More page flipping. She punches a calculator, finally adjusts her glasses, and meets my gaze. "That will be sixty-five dollars and twenty-two cents."

My jaw drops as my brows hit my hairline. "Sixty-five? Dollars? You've got to be kidding me."

She stares back and blinks. "It is what it is, sir. It's three bus tickets, actually, across half of the United States of America." Every time she says the United States of America, the way she says it, I half expect her to slap her hand over her heart and break into a song.

I blow out a big breath. Between all the layovers and the price. "No thanks."

I've had time to think. I'll be damned if I'll beg my wife not to leave me. I'll just tell her I can't afford it. She'll have to get over her mad because, now that I've had time to process this shit, I don't give a flying fuck if it's a direct trip to Austin that costs ten cents. I'm not doing it. I'm not putting them on a bus and sending them away. This bullshit has gone far enough.

BUS

Chapter Seven

BUS STOP

Patsy

AFTER HE FINALLY FOUND a place to parallel park, B.J. made a whole production of growling, slamming his door, and tromping inside.

I get it. You're mad. You don't need to demonstrate.

It's a tall, one-story yellow brick building right downtown, wherever we are. It's busy. Buses pull in and out from a big open bay in front of us.

Where are we? What is the name of this town? I don't even know what state I'm in.

I move to the back and begin gathering things.

When the van door opens, I'm loading cereal and milk bottles into Jim Beau's big diaper bag. "I'm almost ready."

No tears. He wants to get rid of me. I'm going.

With things finally gathered, I turn to leave.

B.J. fills up the doorway. "I don't have enough money to buy a bus ticket to Austin."

"Yes, you do!" Glancing at Jim Beau asleep, I lower my voice. "You've got a van full of pot you're going to sell, so don't tell me you don't have money for a ticket so the baby and I can go home."

He puts one hand on each side of the open door—his arms spread wide like an eagle's wings. He leans inside, his boots on the curb. "I'm not buying a ticket so my wife can take my son away from me. Period. Now get ahold of yourself."

I stare in disbelief.

I didn't expect him to put me on a bus in the first place, but I didn't expect this either.

So, what did you expect, dummy? You're the one who told him to put you on a bus and send you home.

I was hurt when he said he would, and now I'm mad when he says he won't.

I don't know where I am. I don't have any money. And B.J.'s not going to buy me a bus ticket. And if I stay with him in this rolling drug den, we can lose our son.

Oh, God, what do I do?

I sit on the bed, bury my head in my hands, and cry. It's been pent up. Once I start, I can't stop.

He never said I love you. He never said, please don't leave me. He just got pissed off.

B.J. sits beside me, wraps his arms around me, and pulls me tight against his chest. "Patsy, why would you leave me?"

"Because you said, "Maybe I'll leave you out, period."

"You said it first."

I'm stumped.

He grips my shoulders, holding me away, looking me dead in the eyes. "You said you'd rag my ass for the rest of my fucking life if I don't straighten up." His eyes are fiery amber. "And you said for me to leave you and Jim Beau out—which sounds a hell of a lot to me like you'll take him and leave me if I don't do exactly what you say I can do. Which is exactly what you're doing."

I have never seen B.J. as angry at me as he is today. It's more than the Mollies. It's me. He is sick of me.

He says, "I'm your husband, Patsy, not your child. I'm not asking your permission or anyone else's."

We sit in silence for an eternity, my mind absorbing what he said.

I did say that. I didn't mean it the way he took it. I never thought about how my words hurt him.

It's funny how we say things and never think about how our words affect the listener. Who said the pen is mightier than the sword? He left out, "and so is the spoken word." What else can lift your spirit to heaven, chunk your face in the dirt, and pierce your heart like an arrow?

I sniff tears. "B.J., I guess I thought I could rag your ass for the rest of your life because we'd be together the rest of our lives." My eyes meet his, my vision blurred by tears. "I can be mad at you. That doesn't mean I don't love you or that I'd leave you."

He sighs deeply, and I watch sweet relief fill his face, lighting up his eyes.

But it's short-lived.

"I don't want to be in this van with the dope because if we get caught, with both parents in jail, we will lose our son." My voice is kind, but my mind is made up. "We. Will. Lose. Him. The state will take custody of Jim Beau. So, buy a bus ticket and let us go home. You go on to Al's and if you make it back without getting caught, we'll be at home waiting for you."

Pain crawls back into his eyes. Then anger. The anger, I know, is because of the pain I'm causing him.

Seeing so much disappointment in the eyes of the man I love—it's all I can do not to melt into him.

But no. I can't give in. Not on this. He's way past one toe over the line. Hell, he has totally crossed the line, and he dragged me and the baby with him. It could cost us everything.

B.J. flexes his jaw and runs both hands over his face. His gaze darts about the van, his lips mushed together. I know him. He's thinking about doing it.

Then, his eyes lock onto mine. "No. I've taken every precaution, Patsy. We're not going to get busted. Now, I asked you to take my name, and you took it. We have a son. We don't split up."

How did we get here? I never dreamed we'd be talking about splitting up. How do we get back to where we were? We can't—not with the dope in the van.

I start crying all over again.

A moment later, he lifts his hands, ducks out of the van, and leans back through the door. "I don't know what else you want me to say. Yes, I said that, and I'm sorry. But so did you." His face turns hard again. "And I'm not putting you two on a bus. Get that through your head."

Mad again, I follow him out of the van. I can't believe Jim Beau is sleeping through all this. Blurry-eyed, I survey the street. No one is nearby. "Do you love me, B.J.? Or Jim Beau? I mean, you said, 'Maybe I'll leave you out.' You just said you won't buy a ticket so your wife can take your son away. If you could keep Jim Beau but get rid of me, would you? Because right now, I feel like you despise me."

He stares at me with a frozen, unreadable expression for an agonizingly long moment as I stand on the sidewalk waiting for him to finish breaking my heart with something snarly like, 'hell, yeah, I'm sick of you.'

Instead, he emits a condescending laugh. "Did you leave your fucking brain in Texas? That's the stupidest thing I ever heard." He's loud again as he points at the van. "I look at him and I see you! For God's sake, Patsy. How can you question how much I love you? Both of you."

I see him through the veil of tears as a tidal wave of relief washes through me. "Do you?" Even knowing that what I said prompted what he said, I can't get past it.

He cups my face in his hands and crouches low so his eyes meet mine dead on. "Patsy, you're fucking killing me. I love you with everything in me. Everything."

I step away from him and press my fingertips against my eyes. People are passing on the sidewalk. They peer at us but walk on by. "I love you, too." I take another step away so I can see all of him. "But we're so far apart on this." I glance around for eavesdroppers, step back in close, and lower my voice. "I've never fussed at you about smoking pot or selling a bag here or there, or even taking a hit of speed but if you can't see the difference in this? I don't even know what to say."

"I do."

Our gazes still hold. I feel the agony in his brown eyes. His voice is hushed, like mine. After all, people are around, and we're talking about something illegal.

"You do what?"

He closes his eyes and sighs deeply. "I see the differ- ence." He stands straight and lifts his shoulder. "Obviously, I wasn't thinking." He pauses and sighs again. "If I was, I was thinking about making money." He lifts his chin high and glances around the busy area.

My husband is, hands down, the best-looking man I have ever laid eyes on.

His gaze comes back, meeting mine. "Patsy, I work from daylight to dark and we can't get ahead. I saw a chance to make some money and I took it, thinking maybe I could buy you something nice or buy Jim Beau a swing set or something. Hell, just get even. Get a little breathing room. I just—I don't know. I wasn't thinking about anything but making some extra money."

Well, crap.

Everything he says is true. My heart is breaking.

B.J. doesn't sit at a desk. He works physically hard six days a week, and I've seen him work two weeks straight without a day off. And I was the one who told him, 'Leave me and Jim Beau out,' before he said, 'Maybe I'll leave you out.'

He's right about everything—except for bringing the dope.

He says, "I guess your point about the risk to you and Jim Beau, that we could lose him, made me mad. First, I was mad at you. Then at myself. How could I be so stupid? What if I did lose him and you because of what I did? I'd never be able to live with myself." He peers up at the sky and sighs loudly. "Fuck. I'm sorry. For everything."

Tears roll down my face as I peer up at him. B.J. was trying to take care of us. "I'll get a job," I say.

"No! I don't want you to work while he's this little. No!" He grabs me and pulls me to him, and I rest my head on his chest. I love his chest. The strength of it. "We'll make do. We'll figure it out."

"Together?" I blink through tears.

"Yeah. Together." He wraps me in his arms tightly.

I pull away to look up at him again, my palms against his chest. "Promise me, B.J. Never again. We get to Al's and get rid of this stuff and never again."

He rubs his thumbs gently across my cheeks and wipes my tears, his eyes loving me again, and I inhale him. I'm so in love with him. He smiles. "I promise."

When people promise for better or for worse, they tend to gloss over two of those words: 'for worse.' For better, for worse. B.J. and I have shared years of better—the best. Now, we fought through the worst to find our way back to forever.

"I love you, B.J. I will never leave you. Ever."

He pulls me against his chest and runs his fingers through my hair, cupping the back of my head. His voice is gentle like his hands. He leans down and whispers, "Babydoll, I told you the day I put that ring on your finger—we are forever."

His eyes gleam now with a look I know well.

B.J. kisses me right there on the sidewalk with cars and people all around. His hand cups my jaw, holding me in place as his tongue takes all the hurt and fear right out of me. My arms wrap around his neck as all my anger turns to desire, and he stands straight, lifting me off the ground. My feet dangle in the air, and through the endless kiss, he whispers, "You know, Babydoll. Jim Beau's sound asleep."

Chapter Eight

MY BIG MISTAKE

B.J.

SHE'S HAD ME TIED up in knots all morning. Now, I want my wife. No, I need my wife.

Carrying Patsy to the van, I set her feet on the floor. We have a routine. She pulls the sheet curtain that stretches wall to wall behind the front seats, creating a private sleeping cabin while I quietly close the van door. Slow and easy.

She arranges pillows behind the driver's seat, and I transfer Jim Beau from the bed to his soft nest, tucking him in a thin cover. He never wakes up, leaving the bed for us.

When I turn around, Patsy has secured the back curtain and taken off her blouse, exposing her beautiful bare breasts. They are perfect. Her pink nipples are waiting to be kissed. It's in her eyes, on her face: she wants this as much as I do.

This day has been a gut-busting wake-up call. We both need this.

Patsy stretches out on her back, her arms over her head waiting for me—but rather than climb on top, I kneel

50

beside her, cupping a breast, taking it into my mouth. As I pour my passion into nibbling and suckling that sweet tit, her fingers wrap in my hair, holding me to her. She loves it as much as I do.

I free a hand to slide off those hip-huggers. Feeling her little lace panties, she's already wet. I push them aside to stroke her silky slit, and Patsy sighs deeply. As I slide my fingers inside, her head falls to the side, and she hikes her hips, forcing me deeper as she moans, "Oh... B.J."

There's no better sex than makeup sex. But this—I don't know. Somehow, this feels like more than that. It has to be. I never imagined losing her. I'll do whatever it takes. I can't live through losing them.

"Do you want this, Patsy? Here? Now?" I need to hear her say it.

Our gazes lock as she nods and answers, "Yes." Never taking her eyes off mine, Patsy tugs on my belt, her eyes pleading. "I want you inside of me. Now."

It's never been nicer to hear. My tongue darts out to graze her nipples, one at a time. "Patience, Babydoll. I'm not through playing yet."

She becomes breathless as my fingers continue to work inside of her, rubbing her slick clit with my thumb. I love what I see on her face. What I'm looking at is pure pleasure, her nipples taut. "Please, B.J. Now."

I pull out of her to slide out of my jeans—I've got to free my swollen dick—and when I do, Patsy takes control. She slips from the bed to pull off my jeans and boots while I yank my shirt over my head.

Pulling down my briefs, Patsy fists my cock and grins up at me. "You want to play?"

I let out a guttural groan as she slides her tongue around my tip, sucking it into her mouth. "Oh, fuck, Babydoll."

She slides me in deep, twirling that tongue, sucking, massaging my dick until I'm just about to explode. "Slow down. I need to come inside of you."

She looks up, licks her lips, and flashes that foxy little grin again. Her eyes twinkle as she puts her hands on my chest and shoves me onto my back. Then my wife climbs on top. Straddling me, she takes me deep once... twice... She lifts up, holding what I want just out of reach, moving her hips in a circle, barely brushing my tip.

"You need to come inside of me?" She taunts. "You need this?"

Look at that smile. She knows I can't take that.

A part of me wants to play her game, to hold back and not give her what she wants. But the part of me she's teasing says we've already played enough games today. All I want to do is drive inside of her. But Patsy's having too much fun toying with me right now.

God, it's good to see her smile like that. She's keeping her pussy just beyond my reach. Playfully.

I fist my cock, placing it right at her entrance. She's not fooling me. I feel how wet she is. It's my turn to grin and whisper, "Do you need this? Yes? Or no?"

She's biting her bottom lip with her glassy gaze fixed on mine. "B.J. Cole. You better—" She doesn't get to finish.

I grip her waist with both hands and pull her down hard, taking her so deep that she catches her breath and emits a luscious little groan. Oh, God. She is so perfect.

And we begin to move together. We have our own rhythm, me thrusting slowly... deeply... quietly.

She moves with me in perfect sync, always with our gazes locked, our fingers entwined. Sometimes, I think... doing it... silently like this... makes it even more intense, like we're getting by with something we shouldn't be doing... with our little boy sound asleep nearby.

Riding me, Patsy takes my index finger into her mouth, sucking on it seductively, her tongue circling it like the tip of my dick.

Oh, God, Patsy. *Fuck*. I mean, yeah, fuck, it's... always good... but... feeling this, knowing she didn't want to leave, knowing she does love me the way I love her. Finally, admitting I was wrong. That's not an easy thing for me to do... but that guy getting busted right in front of me—the power above was sending me a message to pull my head out of my ass.

I thrust slow and deep with every word in my head. I... was... wrong.

Pulling her to me, I kiss her mouth with all the passion of my regret, and I feel our bodies soaked... in sweat. Both of us.

My hands slide down her shoulders to the small of her back. Cupping the curves of her hips, I begin to thrust harder, deeper, faster. She buries her head in my neck, muffling her cries.

Feel it, baby. Feel it...

She pulls away to sit up straight, arching her back, her beautiful tits right there. A part of me wants to sit up and suck them, to take them into my mouth again—but in this position, she's taking all of me her tiny body can—and I see on her face—this is her bliss.

I know her. She's—yeah, she's right there.

"Oh, B.J.! Yes... yes..."

Sweat glistens on her neck and breasts. Her knees squeeze me, her head falls back, those nipples stand erect—and her inner walls ripple around me. Patsy's body trembles with her satisfaction, and I keep her hips pressed down tight. I am buried to the hilt inside of her as those pulsing walls milk me.

If she keeps that up much longer, I can't last.

Finally soaked in my wife's pleasure, I stop holding back. Three long... deep... strokes—and I explode inside of her. To my surprise, she flutters around me again, both of us lost in our release. *Yes. Oh, fuck, yes.*

She wilts into my sweaty chest, and I press her against me, both arms wrapped tightly around her. Our hearts beat against each other. Neither of us can move. "Twice." She smiles against my skin. "Oh, B.J. That was wonderful."

Brushing her damp hair away from her face, I tilt her chin so her eyes meet mine. "Patsy, you're a part of me. I will love you forever."

Her tears come back, but I know these are tears of joy as she smiles and whispers, "B.J. Cole, you better."

Now, that's an order I gladly accept. Finally. This nightmare is behind us. I will never make that mistake again.

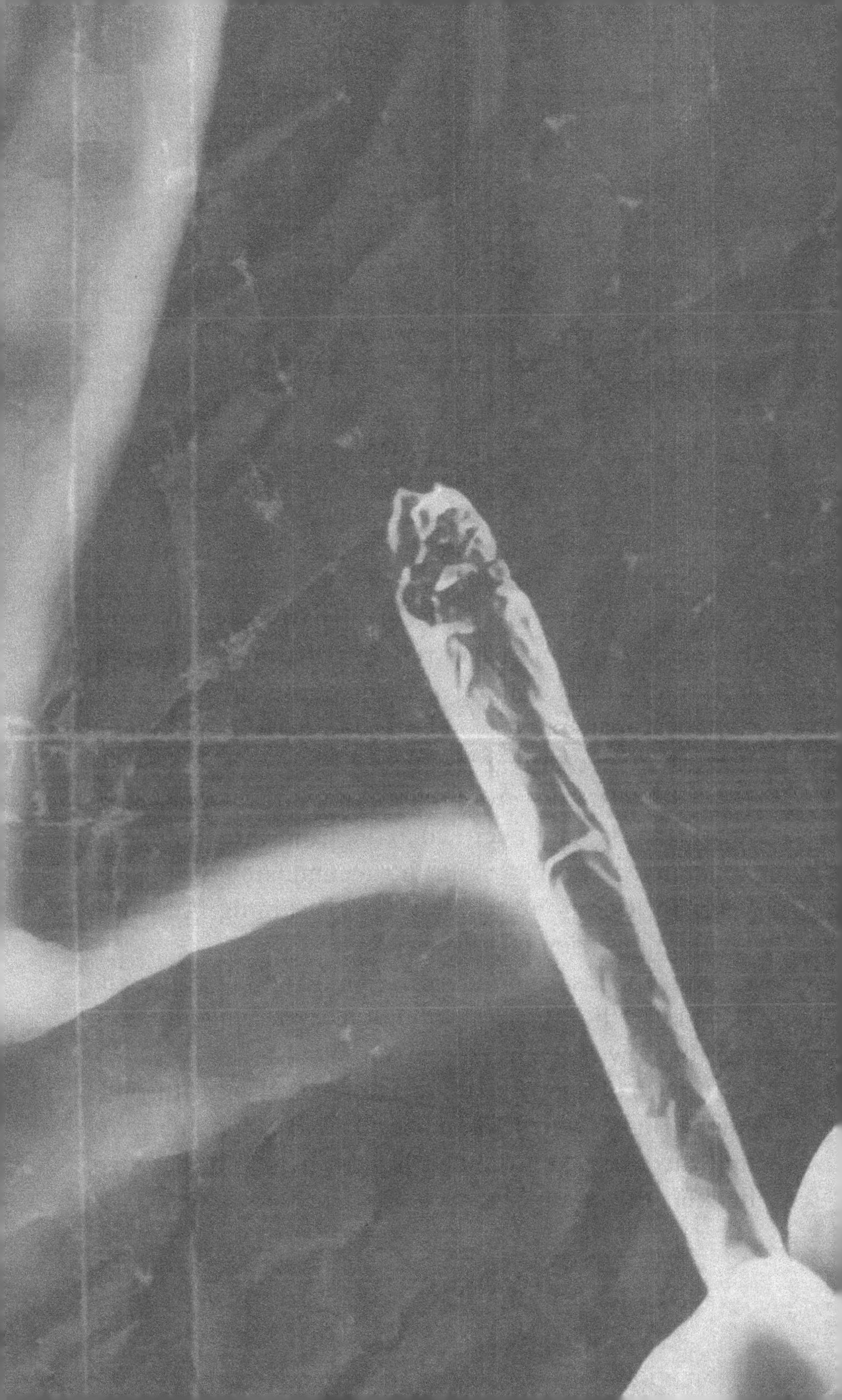

CHAPTER NINE

PARTY TIME

Patsy

BY THE TIME WE get to Al's place, the party is in full swing. His place is on a narrow street in a charming old neighborhood, within walking distance of the university. It is lined with cars parked on both sides in front of big, old houses divided into apartments.

Al's flat is on the ground floor of a brownstone. Judging by the size of the crowd in the front yard, it appears he invited all of the friends he accumulated during two years in Richmond to his farewell shindig. And they invited their friends. It is packed.

Or maybe his friends surprised him. I don't know, and I don't care because I'm still not in a partying mood.

Al has always been sketchy for my taste.

The two of them had quite a reputation going through Austin High—wild boys and best friends. Find them, you find the party, and they both liked living on the edge, bucking the system.

They were two years ahead of me in school, the good-looking, unobtainable upperclassmen every girl I knew drooled over and dreamed about. Back then, I never imagined B.J. Cole would ask me out, much less fall in love with me.

But he did.

If my husband ever gets a tattoo, which I can't imagine he would, but if he did, it would say 'Carpe diem.' Seize the day unafraid. It's just who he is.

It's who Al is, too. It's just too bad Al's sneaky about it.

B.J. is a what-you-see-is-what-you-get kind of guy. I love that about him. No pretense.

I can't say the same for his best friend, and when it comes to Al Mancini, B.J. has a blind spot. He cannot see how manipulative Al is.

After our lovemaking, I asked B.J., "Whose idea was it?"

His attention had been on traffic. It was rush hour when we reached Richmond. "Whose idea was what?" he asked.

"To buy in Austin and sell in Richmond? Was that your idea or Al's?" I always felt like Al resented me for stealing his best friend, something else B.J. was oblivious to.

B.J. took his eyes off the road long enough to meet mine. "I don't know. We were talking and...."

"But Al's the one who would know people pay more for grass over here than they do in Texas. Right?"

B.J. lifted a shoulder. "Yeah, I guess."

"So, it was his idea." It was coming into focus. Al is behind this cluster fuck.

He sighed. "I guess."

"So, this is why we've been scrimping lately? All our money went to buy this?" I jabbed my thumb at the walls of the van. "We're waiting for the return on your investment?"

"Oh, God, Patsy." B.J. wagged his head as he cut his eyes at me, this time with a good-natured grin. "You're like a dog with a bone. Give it up. Please. I promised you never again."

We'd made up. We had maybe the most memorable sex—ever. Another fight was the last thing I wanted. I bit my lip. "You're right. I'm sorry." I leaned across and nibbled his neck as I ran my hand along his thigh, teasing him.

His grin grew deeper as he eyed me up and down. "You want to go again, Babydoll? I'm all in." I kissed him playfully, and yeah, absolutely, we both could've pulled over and romped—again. Jim Beau had fallen back asleep, thanks to the van rocking.

It is hard to explain, but after our fight and after the love we made, I feel closer to B.J. than I ever have, and that's saying a lot. We both put everything out there, and we still love each other. Our foundation is stronger than ever.

Circling the neighborhood, I realize our son will be as wired as his Daddy when we finally park. Maybe I should've napped with him again. But it's too late for a nap or a romp. We're here, and because of the crowd, B.J. has to park around the corner a block away from Al's apartment.

He carries Jim Beau as we thread through a throng of people in the small front yard. He is so excited to see his best friend for the first time in two years—it's in his eyes and on his face.

"Purple Haze" vibrates through the stereo speakers. *...'Scuse me while I kiss the sky...* B.J. yells over the music, laughing, "Who would have thought? Al is having a party!"

If the music is this loud out here, how will we hear each other inside?

I don't guess it bothers the neighbors. Everyone who lives nearby either attends, teaches, or works at the university—birds of a feather and all. Oh, well. I can handle anything for one night.

With the apartment door ajar, we can see the crowd through the thick fog of smoke. Pot and hash and booze and that screaming psychedelic rock fill the room.

"B.J.!" Al's voice booms over everything when he sees B.J. entering the front door. "Everyone! This is my best friend B.J. from Texas I told you about!" His arms are open wide.

The revelers watch as Al rushes to B.J. and grabs him. The two hug and slap each other on the back like men do, shaking each other by the shoulders.

Al turns B.J. to face his friends. "This is the guy I told you about, who put the Volkswagen Beetle in the bed of our coach's pickup!"

Everyone cheers as B.J. and Al high-five each other. "Fucker deserved it." B.J. raises the joint that Al just handed him as if in a toast.

"How did you do it?" someone asks over the music.

"I never said I did." They all laugh, and B.J. cuts his eyes at Al. "If I did do it, I damned sure didn't do it alone."

The crowd cackles as Al and B.J. high-five each other again. The Beetle-in-the-bed-of-the-truck story was one of their claims to fame at Austin High. One night after a particularly grueling football practice, they snuck out and hoisted a convertible Bug into the bed of the football coach's truck. I think it had been in the neighbor's driveway. It was payback. Their way of saying, "You want to work us that hard? You work on this for a while."

They never got in trouble. No one could prove it was them, but everyone pretty well knew, including the coach, who didn't suspend them because he needed them both on the field to win. B.J. was a running back, and Al was a receiver. Neither was good enough to play college ball, but they were good enough to be named All-District, which was a big deal at Austin High.

"So, this is Jim Beau?" Al rubs my son's head and nods politely. "Pat, good to see you."

I smile back as graciously as I can. He's the cause of everything we just went through. "Good to see you, too, Al. It's been a while." Not long enough.

"Two years." He slaps B.J. on the back again, tugging his shoulder. "Damn, I've missed you, buddy."

Okay, I'll admit, Al is a nice-looking guy, but in a different way than B.J.

They're the same height, at or just under six feet tall. Both have brown hair and eyes, but B.J.'s eyes are warm honey. Al's are dark chocolate. Everything about Al—his eyes, hair, complexion—is darker than B.J.

My husband is brawny. Al is scrawny. Whatever strength he possesses is in his brain because I don't see any muscles. But his face is chiseled like a Roman statue. Girls have always flocked to him.

The science of attraction is fascinating. As handsome as I find B.J., it occurs to me some women see Al the same way—like the redhead drooling over him. Go figure. And the size of the crowd attests to his magnetism.

"Congratulations on finishing your master's degree!" I yell over the music, holding Jim Beau, who is turning his head from one side to the other, gawking at the strange new people.

"Thanks." Al and B.J. are passing that joint back and forth.

"What's it in?"

Al cuts his eyes at me. They're bloodshot. "Huh?" He takes a hit and hands it back to B.J., holding his breath for a long second before he exhales.

"Your master's degree? What's it in?"

"Oh, the masters. Poli Sci." He waves smoke with his hand. "I've decided to go to law school."

That makes sense. He is a born politician.

B.J.'s head tilts back as he guffaws. "Damn, man." He takes another toke and holds the joint under his nose, inhaling the smoke before he passes it back. "How many years are you going to stay in school? Only took me two years to get through the University of Texas."

They both laugh heartily.

B.J. wasn't cut out for college. He quit after his sophomore year. It wasn't that his brain was weaker than Al's; he just wasn't interested. He only went because his dad insisted. He preferred working with his hands and being outside.

I dropped out of college during my senior year when Jim Beau was born. I couldn't find peace leaving him with strangers in a daycare center while I was in class, and B.J. wanted me to stay home with the baby. "You can finish your degree when you get ready," he'd said. "Or not. It's your choice."

That's the thing about B.J. He has never judged me for anything.

My best friend married a West Texas rancher. He expects—more like demands—a full-course dinner on the table every evening when he gets home. That man wants Margie to have the table set and the food in proper serving dishes waiting for him—and Joe Don expects dessert, for crying out loud. Homemade.

B.J. doesn't demand anything, and he always comes home after work.

A lot of my girlfriends pace the floor, wondering where their husbands are in the evenings. Are they meeting buds at the bar or hooking up with who-knows-who?

Not my B.J. He always comes home to Jim Beau and me. So, why am I so hard on him? I cannot suppress my smile as I watch him and Al laughing, catching up. Al proudly introduces him to one friend after another. I am so glad B.J. is mine.

I squeeze his hand, and our eyes meet. "Al, where's your powder room?" I ask.

Al points, holding his joint. "Right down that hall."

I mouth to B.J., "We'll be back," and Jim Beau and I head for the bathroom, where I bump, smack-dab, into a great big guy coming out.

It would be more accurate to say he stumbled out. High as a frigging kite. He swats at something, and I dodge. He's mumbling, steadying himself with one hand on each of the hall walls.

I'll be glad when this trip is over.

But then Al will be back in Texas. I never said it to B.J., but I wanted to throw a party when Al moved halfway across the country. It's been nice with him gone for two years.

Al has a line of bullshit as long as the Rio Grande, and you have to sift through everything he says to make sure you don't swallow a load of crap. Like I said, a natural-born politician.

Deep down, I always feared Al might lead B.J. into trouble and throw him under the bus if the going got rough. But maybe I needed to have more faith in my husband.

When Jim Beau and I return to the living room, they're snorting rails on the bar separating it from the kitchen. B.J. is over there with them, which surprises me. I've never seen him snort anything.

"What is that?" I whisper.

"Coke," he answers as he wipes his nose on his sleeve.

Dammit! I've never seen B.J. do cocaine.

I guess it shouldn't be surprising, though. He's back with Al. They're sharing another joint, and B.J. has a glass of what looks like whiskey in his hand.

It's like he's known all these people as long as Al has. He fits right in, everybody laughing, having a big time—as if B.J.'s been the missing piece of this puzzle all along.

And oh, my Lord. *...In-a-gadda-da-vida, honey, don't you know that I love you?...* "In-A-Gadda-Da-Vida" has to be the longest, loudest song in the history of mankind—and every guy I know, including my husband, absolutely loves it. Someone cranks it up even louder. It's a good time to leave.

"Give me the van keys," I shout over the music.

Surprise sweeps across his face. "Where are you going?"

Standing on my tiptoes, I cup my hands to speak into his ear. "I'm going to fix Jim Beau something to eat." We'd refilled the chest with fresh milk and ice, and I'd bought baby food and cereals. "I may find a place to let him run so he can get rid of some energy."

"I'll go with you."

"No, we're okay. Stay here and enjoy Al and his friends. I don't mind. I promise." I kiss his cheek. "But he doesn't need to be around all this."

Al has two women competing for his attention now—that redhead and a tall, thin blonde.

Booze is flowing, along with the blaring music, cocaine, and marijuana, and God knows what that guy in the hall took. "You don't see any other kids here."

B.J. glances around the crowded, smoke-filled room. "You're right. Sorry. Again."

"Don't be." I stand on tiptoes and kiss his lips. "He's your best friend, and you haven't seen him in years. So have fun. Jim Beau needs to eat and run, and I can use some fresh air."

As I reach the front door, a big-chested twit with Carole King hair and red lips sidles up to B.J. and slips her arm around his thick bicep. None of these collegiate types are built like B.J. She bats her eyes at my husband. She knows we're together. He has a ring on his finger. Slut. What a come-on. Can you be more obvious?

I stop and watch. Neither of them sees me.

Give it your best shot, girl. That one's mine.

B.J. smiles at her, takes her hand from around his bicep, and keeps talking to Al like she's not there.

Yes! I want to clap. That's the man I love.

With the van door open, I've got Clapton playing on an eight-track. ... *There's a thorn tree in the garden, if you know just what I mean...* I love Eric Clapton. That man has soul. I love, love, love "Bellbottom Blues." In fact, I'm wearing bellbottoms—hip huggers, we call them. B.J. loves them, too.

It doesn't get any better than listening to Clapton on a summer evening sitting on soft grass with your baby in your arms. Jim Beau and I are on a little picnic blanket I spread on a thick, soft patch of Saint Augustine grass between the sidewalk and the van under a canopy of ancient trees.

They could have been alive when Pocahontas was flirting with John Smith. I think about that, peering up at those beautiful trees. Maybe they were here then. Maybe Pocahontas sat right here, where I am. I smile, thinking of what trees could tell us if only they could talk.

I think maybe they can, at least to each other.

It's not hot, and it's not cold, and there's a soft breeze. There's been no foot traffic or noise where we are. The spot is peaceful and quiet, so I can enjoy my music and my son, who is eating animal crackers and looking at a picture book as two guys walk past.

They don't seem to notice us sitting on the ground. "So, you think this dude's reliable?" one asks.

"Allesandro vouches for him," the other replies.

They're talking about Al.

Allesandro Lorenzo Mancini. Yeah.

My ears perk, and my gaze latches onto them like a heat-seeking missile. I watch them until they round the corner. They're older than we are—maybe in their thirties? Neither man has long hair. Short, cut over the ears, parted on the side, and black. They're both straight-backed, wearing slacks, not jeans. They look more like businessmen than collegiate types.

In the shade of the big trees, I can't get a good look at either, just their shapes and sizes. One is husky, shorter than the other. He's a V-shaped man with broad shoulders and narrow hips.

Sitting on the ground, I get a good look at their shoes. They're wearing city shoes. Laced up, shiny black leather. Not tennis shoes or boots like the men I know.

Al. What is he up to?

I can't ponder it long. Finishing his snack, Jim Beau is restless. He's squirmy. He needs to expend some energy, so I fold up the picnic blanket, close up the van, put the key in my pocket, and hold out my hand. "Let's go for a walk."

Arms outstretched, his eyes glistening, Jim Beau toddles to me, and we head down the sidewalk away from Al's, hand in hand with me bent at the waist. "Let's go explore, baby boy. Okay?"

"'Esplore!" He claps his hands.

I pick him up and swing him in high circles, and he squeals with delight. He is so precious. Chubby little face. His hair is corn silk. He's been cooped up in that van for the better part of two days.

Setting him on my hip, I spot a green space up ahead—a small neighborhood park surrounded by a wrought iron fence. Inside, there are park benches, a fountain, and, yes, swings. And a merry-go-round, teeter-totters, and monkey bars. Perfect.

Chapter Ten

NOT MY STYLE

B.J.

EVEN IF I WASN'T happily married—which I am—this chick's not my style. Big, wild, frizzy hair. Shoved up tits. Red lipstick. No thanks. I peel her hand off my arm before Patsy sees and pulls her hair out.

And mine.

"Al, buddy, we need to talk." I want to unload my van and get that pressure off of me. I promised her I'd get rid of it. I'll keep that promise. She was right all along. There's a risk as long as we've got that weed in the van.

But he's not listening. He's tonguing the redhead. She's tall. Shapely. Right up his alley.

"Al!"

He waves me off. "Tomorrow, bro. Tonight, we party."

"You're not worried about... anything?" I ask.

He pulls his tongue out of the redhead's mouth long enough to meet my gaze and shake his head. "No, man. Nothing's going to happen to it here. It's all copacetic."

Copacetic. An Al word.

"Okay. Just remember, I delivered. I got it here."

"Ease up and take a toke, Al's friend." The now-wobbly redhead shoves a joint in my face. I hadn't noticed how glassy her eyes were. She squints at me. "What'd you say your name was?"

She can't remember B.J.? She is fucked up. The question doesn't deserve an answer. She wouldn't remember it anyway.

I take the joint.

"Come on, B.J. Relax." Al spreads his arms wide. "We've got smoke and blow and booze. Just enjoy the moment. Carpe diem, dude."

Geez. Copacetic. Dude. Groovy. Al's been out of Texas too damned long.

But carpe diem? I get it. Fair enough. Patsy said she was cool with it. I hold the joint in a toast: "Carpe diem."

The redhead is taking another snort. She wipes her nose and passes the straw.

Okay. I'll enjoy the night because I've got that long drive back to Texas tomorrow. And work on Monday. *Oh, shit, man. That stuff is sweet.* What. A. Rush. Wow.

Just look at this room. Man, it is wall-to-wall people. How does Al even know this many people? All kinds. A bunch of them are pretty rough. Scrungy. Man, there are some hard-core dopers here taking advantage of Al and his money and his free drugs. Al's always been pretty free with his drugs. I've never known how he swings the money.

Parents, I guess. They've got lots of it. No telling what his monthly allowance is.

I have to snicker. Al's still getting an allowance.

I've been making my way since I dropped out of college. Yeah, I have to ask Dad for help now and then, but I always pay him back doing odd jobs on the weekends. I built a deck for our landlord to pay Dad back last month. He warned me when I quit school—son, you're taking the hard way.

Maybe I am, but I've had raises, and I plan on more. We won't always struggle.

My attention is pulled to the front door as it swings open wide. Two guys walk in like they own the place. Who the fuck are they?

One is as big as Hoss Cartwright. The other is about my size. Both of them look like fighters. They have black hair and wear slacks and button-up shirts.

The smaller one looks around the room and glowers. He doesn't like what he sees. And he's not hiding it.

My hackles rise as I watch Al lose all color.

An alarm dings inside my head as Al abandons the redhead and rushes to the front door like he's going to block the two from coming any farther. They talk for a minute and step outside.

What the fuck is that about?

CHAPTER ELEVEN

FACE OF A ROMAN GOD

PATSY

WHAT A WONDERFUL LITTLE park. It has baby swings that Jim Beau can't fall out of, so I slip him down into one, pull him back as high as I can get him, and let go.

He giggles as he climbs in the sky, kicking his feet back and forth. "More, Mommy, more!" Jim Beau shakes the chains attached to his swing. He swings so high the wind blows his cornsilk hair.

After a while, we move to the merry-go-round. I hold him in my lap until I get dizzy and decide that's enough. Jim Beau wobbles drunkenly when I set him down. I do, too, and we both laugh.

I try to see-saw holding him in my lap, but with nobody on the other end that's not a lot of fun for either of us, so I put him down, and he takes off running.

I'm enjoying watching my baby toddle free on the grassy square, laughing with his hands outstretched, grasping at flowers and butterflies, when a man behind me asks, "Your son?"

Startled, I turn to face a man with thick black hair, smooth olive skin, and sharp black eyes framed by black brows and lashes. He has the face of a Roman god.

"Yes," I answer, unprepared for his reaction.

As our eyes meet, his mouth opens slightly. Astonishment overtakes his face. He stares intensely with wide, frozen eyes that finally smile as he says, "I didn't think I would ever see you again."

He's not quite as tall as B.J., but he is striking. He blends the best of B.J. and Al—chiseled Italian features with B.J.'s masculinity. He has thick, broad shoulders and narrow hips. And the way he's looking at me, I... I begin to feel... naked in front of a stranger.

With no response from me, he says, "I can't believe you're here."

"Excuse me?" My heart is racing.

He steps closer. "You don't remember?"

I shake my head, but maybe he looks familiar. He feels familiar. I manage to say, "You can't know me."

"Oh, but I do." His eyes drag from my face to my feet and climb back to my eyes. "A man doesn't forget those eyes."

I turn, bend down, and clap my hands. "Jim Beau! Come here!" The baby toddles to me, and I pick him up, hug him tightly, and face the man again.

It's summer, and he's wearing a long-sleeved white button-down dress shirt. The top button is open, and his cuffs are rolled halfway up his thick forearms. He's also wearing black slacks and black leather lace-up shoes.

I smile at him. He's polite and handsome. I don't feel threatened in any way. If anything, I'm intrigued but also a little intimidated. He is so intense. "That's kind of you. Thank you... for your compliment... about my eyes."

"Ice blue," he says.

I stare and stammer. "I'm sorry, there's a mistake. You can't possibly know me." But, again, something about him feels familiar.

His smile moves from his lips into his eyes. "Oh, yes, sweetheart. I do." His smile exposes a dimple in his cheek. His naturally olive complexion is smooth and bronzed. He spends time outdoors, like B.J.

The two of us stand in silence, lost in each other's eyes for a long moment. His gaze has its own gravity. His is the most penetrating stare I have ever experienced. I feel—I'm not sure what I feel—other than unnerved, which confuses me. Why?

I guess because I'm not sure anyone ever looked at me like that. And he is so, so handsome. I glance away.

The man whispers wistfully, "Colpo di fulmine."

My gaze gravitates back, meeting his, and I shake my head. "I don't understand." I'm pretty lame.

I'm as rattled by his forcefulness, his admiring stare, his ungodly good looks, and his insistence that he knows me as he is shocked at seeing me.

He shakes his head with a gentle smile, not deep enough to show the dimple. "It's not important."

"We're not from here. And you are?"

"Oh, I apologize." He offers his hand to me. "I'm Matteo. Matteo DeVecchio. And you are?"

I take his hand to shake it. "Patsy Cole."

He doesn't shake my hand. Instead, he holds it—frozen in place—as he slowly purses his mouth, like a male Mona Lisa. "Cole." He sighs and glances away for the first time since our eyes met. My hand is still wrapped inside of his. "I see." He sounds disappointed as he tilts his head toward Al's apartment. "I guess... I guess you're married to B.J. Cole?"

I nod and feel my eyes grow wide. How does he know B.J.?

He lifts a shoulder and clears his throat. "I hoped you weren't married." Nothing subtle about him. He aims his thumb behind him. "I saw your husband just now. He's working with me."

I'm sure my eyes flash my surprise. "I beg your pardon?" I pull my hand away from him as I step away.

He looks at his hand for a second and tucks it into the pocket of his pants. I feel bad for the insult; it wasn't intentional, but I'm grasping to comprehend what he just said, and besides, B.J. wouldn't appreciate how long he's held onto my hand. "Say that again."

He recognizes my surprise. "I said your husband is working with us. With me." He tilts his head with his brows pulled together. "Your husband is B.J. Cole, right?"

"Yes. But I'm sorry, Mr. De—"

"Matteo."

"Matteo, there's got to be a mistake. My husband has a job in Texas. We're going back tomorrow."

He lifts his brows and tucks his chin, studying me for what feels like a long while. He lowers his head and peers at the ground.

After a long silence, he shrugs. "Well, then, maybe I misunderstood." He keeps his head down for another drawn-out bit, and when he lifts it, our eyes seem to lock together again, and he smiles, this time sadly. He extends his arms wide and bows slightly in some kind of show of chivalry. "So good to see you again. Good evening, Mrs. Cole."

He turns and strolls down the street as I stand there, staring like a statue.

Those shoes. He was the shorter of the two men who walked by earlier. He mentioned Al. Where's the other one?

As it had done early in the day, when B.J. first told me he had weed in the van's walls, my heart pounds wildly. I clutch Jim Beau against me as my head begins spinning, and my gaze darts around.

What's he talking about? How can he know me? How is B.J. working with him?

CHAPTER TWELVE

GOT TO HAVE HER

MATTEO

I CAN'T BELIEVE SHE'S here. I haven't seen her since the summer of 1969. We were at the Mancini house on Lake Austin. I was sitting alone outside by the pool house after getting a call about a problem with a shipment. I was dealing with that, waiting for return phone calls—not in the mood for company. Until she sat down beside me.

It was a moonlit midsummer night. The young woman came from the house, found a chaise lounge, and sat down, her back to me, crying quietly. She didn't know I was there. She buried her face in her hands. Her shoulders shook.

I studied her in silence as I finished my drink.

She was small. Straight, dark hair fell to her shoulder blades. I watched as she collected herself, took a deep breath, and tilted her head to face the moon, whispering something.

I suddenly felt like a pervert intruding on her private moment. But I was there first. I cleared my throat loudly

79

to let her know she wasn't alone. The courteous thing to do.

She startled, stood, and turned—and her mouth fell.

I smiled at her surprise. I couldn't help myself. She was the first thing to make me smile since we landed in Texas for our annual cluster fuck of a family trip. The Mancinis and their parties.

The girl kept staring—and I was as caught off-guard as she seemed to be—at the magnetic force between us. Those were the most captivating eyes I'd ever seen. Ice blue, shimmering through tears in the silver light of the full Texas moon.

She was stunning—a living porcelain doll with that long, almost-black hair and bangs that covered her forehead, falling into her brows. I got lost in those big blue eyes, and to this day, I remember thinking—*fuck. Mother Mary, can she be real?*

I asked her, "What's the matter, sweetheart? This is a party. Why so sad?"

She blinked, I guess gathering her wits. "Yes, it is a party." She wiped her cheek with her fingertips daintily, her chin tilted high. "Why are you out here alone?"

And I thought then, even in her distress, she is composed. Combative. A feisty little thing. I liked that.

Another plus: I didn't detect a drawl. I hated thick Texas twangs.

I nudged my head toward the house and told her, with all candor, "I don't know any of those people. I prefer my own company to that of fools."

Sitting straight, I swung my feet to the concrete, facing her. She warranted a closer look. "I answered your question. Now you answer mine."

She turned away.

"I'm a good listener," I coaxed.

She finally confided that she saw her boyfriend go into a bedroom with his previous girlfriend. She shook her head, peered at the sky again, and swallowed, saying, "I guess, maybe, I'm the ex now." Fresh tears oozed from those eyes.

That infuriated me.

Seeing any woman hurt pisses me off, much less her. My gaze narrowed. "Would you like me to take care of it? I can, you know. It's kind of my specialty." I remember thinking, not saying, "Give me the go-ahead, sweetheart. I can have that cocksucker in a chokehold in three seconds, on his knees in front of you. Just say the word." After the fiasco in Baltimore, I'd have enjoyed hitting something or someone. Very much.

But she shook her head. Her eyes met mine, still glistening with tears, and she said, "No. If he wants her, he wants her. You can't make someone want you."

She surprised me again—so wise to be so young.

She wasn't needy. Not clingy. She wasn't inside, making a messy scene like most scorned women would. And another plus: She wasn't coming onto me like the Texas wanna-be-richer gold diggers who were inside.

No, this girl had class.

Her face was angelic. She was perfect. Her waist was tiny, exposed with her crop top and hip-hugger jeans. I had a vision of my hands reaching around that teeny waist, drawing her to me. That waist. It curved to beautiful hips. My fingers wanted to dig into them and pull her into me.

But I didn't. Instead, I reached across, squeezed her hand, and stood. "Come here," I said.

Surprisingly, she obeyed and came to me. I wrapped my arms around her tiny shoulders, stroking that long, silky hair, breathing her in. My God. The top of her head didn't reach my chin as she rested her cheek against my chest.

She tilted her face to mine, and I kissed her sweet, soft lips. It wasn't enough. Pulling her to me, my mouth mastered hers, and she went soft in my arms, kissing me back.

The taste of her tongue on mine. Fuck. I'm hard again all these years later thinking of it.

I wanted her. All of her. Every way I could have her. No other woman ever did that to me. Not like that.

I lost her that night. The asshole boyfriend stepped outside and called her name. She left me for him. Fucking killed me to let her go.

I won't make that mistake again.

Chapter Thirteen

WHAT ELSE?

Patsy

WHEN WE GET BACK to the van, I pour Jim Beau a bottle of apple juice and scrounge wildly in my purse. Walking back, it hit me: I'm famished. My stomach is growling.

I have enough money for a hamburger. But I'd never be able to maneuver the van out of the tight parking spot B.J. squeezed us into.

Ironworkers supply their tools, and B.J. keeps his in a metal box attached to the back bumper. That's where he stashed the gasoline can. It makes the van even longer. We're wedged between the car in front and the one behind.

Going somewhere isn't an option with me behind the wheel, so I dig desperately for potato chips or graham crackers, something to put in my stomach. We bought them. They're in here; I just can't find them in my tizzy.

The van door slides open. "What are you doing?"

I flinch and turn, staring for a second. Mute.

I want to scream at B.J. What was that man talking about? You're moving us to Virginia and never bothered to tell me? Like you never told me about the dope in the walls of the van? What else are you keeping from me?

His Mollies have worn off. They don't last that long, but now he's got cocaine in him—how much I don't know, nor do I know how cocaine will affect him. And he's been smoking pot, and I saw him with whiskey. This isn't the time or place for another fight.

I hold my tongue. "We're just... hanging out here. There's a park down the street. We played on the swings and merry-go-round, and Jim Beau got to run a while. You'll thank me later when he falls asleep."

He's leaning in with a hand on either side of the door. "Are you coming back?" That's disappointment in his eyes. I think his feelings are hurt that I left him alone at the party.

I can't believe it.

Jim Beau is curled up on the bed with his bottle of apple juice. "Appy joo," he calls it. He's content to lay still for a few minutes after his playtime.

I stroke the baby's head. "B.J., we can't have him at a party like that. With all those drugs." I give up on finding something to eat and rest my forehead on my hands. "I'm pretty sure at least one guy is tripping."

The guy in the hall was high on acid or mushrooms, or peyote. Some psychedelic.

That idiot could have dropped some tablet on the floor that we didn't need Jim Beau to accidentally find and put in his mouth.

B.J. shoots me a scowl. "Exactly what does it look like when someone's tripping?"

Ooh. That's the wrong thing to say. "Really, B.J.? You're going there?"

B.J. stares blankly—gradually, I see—there it is. He remembers.

I earned my merit badge taking care of him through a bad acid trip in our early days. He and another friend, Dan McCullough, ate some kind of cactus they thought was peyote. It wasn't.

They stayed high for two full days. They were out of their heads. At one point, B.J. wandered into a stranger's apartment and those people would have called the cops had I not been right behind him.

Dan's girlfriend said he mumbled about roses vining around elephants and dogs in trees.

Acid is another drug I want no part of, and B.J. Cole, of all people, should have remembered that. "I had no idea Al was going to be having a party when we got here, especially not one like this."

He sighs. "Neither did I. But, I guess, knowing Al, I should have known."

"Well, you seem to fit right in."

That was hateful. *Why did you say that, Patsy?* My frigging tongue. Maybe I should just cut it off.

I press my fingertips to my eyelids. "I'm sorry, B.J. You didn't deserve that. I know you didn't expect this either. I guess I'm just—I don't know. I'm tired. I'm hungry. I'm sorry."

He sits down in the open van door, his back to me, boots on the curb, elbows on his knees, and slowly rubs both hands over his face.

His shoulders bulge under that brown T-shirt as he unties the ponytail, rolls his neck, runs his fingers through his hair, and pulls it away from his face. He re-ties the ponytail.

For the first time, watching him, I realize how tired he is. Before we left Austin, B.J. worked a long day in the Texas heat, and he'd done all the driving except for those few hours when I relieved him. He'd just been eating Mollies and driving until we got here.

"Daddy!" Jim Beau chunks his empty juice bottle and scrambles into his father's lap.

"Hey, buddy." B.J. holds the baby up high, then sets him in his lap, stroking his head as we sit in silence for a moment. "What do you want to do?"

"I want to go home."

A deep sigh later, he says, "Well, we can't do that tonight." He stands, holding Jim Beau in one arm. "I made a commitment to take Al home. We're going to do that. Besides, I can't unload the pot while the party's going on."

"Who's he selling it to?"

"I don't have a clue." He holds out his free hand to me. "Let's go for a walk."

I'm so tired. We haven't eaten. Just being in Al's smoky apartment, inhaling all that pot and hash, makes me want to go to sleep. But I'm not about to tell him no—not if he wants to be with us over that party crowd.

I climb out of the van, and he closes the door. I give him the keys. He locks the van, tucks the keys in his jeans pocket, and takes my hand, holding it tightly as we walk back to Al's apartment.

B.J. carries Jim Beau in one arm and holds my hand with the other. I'm so glad he's mine.

At the apartment, he passes Jim Beau to me. "Wait here."

Jim Beau reaches and cries for his father, and I tell him, "Daddy will be right back."

I know my son loves me, but if he was old enough to choose? Hands down, he is Daddy's boy.

A few minutes later, B.J. emerges with Al—who is drunker than he was the last I saw him. "Yeah! Let's get some fresh air and take a walk!" He is so frigging loud. "Let me show you around the neighborhood!"

Al is so obnoxious. Slurring and wobbly. What else can he be after smoking pot, snorting coke, and drinking whatever? He's consumed a lot more of everything than B.J., who is maintaining nicely.

I can't tell that the cocaine or whiskey has had any effect on my husband, but getting high and staying high seems to be Al's sole objective, at least on this day.

Six years of college education. He might become the most brilliant lawyer ever, but Al hasn't got an ounce of common sense.

But I argue with myself. Cut him some slack. It's his farewell party after two years here. Stop being a bitch. And cut B.J. some slack while you're at it. For God's sake, let him enjoy this night with his best friend.

We take off walking in the opposite direction from our van and the park I found. It's twilight on one of the longest days of the year. The Virginia sky is showing off a beautiful shade of violet with swirls of pink and orange.

B.J. carries Jim Beau. Al is like our tour guide. His narrative drones on and on about the history of this house and then that house, the Civil War, and the Civil Rights Movement.

Any other time, I'd have appreciated this storied neighborhood with its enormous trees, quaint houses, and antique-looking streetlights.

But perspiration begins beading on my face and upper lip.

I'm woozy-headed.

My ears are ringing.

Oh, I'm... dizzy. They're... getting... ahead... of me.

"Momma!" I hear my baby's voice.

"Pat?" A big hand taps my cheek. "Pat." It's B.J.

I open my eyes. His face comes into focus over me. I see fear in his eyes. "Pat?"

I blink. My gaze roams the sky. It's twilight, and there is a canopy of trees. *Where am I?*

B.J. runs his hand across my forehead, sweeping my bangs back, and wipes perspiration on his shirt.

A street light. I'm on my back. On grass.

B.J. hollers, "Al, get Jim Beau!" He slides his arms underneath me and lifts me like a child, running down the sidewalk, carrying me in his arms.

I hear Jim Beau crying, "Momma! My Momma!"

B.J. leaps up the steps of the brownstone two at a time and kicks open Al's apartment door, which is ajar. He weaves through the crowded living room, me in his arms, people dodging to get out of his way.

He lays me on a bed.

I guess Al was right behind him, because Jim Beau is on the bed. My baby crawls on top of me, sobbing, "Momma."

He buries his head in my breasts, and I wrap my arms around him.

B.J. sits on the edge of the bed, stroking my face. It's still clammy. "Pat?"

Our eyes meet, and I ask, "What happened?"

"You fainted."

I try to push up on my elbow. "I guess, we just haven't eaten." I lay back down, rest my head on the pillow, and close my eyes. Jim Beau crawls higher and nuzzles his head under my chin and I stroke his back, whispering, "Momma's alright, baby boy."

But he's still whimpering. It terrified him, I guess, seeing me crumble and watching his father running with me.

I'm so tired. I'll just... go back to sleep.

B.J.'s voice brings me back. "Al, have you got anything to eat?"

Al. My eyes open.

He's standing in the bedroom doorway, his party guests behind him, gawking over his shoulder. At me.

Al lifts his hands with a grin. "Sorry, man. I've got nothing. I'm packed and ready to go as soon as we clean up the party mess."

Abruptly, B.J. rises. I've seen that menacing stance before. "We your ass, Al. Y'all clean up the damned party mess while I get my family something to eat." He points at me. "She doesn't do drugs. The smoke's so thick in here, she might as well have smoked a joint. She can't handle it."

Al snickers and glances over his shoulder at his leering friends, who are all chuckling. Again, at me. "Damn, bro. You married a lightweight."

They all laugh, and some chick, I think the frizzy-haired blonde who was all over B.J., earlier says, "Little bitch can't hang with the big dogs."

And, again, the group laughs. At me.

My focus is on my husband. Someone should've known B.J. Cole better than that.

One big step and he shoves Al into his friends.

The whole bunch of them stumble backward as B.J. closes the bedroom door behind him and yells. "Get out! The party's over!"

"Fuck you, B.J.! This is my fucking apartment!"

It sounds like something or someone is shoved. Something breaks. Furniture shuffles, and one more time, B.J. shouts, "Out! Everyone! You, get the fuck out! Take this party somewhere else!"

Finally, the music dies. The front door slams. Everything is quiet.

I can't remember B.J. attacking a crowd like that. That—that must be from the cocaine. I don't know. Maybe my fainting scared him, and he overreacted. I'm too weak to worry about it.

He's right. The fainting was from inhaling all of the drugs. And not eating.

I'm sitting up in the bed, my back against the headboard, still holding our son in my arms when B.J. comes back into the room. The best I can tell, he doesn't have a scratch on him.

He says, "I'm going to get us something to eat."

I sit up straight, holding Jim Beau to me. "We can go with you."

With concern on his face, B.J. asks, "Are you okay to walk to the van?"

"I think I'm okay now. Are you okay with Al?"

B.J. looks over his shoulder and sighs. "I'm not sure."

My knight. "Thank you, baby. For taking care of me."

He strokes my cheek and smiles. "I always will, Baby-doll."

———

I haven't the heart or the energy to confront him about what Matteo DeVecchio said.

It makes no sense, anyway. It's a mistake.

We leave the apartment and find a little café not far away, where we eat a real meal. Chicken fried steak, mashed potatoes, and gravy. It's B.J.'s favorite. He devours his food, and so do I.

Jim Beau shares our mashed potatoes and gravy, and we spoon-feed him smushed-up green beans. It's good to sit at a table, eat a real meal, and drink sweet, iced tea. I'm hooked. After tasting this, I will never drink unsweetened tea again.

When we get back to the apartment, Al has the place picked up and straightened. Amazing. I don't know where he is. We don't see him.

We sleep in that front bedroom, in the bed where B.J. set me down.

Chapter Fourteen

His Gift

Matteo

HER NAME IS PATSY. I never knew. The pull to her is—I don't know—overpowering. I once felt her lips on mine. I want to take her into my arms again. I want to inhale her. And this time, when I do, I want to make love to her—mad, passionate love—and I want to feel her love me back.

I want her to give me a son like the one she loves so much. I would love that little boy, too, because he's hers. His eyes are her eyes. I don't care who his father is. I'd love him. Raise him as mine. And we would have more—a house full of children that are from me and her. *She is the one.*

The way she looks at me. A man knows when a woman is attracted to him. I felt it five years ago, and seeing her expression as she took me in this afternoon, I know she felt what I did. I saw it in those ice-blue eyes. She feels the pull, the sparks. But she's shackled to that long-haired loser I saw snorting cocaine in Al's apartment.

Al told me who the driver was.

How much can he love her, bringing her and his son on a drug run? Partying, snorting coke while she and his child are alone at a park. Hell, anyone could steal both of them. If he loves her, he's a stupid idiot. She deserves better.

Pop and I sit in his study and visit over drinks. I prefer Scotch, but Pop always sips sherry after dinner. When I left the park, I headed here to seek my father's counsel, but we couldn't speak privately until after dinner.

In 1969, our business was pressing. My father is capo-famiglia. He had just made me his underboss, running the day-to-day operations, answering only to him. When I returned to Baltimore from Texas, I had to get her out of my head if the family was to survive. I did what I had to do. I shoved that beautiful memory away—until today. It found me. That's got to mean something.

Pop sets down his glass of sherry. "So, this girl, you call her Patsy. She is married?"

"Yes."

He purses his lips. "Marriage is a sacred institution, son. It would be bad fortune to interfere in her marriage, no matter how much you want her."

That's not what I wanted to hear.

"I watched him snort cocaine while she had their baby at the park. Alone. A tiny thing like that—by herself—handling that little boy. You should see her with him. She has so much love inside of her."

Pop scowls and knits his heavy white brows. "So, her husband is a druggie?" He ponders a long moment, his chin on his fist.

"It would appear."

His gaze meets mine. "Is she?"

"She was at the park with her son, not at Al's party. She's been sober both times I've seen her. Her husband is a close friend of Allesandro."

Pop groans. "Allesandro is becoming a problem. Capiche?"

"He was fucked up when Tommaso and I went to his apartment earlier. I told him—we're going to have a talk tomorrow."

Pop repositions in his chair. "And this girl's husband, Al's friend. He uses drugs and drives our product?" His cheeks glow red.

"I don't like it either."

He pounds his fist on the side table. "Our drivers must be sober."

"Agreed."

Pop's gaze dances high above me as he rubs his hand slowly across his jaw. "Allesandro." He tweaks his mouth to the side. "I worry about my sister's son." He aims his drink at me. "You have a lot of work to do if you are to salvage him from this path he is on."

"I'll make that clear tomorrow. That party he has going on—as we speak—could jeopardize this load. If someone calls the cops because the music and crowd are so loud... if the cops arrest his driver... they could impound his van."

Walking to the decanter, I refill my glass. "Are you ready?"

Pop nods and holds out his empty glass. "One more. Do you want him eliminated? The driver?" he asks. "It would be business—not about the girl, but about his not being fit to drive. He agreed to the arrangement. I assume Allesandro told him the rules."

"I'll get a feel for him tomorrow when we pick up the delivery. The delivery we couldn't pick up today, because of Allesandro's party."

Refilling for both of us, I offer his glass back.

Taking it, Pops says, "I leave it to you, son. As far as the girl is concerned, I told you five years ago when you first told me about meeting her—if no one has ever made you feel the way she does—if that chemistry is there—perhaps it is meant to be."

He sips his fresh drink and goes on. "The fact that she showed up here—again? Out of nowhere? Maybe the gods have brought her back to you as a gift." He aims his glass of sherry at me again and raises it high. "If it was me? I wouldn't let her get away."

Yes. Now, that's what I wanted to hear.

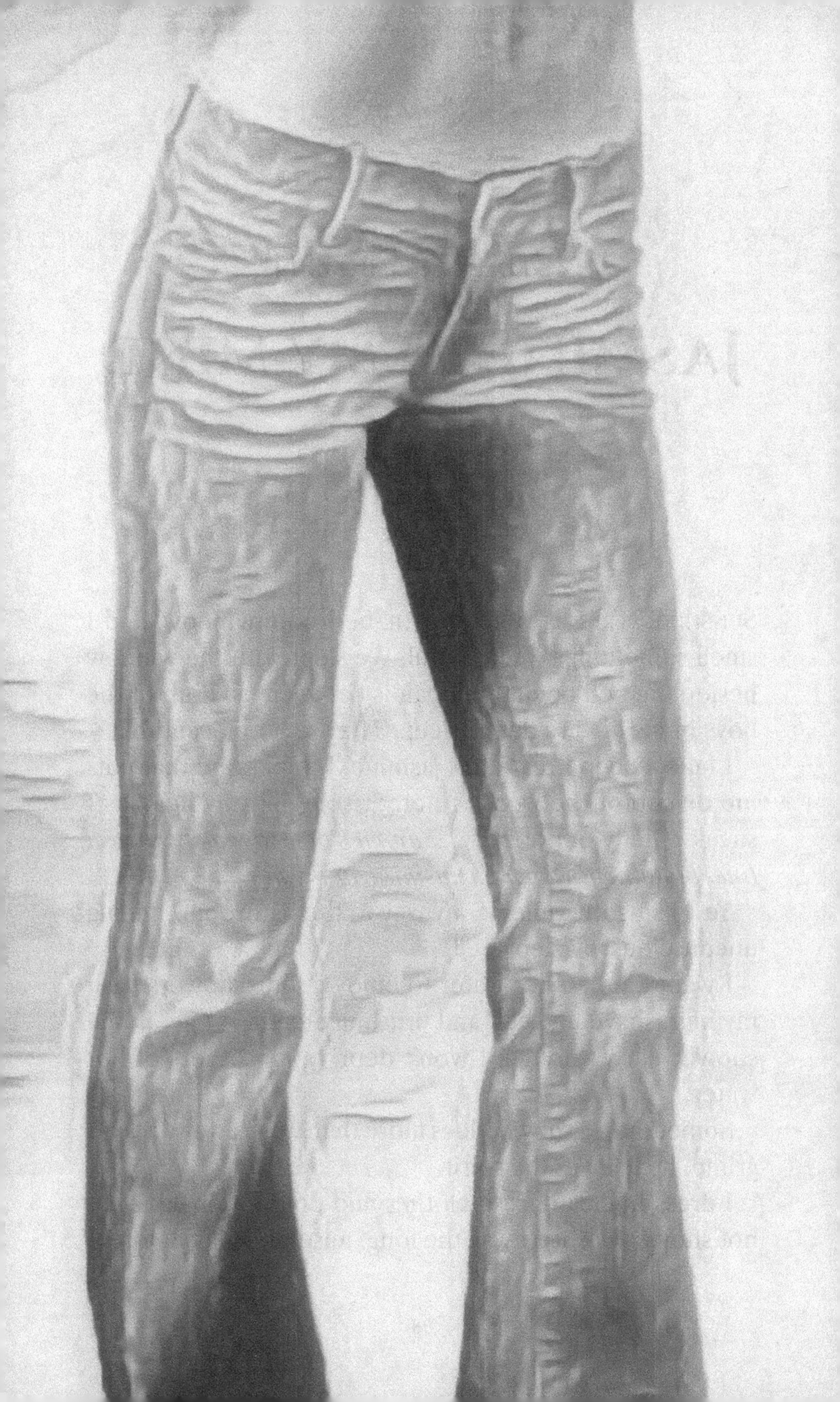

Chapter Fifteen

Jasmine in my mind

Patsy

Sunshine streams through the bedroom window, and I smell something sweet. Floral. We slept with the window beside the bed open. Jim Beau is between us. Both of the boys in my life are deep asleep. They're both beautiful.

I take a deep breath. It's jasmine, I think. And that puts me on top of the world. Another song fills my head as I sneak quietly out of bed. ...*Summer breeze makes me feel fine, blowing through the jasmine in my mind...*

Yes! I sing the tune on my way to the bathroom, smiling unconsciously. I slept well.

I want enough hot water to enjoy a long shower, wash my hair, shave my legs, and brush my teeth. If I get in the shower early enough, I won't deprive the others of hot water.

Sometimes, a shower does more than wash away dirt and grime. It cleanses the spirit.

I dress in clean, fresh clothes and doll up for B.J. That hot shower washed away the long, miserable day before. I dry my hair as best I can with a towel and brush it out. It's going to have to dry the old-fashioned way. I didn't bring my hair dryer on this trip.

I dab on my coconut perfume and even slather on lipstick because this is a special occasion. We're heading home! Yay!

Someone's in the kitchen.

Not B.J.

He's asleep beside Jim Beau.

I close our bedroom door and sit beside him on the edge of the bed, running my hand over his cheek, feeling his two-day stubble. He is so damned sexy.

I kiss him awake softly. His ponytail is loose, his long hair falls around him, and his brown eyes open sleepily.

B.J. smiles and pulls me on top of him. "Get in here with me."

I love his orders. I follow them as long as I want to—and this morning, I very much want to.

His arms engulf me, and he kisses me deeply, his hands already exploring underneath my blouse, caressing my skin. He's already rock-hard against me. "Babydoll, you feel so good." He smacks his lips. "But I need to brush my teeth."

That shower. I'm feeling frisky. I nuzzle his neck and whisper, "You taste fine to me."

That's all the encouragement he needs. Oh, there he goes. His hands are everywhere. They slide down the small of my back into my hip huggers, slipping them off. B.J. has magic hands that make me ache for him inside. He moans into my mouth as I straddle and stroke him against me, and he murmurs, "Babydo—"

Knock! Knock! "Hey! I made coffee!"

We both freeze.

Al is on the other side of the door. "Come and get it!" he yells.

"Dammit," B.J. mumbles through his kiss, but he doesn't stop, and I catch my breath as his hands go exactly where he knows I want them to go.

I come to my senses and pull away. "Al is right there."

"He'll leave." Those hands aren't taking no for an answer. His fingers find my panties and move them aside. "You're wet," he notices.

Uh. Yeah.

But... I force myself to say, "Baby, wait. We'll be home soon."

Of course, that makes B.J. even more determined. He pulls me higher, cups my breast, sucking my nipple into his mouth as he strokes between my legs.

I melt into him. "Oh, B.J."

I don't want to make him stop, but I pull away. Again. I mean, Al is right there.

B.J. growls, accepting defeat and frowns. He sits up on the side of the bed. "I need a shower, anyway. You're all clean."

One intense eye exchange, and we're right back at it. He's got me wanting it as badly as he does. As he flips me onto my back, I wrap my legs around his waist, kissing his neck as he—

Bam! Bam! The door vibrates. "For crying out loud! Coffee's getting cold! And I'm not deaf!"

B.J. sighs and rests his head on mine, chuckling. "He's an only child."

I ogle him as he slips into his jeans, pulls his hair back, and wraps a rubber band around it. He's still bare-chested. *I was so wanting him...*

I sigh deeply and glance at Jim Beau, still asleep on the far side of the bed, as I pull my top down and my jeans up. We are so lucky our baby sleeps so deeply.

B.J. glances over his shoulder to be sure I'm decent, winks and opens the door. Al is standing in it, I guess holding a coffee mug because B.J. says, "Thanks, man," and closes the door behind him.

Al couldn't possibly have seen me. B.J. blocked the doorway with his broad self.

No mention of last night. Knowing those two, they'll let bygones be long gone. Let's duke it out tonight, bro; we're still best friends in the morning.

I take a moment in privacy to straighten myself after our near romp. It doesn't take him long to make a mess of me.

When I walk into the kitchen, they're both at the bar, the same one that had cocaine spread on it last night. Cocaine is something I've never been around, and it was unnerving to see B.J. snorting it. But, oh well. It was a special occasion.

"Good morning, Al." I smile at him. "I'll take some coffee, too, please. Your dishes aren't packed?"

"Dishes came furnished with the place. Pots, pans, and silverware, too. All I furnished were towels and bedding and books." He reaches into the overhead cabinet, pulls out a coffee mug, and pours the steaming brew.

I became hooked on coffee while working on the college newspaper. I was a journalism major. Strong black coffee is a legally acceptable mild form of speed. It never made me grit my teeth and I love it. "It smells good. Thanks."

I'm pleasant to Al. He's not nearly as obnoxious when he's sober as he is when he is drunk and high like he was last night. I'm not letting anything spoil my good mood today. We are going home with an empty van. Woo-hoo!

Except for Al. Ugh.

Nope. Not going there.

"Do you want anything in it?" Al asks.

I was mistaken. He got the first shower. Al is clean and dressed and smells good. I smile at him. "No, I'm good, thanks."

B.J. downs his coffee and kisses the top of my head. "I'm going to clean up." He hands his mug to Al. "Thanks, man." He grabs his shaving kit and a change of clothes from the bedroom and heads for the bathroom.

CHAPTER SIXTEEN

BAD MOON RISING

B.J.

THE SOLITUDE OF THE shower and hot running water is conducive to clearing your head.

Mine needs clearing. That long drive, the Mollies, the coke, the booze, that ungodly fight with Patsy—her fainting, the fight with Al.

Geez. Now I'm like Patsy. I just want to unload this dope and get home, back to our lives.

But... something's off.

What is going on with Al? He's acting strange. It's like I don't even know him, even though I've known him all my life.

He hasn't said a word—not one friggin' word—about the load of weed. I mean, nothing.

He hasn't asked me how it went in Seguin. Hasn't asked me if they weighed it out, if they gave me a receipt. Nothing.

That surprises the shit out of me.

If I paid for a load of weed, I'd want to know I got what I paid for. Is it good shit or stems and trash?

And I'd be damned if I'd let it sit out on the fucking street all night. I'd get it unloaded as fast as I could.

He hasn't said anything about unloading the van.

I want it out.

Where am I supposed to take it? Who is he selling to? Where's the money? I'm out a couple hundred dollars on gasoline and food that I can't spare, and he hasn't offered a dime.

And what was with the fucking party last night? Yeah, everyone knows Al likes to party—but not when you've got a truckload of dope coming in that needs to be unloaded.

Half of those people he had here last night? They weren't in college. Some of them looked like the dregs of the docks. Mainliners. Who is he running around with now? Is he getting too deep into drugs?

God, I hope Al doesn't end up like Danny and John. One is in the pen, and the other is constantly in and out of rehab.

Al is too smart for that.

He didn't spend the night here. I got up a few hours ago to take a whizz, and Al wasn't in the apartment—his bedroom door was open. Bed empty.

I'm guessing he spent the night with the redhead. Maybe she lives in this same building. They fucked all night, high on coke. And I don't care what they do. Except something's not right about our deal. I feel it. Like the other shoe is going to drop.

It's not just last night.

Normally, Al doesn't drag his ass out of bed before noon unless he has a class, and he works damned hard to make sure he has late classes. Eleven o'clock at the earliest.

So, I know my best friend: if he wasn't wired to the gills, he wouldn't already have showered and made coffee, and he damned sure wouldn't be pounding on our bedroom door all antsy at this hour.

Ten bucks says he has a shot of whiskey in his coffee. I smelled it on his breath.

I don't know. And like I said, I don't give a fuck who he does or what he does, except for how it affects us: me, Patsy, and Jim Beau.

I took this risk for money. Yeah, and to bring him back to Texas, but the fact that he hasn't said a word about our deal or going back to Texas—man, it doesn't feel right.

And it hit me, eating dinner last night. Those guys who came into the party—the ones who didn't belong—the ones Al disappeared with outside for a while: the smaller one is his cousin. I forget his name but I've seen him before at the Mancini house.

And if my memory is right—and I'm pretty fucking sure it is—that guy's father is the head of a crime family.

Now, what the fuck was he doing here last night?

Chapter Seventeen

WHO IS HE?

Patsy

WHEN I HEAR B.J.'s shower water running, I waste no time asking Al, "Who is Matteo DeVecchio?"

Al stiffens with his coffee mug in hand. Our eyes are locked. He doesn't answer, which I don't understand.

I repeat. "Matteo DeVecchio."

He averts his eyes, takes a drink of coffee, and peers out the front windows. The wooden blinds are open onto the street.

I push again. "He introduced himself last night and said B.J.'s working with him. B.J. hasn't said anything to me about working for anyone."

Nothing. Al acts like he doesn't hear me.

"Al?"

His black eyes meet mine. "Matty is my cousin. My mother is his father's sister." His gaze narrows. "His dad is Francisco DeVecchio." He pauses as if waiting for a reaction.

I've got nothing.

"Franco DeVecchio," Al repeats emphatically.

Am I supposed to know that name? "Well, Matteo said he knows me. How could he know me?"

Al tilts his head and lifts one shoulder, genuine surprise in those dark eyes. "Hell, if I know, unless you and B.J. came by my parents' house while he was there. Do you remember meeting him?"

I never went to the Mancini house without B.J., so if I met Matteo there, so did B.J.

I sift through memories. Al had plenty of parties when his parents were away and some when they were there. The Mancinis—his father is some kind of famous surgeon—are social, country club party people. His mother plays bridge with B.J.'s mom.

"He called himself Matteo. Is it Matty or Matteo?"

"Matty to his family. Matteo to everyone else." Al rakes his fingers through his hair. He's fidgety. Probably hung over. He rubs his thumb across his lower lip nervously as he says, "Matty was a Golden Gloves champion when he was young. He could have gone pro, but Uncle Francis wouldn't let him get wrapped up in the professional boxing world." He snickers and flicks his brows. "He says boxing is too corrupt."

I polish off my first cup of coffee and help myself to a second, agreeing with Al. "Maybe he was at some event we went to. I don't know. He does seem kind of familiar, but he's older."

"Matty is six years older than I am. What does that make him to you? Eight years older? Yeah, he and his folks could've been at my parents' house when you and B.J.

stopped by. Maybe he saw you there, and you were too starry-eyed over B.J. to notice."

Okay, that could make sense. "What does he do for a living? Why would he say B.J. is working with him? Is he in construction?"

Al chokes on his coffee. I think he must have sucked it down his windpipe. He sputters, then hacks, but he finally clears his throat. "Construction?" He shakes his head and coughs again. "No, I wouldn't call what he does construction."

I'm baffled. "If it's not construction, what is it? Why does he think B.J.'s working for him? Does he need something built?"

Al appears to ponder momentarily, peering into his mug of coffee and then out the window again. Finally, he looks at me and says, "He runs DeVecchio Imports. The family owns an import business. Matty runs the day to day business. Uncle Francis oversees the big picture."

"Oh. Okay, he's a businessman."

"Yeah." Al pours himself another cup of coffee. "A businessman."

Is he smirking?

"Well, that still doesn't make sense. Why would he think B.J.'s working for him?"

"Who thinks I'm working for him?" B.J. rounds the corner from the hallway. His damp hair is pulled back tight in a ponytail at the base of his hairline. He's clean, and he shaved, and he's wearing clean jeans and a fresh T-shirt. It's olive green, which makes his eyes even more striking, and he fills out a T-shirt like no one else.

His eyes are on me, glistening. My husband and I share a covetous glance. If only we hadn't been so rudely interrupted—right now...

I regain my wits, answering B.J. "Matteo DeVecchio. I met him last night. He said you were working for him."

B.J.'s gaze travels to Al. The twinkle is gone. "What's she talking about?"

Nothing. Al's face is as blank with B.J. as it was with me earlier.

What is he hiding?

B.J.'s eyes come back to me. "How did you meet him?"

"In the park, when I was playing with Jim Beau. He came up to me and introduced himself and he said he knew me. And then he said you were working with him."

B.J. faces Al with a scowl. "Isn't he like, your cousin or something? Why did he stop by here last night? He didn't stay and party."

Still nothing.

B.J. and I exchange suspicious glances.

"Al!" B.J. barks. "What's going on?"

"Matty stopped by to check on things, that's all. He was just in the neighborhood."

"Why would your cousin think I'm working for him?"

Al responds with a shoulder shrug. "I told him you'd help him out."

"Okay. I'll help him. How?" B.J.'s thinking the same thing I am. Matteo needs him to build something.

But that's not the way it feels.

Al's gaze shifts from B.J. to me and back to B.J. "Can we talk? In private?" he asks.

B.J. cuts his eyes at me.

I lift my hands, showing them my palms. I couldn't care less. Al is not spoiling my day. "Talk all you want. I've got to get Jim Beau up and bathed so we can go home."

I grab a bottle from the fridge. The cereal is still in the diaper bag.

B.J. pours a fresh cup of coffee. "Okay, Al. What are you not telling me?"

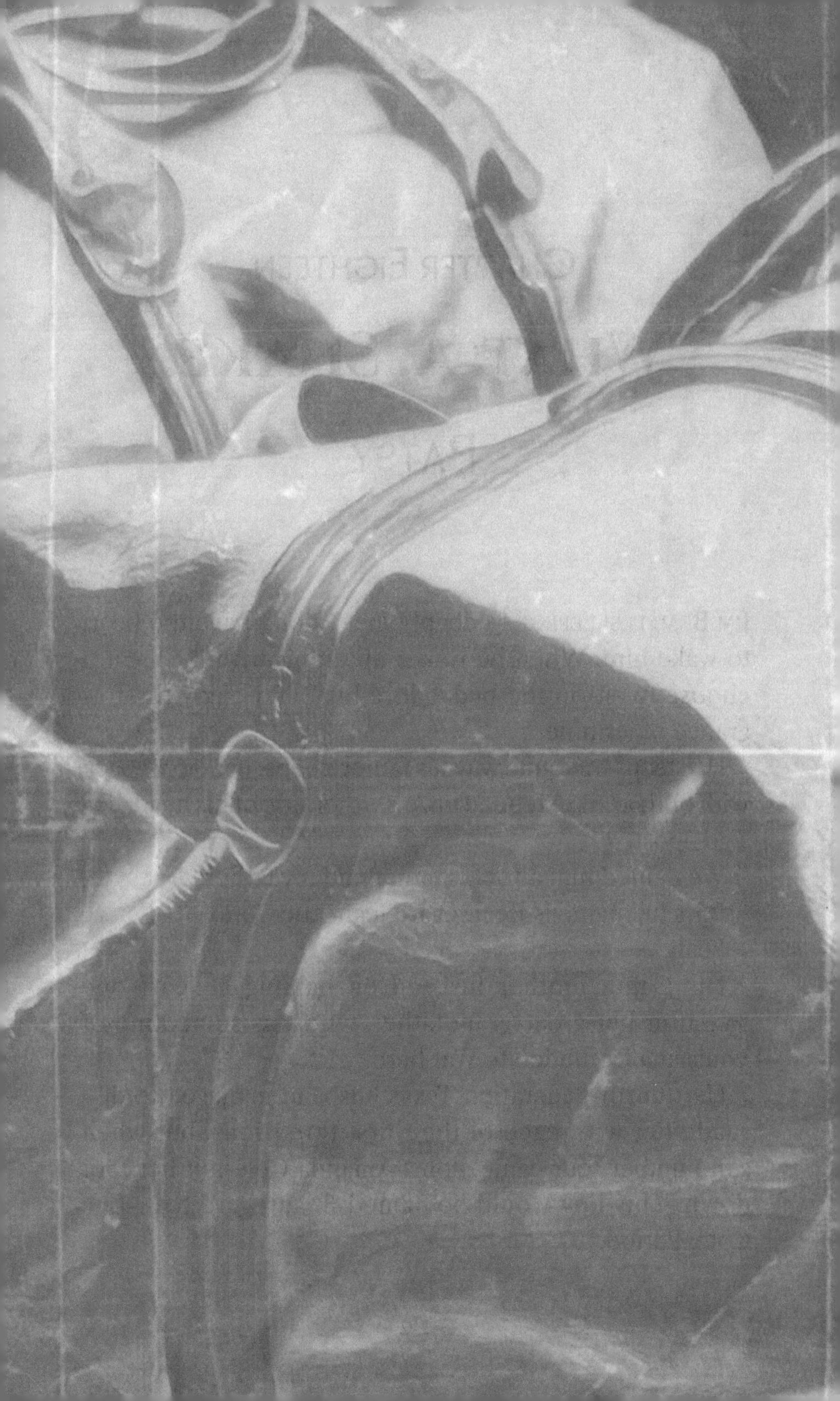

CHAPTER EIGHTEEN

WHAT. A. SNAKE.

PATSY

JIM BEAU IS SLEEPING so deeply that I don't have the heart to wake him. When he wakes up on his own, he'll eat. I choose to sit on the bed, adore him, and enjoy the fragrance of jasmine.

He sleeps the same way his father sleeps: flat on his back with both arms extended up, on either side of his head, like a goalpost.

We named him after his father and my father.

B.J.'s full name is Beauregard Jean-Luc Cole.

Yeah.

His Cajun mother insisted on naming at least one son after her great-grandfather, who was some kind of Louisiana Confederate War hero.

Her fourth-generation Texas husband managed to dissuade her with each of their first three sons, but when son number four came along, Amanda Cole put her foot down. This boy would be named Beauregard Jean-Luc Cole. Period.

I've often wondered if that's not why he is the way he is: named after a famous rebel, how can he be anything but a rebel by birth?

Mr. Cole finally acquiesced, stipulating his son would be called B.J., never Beauregard.

Amanda agreed—until she became furious with her youngest son, at which point he automatically became Beauregard.

My father's first name is James.

So, our son is James Beauregard Cole. James Beau. Jim Beau. I like it. I can guarantee there will not be another Jim Beau when he gets into school. He will grow up to look like his father, I think, only with my light blue eyes, which I got from my father, who got them from his father. I'm not sure who had them before that. Genetics are interesting.

Petting on my baby's face, admiring his beauty and innocence, I'm jolted when the kitchen erupts.

I glance over my shoulder, straining to hear. It's B.J., and he's loud.

I slip out of the bedroom, closing the door behind me so the yelling won't wake the baby.

"I fucking knew something wasn't right." B.J. slaps the countertop. "Dammit, man!" He gets even louder. "Do you have a clue how much money we spent just for the gasoline to get here? It's fourteen hundred fucking miles from Austin to Richmond!"

Al's voice is quieter. "I'm sorry, bro."

I rush into the kitchen. They're standing at the bar, one man on either side, eyeball to eyeball.

"What are you sorry for, Al?" I ask.

They both jump and turn to face me, and I'm transported back to that little park, hearing Matteo DeVecchio say, "Your husband is working with us. With me."

Before that, when I was sitting on the ground as he walked by with the other man who asked, "So you think this dude's reliable?" And Matteo answered, "Allesandro says he is."

I jab my finger at Al, trying to put the pieces together. "Allesandro Mancini, what have you done?"

The two men exchange glances.

Al answers me with his focus on B.J. "Nothing for you to worry about, Pat."

What is it?

"You still haven't said exactly what he expects me to do," B.J. says.

Al flashes a malicious glare. It takes a drawn-out moment to come out, but he finally mutters. "I told him you'd make a couple more runs."

"What?" We say it together, B.J. and me.

Al hangs his head and fidgets on the countertop. He can't even look at us—until he finally does. Al lifts his head defiantly; his dark eyes meet B.J.'s glare, which demands an answer. "I told him you'd make a couple more runs for him."

He said that plainly enough. I still don't know what he's talking about.

"Well un-tell him," B.J. says. "I didn't know this run was for him."

Oh. So, we just made a run.

B.J.'s Italian friend from childhood chews on his lower lip for a moment. Their gazes hold as Al says plain as day, "I can't."

"What do you mean, 'You can't?'" B.J. demands.

Al gets louder. "I mean you don't renege on a DeVecchio. It would be suicide."

What? I'm trying to get my head around this. What on Earth are they talking about?

B.J. lifts his hands. "He's your family, Al. He's not going to hurt you."

Al snorts. "That doesn't make any difference when it comes to this kind of money."

The tendons in B.J.'s neck begin to strain. "Did you lose your fucking mind? You can't commit me to do anything." He slams his palm on the counter again, leans in, and jabs his index finger at Al. "You make a couple of runs. Yourself."

"I don't have a van."

"Buy one. Rent one. I don't give a shit."

Al's arms swing high and wide. "Come on, B.J., it's two trips from Brownsville. Then I'm off the hook." He's as loud as B.J.

"What are you on the hook for?" I ask.

Maybe they forgot I'm still here. Both of them startle again, hearing my question.

With his focus still on his friend, B.J. says, "Tell her, Al, what you're on the hook for."

When Al looks at me, there is no mistaking the loathing in his eyes, having to answer to me. "Twenty grand."

I'm stunned.

B.J.'s voice has a new edge to it. "Now, explain to my wife what kind of runs you told him I'll make."

"Fuck you, B.J."

"Tell her."

Al faces me again. "He's going to make a couple of drug runs."

I feel my eyes about to pop out of my head. "Oh, B.J. I don't want you driving pot again."

B.J.'s gaze is still trained on Al as his upper lip curls. "He's not talking about pot."

It's not sinking in. I've got nothing.

I stare at Al, who sighs in apparent disgust at my ignorance. "A load of weed sells for a fraction of what blow or smack can bring."

I turn to B.J. for an explanation.

"Cocaine and heroin, Pat."

My scalp tingles. I feel numb. *Cocaine and heroin.* How could a man as educated and sophisticated as Al get mixed up in that world?

And the handsome man in the park—he's part of it, too?

A horrifying thought flashes through my mind, followed by an equally paralyzing fear. My husband, that man I love, the father of my child who I was just wallowing with in bed—the guy who snorted cocaine with Al last night—has one foot inside a heroin and cocaine world. *Oh. My. Lord.*

And he's dragged us in here with him.

I may be sick. It's not just pot. It's heroin and cocaine.

Okay, drugs are a part of our world. They just are. Weeds, whites, and wine. B.J. calls them recreational drugs. But cocaine and heroin? They're in a different sphere, as bad or worse than crystal methamphetamine.

Those hard drugs ruin lives. Destroy families. Using them, transporting them, selling them? That's serious prison time. I mean, like, a life in prison time.

Al twists his neck and shifts his shoulders as if they're sore, maybe from their scuffle last night. He throws a nasty sneer at B.J. with his eyes narrowed into slits. "Who the hell do you think furnished last night's blow? Do you think it grows on trees?"

B.J.'s absorbing the remark when Al throws a second punch—verbal—the only kind he's capable of throwing. "That was Matty's reward for a job well done—a clean delivery. Seems I noticed you enjoying a snort or two, bro."

B.J. cuts his eyes at me, and his face flushes.

My mouth. I can't keep it shut. "Do you honestly think your cousin would hurt you if B.J. doesn't do whatever it is you're talking about?"

This has become terrifyingly preposterous.

Al scoffs at me. He moves his head slowly back and forth and runs both hands through his black hair. "I'm not taking any chances. You two don't know my family."

I guess my face is blank. It's such a contradiction to the man I thought I met in the park. "But he seemed so nice."

Al snaps. "My aunt's husband's family—the DeVecchio family," he stresses the name again like it's supposed to mean something to me. It doesn't. "They run the mid-Atlantic. Do you understand?"

Clearly, I don't.

Al tries again. "De...Vec...chi...o." He closes his eyes and shakes his head.

B.J. clears his throat. "They're the Mafia, Patsy."

The Mafia. Now, I feel nauseous. That good-looking man is part of the Mafia? And he hurts people?

Al is still looking at me. "Maybe I got in over my head a little."

"That doesn't explain why you'd commit your best friend to do something without asking him."

For the first time, Al hurls his frustration at me as he points to B.J. His normally handsome face twists as he rants. "Because he's been my best friend since the fifth grade, and I thought I could count on him helping me out of a jam."

"A jam you got yourself into." I turn to my husband. "B.J., you won't run illegal drugs for the Mafia. Please tell me that's not crossing your mind."

B.J. holds up his palm, cutting me off. Our eyes meet. "It's not," he says, "But I need a minute. Just let me think."

Al snickers. "What are you going to think about? About how to bury me?"

"You dug your own grave!" I know. I'm loud. My worst fears about Al Mancini are real.

"Pat, I'll deal with it." Oh, my. That fast. B.J.'s tone makes me feel like I dove into ice water. I shiver as B.J. looks from me to Al and clenches his mouth. "Both of you just give me a goddamned minute."

He walks out of the apartment and closes the door tightly. Not with a slam, just a firm tug.

I open the bedroom door and peek in. Jim Beau's still asleep.

As I close the bedroom door and return to the kitchen, I discard the disingenuous cordiality I'd draped myself in since we got here. "You snake in the grass." I point at the door B.J. just closed. "He drove across the country to bring you home and this is how you reward him? He spent our money for all—"

"Excuse me?" Al's brows are high, his eyes wide, like he's looking down his nose at me.

"He said—"

Al shakes his head with his know-it-all snarl. "I don't think you get it, sweet cheeks. Matty paid for the marijuana. B.J. just delivered it."

So that's what he was talking about when he said B.J. was working with him. The wind goes out of my sails. I sink into the couch. "Did B.J. know that?"

"He does now." Al kicks the cabinet under the bar, and I flinch as a door bangs loudly.

He shouts, "Son of a bitch!" And as if in punctuation, he slaps an overhead cabinet door with his palm. It bangs, too. "This is so fucked up!" He grips his head as he turns in a frustrated circle and kicks the bar again.

It bangs like before. "It's because of you!" Al points at me. "If it wasn't for you, Little Miss Goody Two Shoes, this wouldn't be happening. If it wasn't for you, B.J. would help me."

Now, I am flummoxed. My mind is still back on our van being full of Matteo's pot. "B.J. thought he'd make money. Right?"

"Of course. I told him we'd split 50/50 when we sold it. And we will."

"But if Matteo paid for it, how do either one of you get 50/50?"

He lasers me with his glare. "B.J. gets half of my share."

"And what's your share?"

He lifts his hands. "I'm not sure, Pat. I set up the deal because I was in a bind. I got in too deep, okay? Matty promised me a fair share when it's sold."

He moves around the bar toward me. His gloves are gone, too. "I never dreamed I'd see the day B.J. Cole would let himself be henpecked." He aims his arm at the door. "We were brothers, for crying out loud! Before you, he wouldn't have thought twice about making a couple of runs to help me out. Now? You've got him so fucking pussy whipped it makes me want to puke."

If anyone is upstairs, they could be taking notes.

Al is getting louder with each breath. "For the life of me, I can't understand the decisions he's made." He's still pointing at the door. "B.J. could have been anything he wanted to be, had any woman he wanted—and what does he do? Drops out of college, goes to work like a fucking laborer, and marries you. Fuck!"

He slaps the countertop and aims at me. "And you start spewing out kids to make sure you keep him tied down. What's he got to look forward to the rest of his life but working his ass off all day every day and coming home to a house full of crying kids and a nagging little..." He bites his lower lip, glaring at me, deciding whether to say it, then spits it out: "Bitch."

Let the name-calling begin.

"You condescending son of a bitch. You think because you have all these degrees, and he doesn't—because you push papers around while he pushes steel—that he's less than you?" I jab my finger at him as I step closer. "You don't hold a candle to B.J. You can't do anything but run your mouth. You can't fix a faucet or a light switch—you have to hire someone to do it for you. You lawyers and doctors and bankers wouldn't have buildings to work in if men like B.J. didn't build them. You idiot. He is exactly who he wants to be—because, unlike you, he has a backbone."

I can't resist. My snide takes over. "He told me you wanted to be a musician, but Daddy wouldn't allow it. That's probably why you're such a fucking drunk. And yes, I'm sure he could have married someone prettier or more glamorous—but he didn't. He chose me, and we were doing just fine until you came back into our lives. You—" I stop myself, hearing the front door swing open.

We both turn to see B.J. carrying two oversized canvas duffle bags.

It is easy to see by the way he handles them; with his forearms and biceps bulging, they're heavy. Maybe he emptied the van.

"Here, Al." B.J. slings both duffle bags on the kitchen floor and tilts his chin at them. "Unload that shit and I'll get the rest."

The rest? My Lord, how much pot is in our van if it won't all fit in those two gigantic canvas bags?

B.J. demands, "Exactly, how much do you owe them, Al?"

"I told you. About twenty grand." He's not looking at B.J.

"About? More or less?" B.J. barks.

Angry eyes meet angry eyes. "Not more," Al hisses.

B.J. peers at me. "Okay. We'll get a loan from the bank." He turns back, speaking directly to Al. "You can pay me back."

I gasp loudly. "B.J., if we could get a loan for twenty thousand dollars, we'd buy a house!" Yes, the neighbors are getting an ear full of me, too.

"Dad will co-sign for me if he has to. I know he will."

My voice gets an octave higher and louder. Listen up, neighbors. "Why can't his parents get a loan for twenty thousand dollars?"

B.J. snaps at me hard and cold, but the thing is, he's not loud. It feels more dangerous than the shouting. "Pat, it's like he said. He's been my best friend for as long as I can remember. I'm not going to let my best friend get killed if I can stop it. This is the only way I can think of to stop it."

I open my mouth to protest, but when B.J. holds up that hand, I know there's no point.

He says, "I'm not going to work for them. I won't risk going to prison hauling drugs." He aims his arm at Al with his eyes on me. "But I'll never forgive myself if he gets killed, and I could've stopped it."

Al and I exchange glares, and I want to wipe that cocky smile off his face.

There you have it. The room is filled with an uncomfortable silence, which Al finally breaks. Maybe B.J.'s words humbled him. "I appreciate the offer, bro, but I'm not sure they'll agree to that."

Maybe it was B.J.'s declaration of friendship. I don't know why, but Al's tone is softer, and I catch a flash of humanity in those dark orbs as he says, "I'm sorry, B.J."

Are you? Or are you just playing on B.J.'s sympathy? I don't trust a word that comes out of Al Mancini's mouth.

B.J. draws up to his full height, tall and straight, his face like stone. "I'm sorry, too, Al, because I'm not driving drugs for you or them. I thought this trip was for us." He moves his hands between them. "Fifty-fifty. I never planned on another."

I knew it.

Al breaks out his trademark patronizing sneer. "Now, how the hell did you think I'd get enough money to pay for that much dope?"

B.J. shouts at Al. "The same way you get everything else. From your fucking parents. I had no idea I was hauling somebody else's weed for pennies to be paid in the future. Hell, we're going to have to coast back to Austin on fumes."

Al presses against his eyes with the heels of his hands and tilts his head back like he's thinking. "Maybe I can use your van."

What a horse's ass.

Did he not just hear what B.J. said? Thanks to his double-cross, we might not have enough money to get home. We at least have to feed the baby, even if B.J. and I don't eat.

"Rent your own van. I didn't sign up for this." B.J. is his unmovable self. "I'm not doing it. Now hurry up. I want to get everything out of the van so we can get out of here."

Desperation crosses Al's face. His dark eyes dart about the room, settle on B.J., migrate to me, and then back to B.J. He's like a cornered animal. For the first time, Al sees his plan is falling apart. B.J. is not going to make another run like this.

Al slaps the bar top with his open palm. "You don't understand, man. They will kill every one of us over twenty thousand dollars."

I've stopped trying to hold my tongue. "I just don't see Matteo DeVecchio as a killer."

My remark paralyzes Al.

Slowly, his hateful gaze leaves B.J. and travels to me, staying there. "Are you that naïve or just ditzy?"

I might be naïve, but no one ever called me ditzy.

B.J. raises his hands in exasperation. "What do you want me to do, Al? I'm not getting in bed with the Mafia. How do you not understand that?"

"Buddy, you're already in bed with them."

Fast as a whip, B.J. grabs Al by his shirt and draws him close.

Al keeps blabbering as he tries to push B.J. off of him. "You got in bed with them when you loaded that weed in your van."

B.J. shoves Al, who loses his balance and stumbles backward over the duffle bags. B.J. saves him from falling by snatching his shirt again. He lifts Al and slams him against the wall. "Get your shit. We're getting out of here."

"They know your name, B.J. They can find you, even—"

Whop! A thunderous right hook hammers pretty boy's jaw. Did B.J. take more Black Mollies? Maybe. Maybe not. Finding out your best friend Shanghaied you into working for the mob—that alone could do it.

B.J. glances at me. "Get everything. We're getting out of here."

I run to the bedroom, gather Jim Beau, waking him abruptly, grab the diaper bag, our clothing bag, and my huge purse, and run back into the living room.

B.J. holds up his hand. "Wait. We can't leave until I get the rest of that shit out of the van. Hurry up Al, get that unloaded."

Al leans with both hands on the bar.

B.J. yells at him, "Come on!"

Al wipes blood from his mouth with the back of his hand and shakes his head, trying to get the cobwebs out, I guess. He seems dazed.

An undeniable sadness tinges his face, darkening his eyes. He's defeated. "Give me a minute." Al looks around for something he can use to wipe blood dripping from his mouth.

I grab a clean cloth diaper from the bag and offer it to him.

He dabs his lip with it, opens the freezer door, reaches in, and drops a handful of ice cubes into the bloodstained diaper, holding it against his lip and jaw. "Matty likes me," he mutters. "He'll probably let me do something else if he can convince his old man. Which he probably can. Like you said, I'm blood."

"Do something else like what?" B.J. asks.

Al flicks his brows and flashes that familiar grin, only this time he has blood on his teeth. "Hey, the family always needs good lawyers."

CHAPTER NINETEEN

A FORGOTTEN MEMORY

PATSY

WHEN B.J. GRABS THE two empty canvas bags to return to the van, he tells me, "I've got about two more loads, and we'll get out of here."

That prompts another wave of nausea. I had no idea we had that much in our van. What would have happened had we been caught?

He swings open the apartment door to leave, and I almost lose the contents of my stomach—gagging on bitter coffee—seeing Matteo DeVecchio standing there with his fist raised, about to knock on the door.

Two goons flank him, each a head taller than Matteo and even wider. Both are dark and ominous, like thunderheads rising behind the lightning.

Both are wearing shoulder holsters with guns. Never in my life have I seen anyone wearing a gun, certainly not someone at my door. The only people I know who wear guns are policemen.

The men behind Matteo aren't policemen.

Not one of them smiles until Matteo flashes B.J. a disingenuous grin. "Good morning. May we come in?" His mouth is smiling, but his eyes are not—and that's not a question.

I never knew Al could move that fast. He's out of the kitchen, across the living room, shoulders past B.J., jerks the door out of his hand, and swings it open wide. "Come in."

Matteo steps inside the apartment and surveys the room. His gaze lingers on the cellophane-wrapped bricks of pot stacked on the kitchen counter. I guess that answers B.J.'s question about why he was here last night. He came by to make sure his product arrived. Today, he's here to collect.

One of the bodyguards steps inside behind him. The other remains in the doorway, stone-faced, arms crossed over his chest, blocking our exit.

I study Matteo DeVecchio, trying to reconcile the gentle, well-mannered man I met in the park yesterday with this man, whose persona is suddenly so intimidating.

Unlike yesterday—here, inside this room—his presence is menacing.

I lean against the arm of the couch as my knees tremble.

I'm not sure what I see cross B.J.'s face, but I don't read it as fear. He snatches the door away from Al and closes it in that third man's face. B.J. sets the canvas bags on the floor and faces Matteo squarely.

They are both thick through the shoulders. B.J., with his long hair, T-shirt, and jeans, stands eye to eye with Matteo, who looks like he just stepped out of Neiman Marcus, dressed in tan from head to foot.

B.J. doesn't flinch. "I don't care who you are or who told you what. I'm not a drug mule. I have a family, and we're not a part of your world."

Matteo is like ice, glaring at B.J.

Dry ice inflicts a wicked burn.

"Yes," he replies. "I met your family last evening." His face betrays no emotion. His gaze strays from B.J. and settles on me as I stand near the couch, clutching Jim Beau, who is still not fully awake.

I'm frozen, staring back at him.

"You married above yourself, Mr. Cole, if you don't mind my saying so." Matteo drags his eyes from my face to my feet, and I feel naked in front of him. Again.

I look to B.J. for help as Matteo's black eyes devour me like he's dragging me into a black hole. "Beautiful. Petite. And those eyes. My, my, my." He scratches his neck under his left jaw and flicks his fingers. "Colpo di fulmine."

He said that yesterday. I still don't know what it means.

The bodyguard and Al exchange glances, and neither hide their surprise at hearing it.

Al cuts his dark eyes at B.J. That is bonafide fear I see on Al Mancini's face. He is most definitely afraid of his cousin. He was not bullshitting about that.

I see no fear in B.J. My husband's eyes flash, and I can't breathe, seeing his rage, but I know, if there's ever been a time to keep my mouth shut and trust him, this is it. He is a foreboding figure himself. "What did you say?" B.J.'s brows draw tight as he glares at Matteo and points at me. "What did you just say about my wife?"

Matteo shakes his head slightly, dismissing B.J., and he repeats what he said yesterday when I asked the same question. His eyes still on me, he says, "It's not important."

"The hell you say." B.J. tilts his head at Al. "I saw how they reacted. What did you say? What does that mean?"

Al mumbles through his swelling jaw, "Colpo di fulmine. It's the Sicilian thunderbolt... Matty's saying... he's in love with Patsy." He stares at his older cousin in disbelief.

Matteo snaps around and scowls at Al, who tries to clean up his mess. "Maybe you two met at my parents' house. Maybe at some party."

No one speaks.

All eyes are on Matteo as he nods slowly. "Yes, Allesandro, she was at your swimming pool, alone and crying." He turns back to face me and tilts his head to the side. "Now, do you remember, sweetheart?"

As I gasp, my eyes grow, probably wider than Al's. "It was you."

Yes. I remember. No wonder he feels so familiar.

Matteo approaches me and says, "I held you in my arms. I wiped your tears. I asked you what was wrong, and you said your boyfriend was with another girl."

I'm too stunned to respond. I never told B.J. about that. He's hearing this for the first time—from someone else.

My hand covers my mouth, my eyes wedged wide, locked on Matteo's.

B.J. and I hadn't been together but a few weeks, but I was already crazy about him. We went to a party at Al's parent's house. B.J.'s former girlfriend was all over him, and it didn't look like he was fighting her off. They disappeared into a bedroom, and I just knew she was going to give him what he wanted. What I wouldn't give.

Numb, I slipped into the backyard, trying to breathe.

I was startled by a sound behind me and turned to see a man so gorgeous that I thought he was a dream. I could see him clearly in the full moon, stretched out on a lounge chair, one arm tucked behind his head, watching me.

"What's the matter," he asked. "This is a party. Why are you outside alone, crying?" Something about him oozed authority, wealth, and sophistication, like some European prince—and he could've been one, given the way he was dressed and the rich people in Dr. Mancini's circle. "I'm a good listener," he said when I didn't answer.

We ended up talking, and I told him what I had seen.

He offered to 'take care' of it for me, and I remember wondering, at the time, what he meant by that. Now I know.

I told him no. "If he wants her, he wants her. You can't make somebody want you."

He stood and opened his arms. "Come here," he said, and I did. I let him wrap his arms around me, and to my surprise, it felt wonderful. My world had just crashed down around me. B.J. had cast me aside, and out of nowhere, this handsome man made me feel desired.

Resting my head on his chest, as I had B.J.'s, I realized—his was the wrong chest. "I need to go back inside," I said.

"Why?" The handsome man gripped me by my shoulders, lowering his eyes to peer into mine. "If he was worth your tears, he'd be out here right now looking for you." He paused, those mesmerizing eyes searching my face as if waiting for a reply that didn't come. He whispered, "I would be. A beautiful girl like you."

I knew he was right. If B.J. wanted me, he'd be looking for me, and just like that, I wasn't hurt anymore. I was furious. I had to find B.J. He owed me an answer.

I stood on tiptoes to kiss his cheek, to say goodbye, but when I did, he turned, and my kiss landed on his lips.

He pulled me into him with a hunger I never felt with anyone but B.J. His kiss was ravenous but sensuous. *Truth?* I didn't just let him kiss me. I kissed him back, lost for those seconds in him.

To this day, I'm not sure why. Did I kiss him because I was mad at B.J.? I don't know. He... just felt good.

But B.J.'s voice shattered the handsome prince's spell. "Patsy!" he yelled.

Stepping into the darkness, B.J. couldn't see me in the arms of someone else. "Patsy, are you out here?"

My heart leaped into my throat at the sound of B.J. calling for me. I pulled away from the kiss, glanced over my shoulder at B.J., and turned back to this sexy man who appeared out of nowhere. "He is looking for me," I said. "But thank you."

And I ran to B.J. That was it.

I didn't know his name, and he didn't know mine. We simply shared a moment of—*what?* Why had I never told B.J. about him? Why did I kiss him?

"Patsy?" B.J.'s voice does it again, pulling me back to reality. He peers at me, bewildered by our remarks and my subsequent silence as I recalled the chance encounter.

Breaking free from Matteo's gripping gaze, I see astonishment and hurt in my husband's eyes. My cheeks flush with shame for what I felt that night five years ago and maybe what I felt yesterday.

They were fleeting moments, yes, but I had been intrigued by and mysteriously drawn to Matteo DeVecchio on two different occasions. And I hid it from B.J. both times.

Instinctively, I do what I always do with B.J. I confess. "It's true. I forgot. Remember? It was when you and Linda went into a bedroom."

Shock sweeps across B.J.'s face, replaced by full-on anger. "We straightened that out," he says loudly. "You misread what you saw, remember? It was all a misunderstanding."

His face. His eyes. They are filled with confused indignation.

Our eyes are locked now, mine and B.J.'s, and all I have to offer is, "I'm sorry, baby. I know." We hashed that out years ago.

He's defensive. "I wasn't interested in Linda. I told her—that night—and I told you, too. I married you, Patsy."

Matteo smirks at me, his brows lifted high. "So, you never told him, did you, sweetheart? You didn't tell him you fell into my arms? Or that you kissed me?" He turns to

B.J. and snarls. "And you—you took another woman into a bedroom at a party you brought her to." His eyes come back to mine. "That would never happen if you were with me. I told you then that you deserved a better man."

B.J. goes on the offense. "The only reason I took Linda into the bedroom was to make it clear to her that I was with you, Patsy. I didn't want a scene in front of other people. And trust me, it was the right move. She made a scene."

Matteo continues to ignore B.J. as he steps toward me. "Patsy, men don't take women into bedrooms to talk."

I'm stunned. Speechless. Never in my wildest dreams...

B.J. interrupts my thoughts again, crossing the room. "Maybe you don't. But I did." He wraps his arm around my shoulder, pulling me to him tightly. His eyes are locked on Matteo's. "You missed your chance, bud. We're married." He gestures at Jim Beau in my arms. "And he is our son. Now butt the fuck out."

Jim Beau is amazingly quiet for a baby who'd just been so abruptly awoken. Maybe even at his age, he senses the tension.

His little blue eyes are glued to his father, who says, "Let's get back to today. Al says he owes you money. I'll pay you what he owes. He'll pay me back."

Matteo's brows lift slowly, and he keeps them high as his stare migrates slowly from B.J. to Al. "Now, Alessandro, that's what I call a good friend."

He has the same condescending laugh as Al, as his black eyes return to B.J. "I'd say that's a very... friendly... gesture... *bud.*" His gaze narrows threateningly. "But we don't work that way. An offer was made. An offer was accepted."

It is becoming clearer to me why Al is afraid of him.

But still, B.J. isn't. He responds with angry dismay. "A man like you. You're telling me you can't find anyone but me to move drugs for you?"

Matteo holds up his index finger and wags it, clicking his tongue. The gazes are locked like horns. "No. I did not say that. I said an offer was made. An offer was accepted. Arrangements have been made."

B.J. swings his free arm and points at Al. "He didn't have the right to make that offer."

"That's between you and him." Matteo's gaze returns to me, lingering there.

B.J. steps in front of me, shielding me from Matteo's eyes as he growls through clenched teeth. "Keep your fucking eyes off my wife."

Before I can blink, Matteo's goon whips his gun from the holster and aims it at B.J.

"Think twice before you threaten me." Matteo's icy tone terrifies me, but still, I do not feel fear emanating from B.J. No, his body trembles with rage.

A quick step and the big goon shoves the gun barrel against B.J.'s temple as Al yells through his clenched jaw. "Dammit, B.J.! Stop it! I tried to tell you. You wouldn't listen."

Not an hour earlier, I said I didn't see Matteo DeVecchio as a killer, and Al called me ditzy.

I was.

I quiver, witnessing the reality of who this man is.

Another thick silence blankets the room. My forehead is buried in B.J.'s back as I clutch our baby, but over his shoulder, I see that silver gun barrel pressed to the side of my husband's head.

CHAPTER TWENTY

THE DEVIL'S DEAL

PATSY

MATTEO MOVES TO THE couch, starts to sit, then stands and shifts his gaze to Al. "May I?"

Al nods. His eyes are still saucers.

As he sits, Matteo addresses B.J., "Let's all calm down and assess the situation. Tommaso, you can lower the weapon."

The goon, Tommaso, steps back and slowly lowers his gun, his gaze glued onto B.J. Tommaso is a monstrous man with shoulders as broad as the door, and he glares at B.J. as if my husband was a cobra ready to strike his boss.

He would be—if it weren't for that gun. It's hard to ignore.

Matteo coaxes. "Let cooler heads prevail."

Nobody moves.

"Please." He waves his arm across the room. "Have a seat."

The way he says it. That's no request.

Outside, people stroll down the sidewalk on a sunny summer day, laughing and smiling, oblivious to the nightmare playing out inside this room.

I am terrified for B.J., and I am ashamed to face him.

My heart is in my throat. I caused this. This is all my fault. I have given Matteo the wrong impression. He is unnervingly handsome, yes. His piercing gaze and insistence that he knew me were—I don't know what. Unsettling? Intriguing? Almost overpowering.

But I never imagined him in B.J.'s place—not in 1969, and not yesterday.

I need to clarify this.

Slowly, I move and sit in the wingback chair by the window, holding Jim Beau in my lap as B.J. moves and stands behind the chair. "Matteo?"

His black Italian eyes meet mine. He has the same cupid lips and chiseled face as Al, but his jaw is stronger.

I have to make him understand: "I love my husband."

His expression is stoic, but I swear disappointment sweeps through his eyes for a nanosecond. Pain and disappointment are not emotions Matteo DeVecchio will allow anyone to see.

He lifts one shoulder nonchalantly. "Quello ciò che sarà sarà."

I cut my eyes at Al, who does not translate, so Matteo says in English, "What will be, will be." He bends forward, his forearms on his thighs, his hands clasped in front of him.

With his penetrating gaze, I feel like he's trying to crawl inside my head as he says, "Sweetheart, I will give you anything and everything your heart desires."

B.J. growls. "That's fucking enough."

Matteo flashes him a malicious grin. "Just so there are no misunderstandings."

He hides his pain and disappointment but has no problem admitting desire. Him—a Mafia boss. He says things most men are afraid to say. He just puts it right out there, unembarrassed and unapologetic. I've never seen or imagined anyone like him.

And poor B.J. is having to watch it. Hear it. Endure.

I peer over my shoulder at my husband and see murder in his eyes.

What would I do if I were in his shoes? How would I behave if some woman fawned all over B.J. in front of me, telling him she'd do anything to have him? Even worse, if I learned of some connection between them that B.J. hid from me?

I'd pull her hair out and give him a piece of my mind.

For the sake of my marriage, I've got to clean this up.

My eyes leave B.J. and return to Matteo. "Matteo, I'm sorry if I gave you the wrong impression. I love B.J. He and I—we're together. Forever."

"Forever?" His snicker is almost a laugh. "I don't think so."

Realizing I'm not getting anywhere, I pivot. "If it's okay, I need to change the baby. He hasn't eaten."

He presses his thumb and forefinger against his eyelids. "Patsy, you have nothing to fear from me. Tend to your child."

He doesn't understand. I have everything to fear from him. If he hurts B.J., he hurts me.

But I'd be overstepping to interject myself into what's happening between them any more than I just did. I've made it clear to him and everyone in the room: I'm not interested. I love my husband. Now, it's between the two of them.

"Thank you." I glance over my shoulder and up at BJ., trying to tell him I love him with my eyes, but he's not looking at me. His gaze is fastened onto Matteo, who glares back at him from the couch.

I grab the diaper bag from the floor beside me and carry Jim Beau into the bedroom, leaving the door open so I can hear.

It sounds like B.J. takes the empty chair, sitting directly across from Matteo. Even through the bedroom wall, I feel the ungodly strain, like the room might explode any moment.

They are two bull elk circling each other, heads down, antlers threatening. One is trying to claim the other's mate. Those battles always end in death, and I have no doubt B.J. would like to see Matteo dead just as much as he wants B.J. gone.

But B.J. Cole is not a killer.

I know now—Matteo DeVecchio is.

How could I have misread anyone so badly? He seemed so kind and gentle. Seemed. Past tense. Matteo DeVecchio is exactly how Al described him.

I listen to their conversation as I change Jim Beau, wondering how I let this happen. I never intended to convey to Matteo that I was interested in him that way.

"So, you're a Texas cowboy." It's not a question but rather a declaration by the mob boss.

B.J. emits a condescending snort. "Not everyone in Texas is a cowboy."

"You wear boots."

"Work boots. I'm a common working man," B.J. says.

"Well, your wife certainly deserves more than a common man."

"Damn, man, leave my wife out of this." B.J.'s not loud anymore. He has turned as cold as Matteo. "She just told you she loves me. Now get the fuck over it."

"But do you love her? Are you good to her?"

Leaving Jim Beau on the bed drinking his bottle, I move into the hallway to see B.J. bristle. "Who the fuck are you to ask me that? Yes, I love her and our son. And get this straight, motherfucker: There's no room for you in our lives."

Matteo snickers wickedly. "That's your mistake, bud."

I close my eyes at the ominous way he emphasizes the word bud, throwing it back at B.J.

"I'm in your life whether you like it or not." Matteo waves his hand. "Women aside. We're talking business. Allesandro offered your services. He said you were reliable. That's binding in my business."

"He had no right to do that."

Matteo lifts his chin. "Why would I take your word over that of my family? I... made... arrangements."

B.J.'s gaze narrows. "I never agreed to anything involving you."

Matteo offers his dismissive shoulder shrug. "I said, that's between you and Allesandro."

"You're damned right it is." B.J. glares at Al until his gaze travels back to Matteo. "I have a job. I told you. I connect steel."

Matteo tilts his head back with an evil laugh that makes me cringe. "A connector, huh? Well, you'll connect for us, also. You'll connect the product to the supplier."

He leans forward, and his tone changes. "Let's put the personal distaste aside. We take care of our people. If you work for us, should you have the unfortunate experience of," Matteo clears his throat and lifts his hands, "let's say, being accused of some wrongdoing in the eyes of the law, your legal services would be furnished. One hundred percent."

B.J. squints at him. "Are you going to serve my jail time? My prison time?"

"That's why we have the best lawyers in the country. So our people don't spend time behind bars."

The bodyguard's eyes remain on B.J., and he's still gripping his pistol. It's aimed at the floor, but his finger remains on the trigger.

Al still stands by the door, nervously glancing from Matteo to B.J. His lips are purple and swollen, as is his jaw. Al should probably see a doctor. Why hasn't Matteo asked about his cousin's injury? It's not like he could miss it.

The answer comes to me: smashed-up faces are not uncommon in the DeVecchio world.

"I don't understand why it has to be me." B.J. gestures at Al. "Buy Al a van and let him do it."

Matteo lifts his hands, glancing left and right. He's getting frustrated. "How many times must I say it? Arrangements have been made based on Allesandro's offer."

He tilts his head toward the kitchen. "The first delivery is done." His eyes linger over the stacked bricks of marijuana on the kitchen counter. "That's not all of it."

"I was headed out to get the rest when you showed up. Remember?"

"Give Allesandro your keys. My men will take care of the rest."

B.J. reaches into his jeans pocket and chunks Al the van keys. "It's behind the paneling around and over the bed, and in the back door." He adds as an afterthought, "Tell them to put everything back the way they find it."

Al steps outside the apartment, leaves the door ajar, and hands the van keys to the goon outside, whispering.

Matteo draws my attention back, telling B.J., "As I said, you completed one delivery. Why wouldn't you fulfill the rest of your obligation?"

B.J. cracks back snidely. "How many times must I say it? Because I didn't know I was making this delivery for you."

Matteo cuts his eyes at Al, who is back inside, in what appears to be his safe place, near the front door. He doesn't want to be between B.J. and Matteo.

I have a new understanding of the term 'shifty' as Al moves his weight from one foot to the other, squirming under his cousin's lingering scrutiny.

I think Al sees that his cousin realizes B.J. is telling the truth. Al finagled him.

But Matteo doesn't care. He just wants his drugs delivered on time.

He says, "Again, that's between you and Allesandro. He's not suited for the task." Matteo rubs his thumbnail over his lower lip, studying B.J. "Like you or not, you have moxie." He tilts his head toward Al. "Allesandro will be a fine attorney, but he's not suited for this."

The gangster shifts on the couch, turning to face Al squarely. "Besides, Allesandro likes the product a little too much for my taste—and for my father's taste—which is why he finds himself in his current predicament. Drugs are for the weak-minded and the weak-willed."

Silence.

"Alessandro?" Matteo's voice is louder, demanding as his eyes bore into his cousin. "Do. You. Understand. Me? From my father and me: Enough. Last night was the end. Capiche?"

Al nods.

Seeming satisfied with Al's acknowledgment, Matteo turns and extends his arm toward B.J. "You like the product yourself. You enjoyed a snort or two last night, didn't you, bud?"

Every time he calls B.J. *bud*, I get madder. He's intentionally goading him.

B.J. leans forward in the chair, his hands folded together, his knuckles locked tightly in front of him. He doesn't answer.

Matteo prods, "Good stuff, huh?"

B.J. peers over his shoulder out the window. The morning sun is bright, filtering through the window blinds. He stares out the windows for a long moment before he turns to face his tormentor. "You know what?" B.J. stands, glaring at the smug mobster, then jabs his finger at him. "Fuck you. Fuck your dope. Fuck your deal."

Matteo stands with him and straightens the cuffs of his long-sleeved shirt. He clears his throat loudly, glancing at the big thug Tommaso. "You have an impressive vocabulary, Mr. Cole."

"Who's trying to impress anyone?" B.J. takes a step toward Matteo. "Why don't you be a man and stop hiding behind his gun? Let's settle this—man to man."

Matteo tilts his head back and guffaws—loud and haughtily. "You want to fight me?" He keeps chuckling and shaking his head. "You—want to fight me?"

Al steps forward, yelling. "Dammit, B.J., he's a fucking boxer."

Yes, that is fear I see in Al Mancini's eyes. Does he actually care about B.J.?

My husband's focus isn't on Al. B.J.'s eyes are on Matteo as he snarls, "I'm not afraid of you."

Matteo cuts his eyes at the bodyguard and then back to B.J. "You should be." He dismisses B.J. with a wave of his hand.

"You're a druggie. You indulged last night with your wife and son present. You stay at a party snorting cocaine, smoking pot, drinking whiskey, while your wife and son are alone in the park. What kind of man are you?"

B.J. recoils. It's as if Matteo DeVecchio stuck a knife in his chest and twisted it, shaming him that way. B.J. has no response.

My fear turns to hatred as I think about the hypocrisy. I'm ready to go in there and give him a piece of my mind, but something holds me back. It is not fear of Matteo DeVecchio. It's B.J.

I know my husband. He intends to fight this battle. It's a man thing.

The problem is he can't fight with that giant thug still leering at him with a gun in his hand. It is clear: with a nod from his boss, Tommaso will pull that trigger.

Amid the silence, Matteo says, "So, it's settled. You will fulfill—"

"I will not."

My stomach churns with a mixture of pride and angst as my husband stands his ground. Has anyone ever defied Matteo DeVecchio this way?

B.J. leans toward Matteo, his gaze narrow. "Do you really want to kill me?" He tilts his head to Al. "Him and my family over this?"

The mob boss scratches his brow, eyeing B.J. with that wicked gaze. "I don't plan on killing anyone. Certainly not my cousin or your wife or her son."

"My son!" B.J. shouts.

"As I said, I don't intend to kill anyone. Might someone have an unfortunate accident sometime in the future should an agreement not be honored?" He lifts his hands and shoulders. "I cannot predict the future."

B.J. squares off with Matteo. "I'll take my chances on the future."

Something incendiary moves across Matteo's face and into his eyes. It's like he's tired of messing with B.J. If looks could kill, I'd be a widow already. I grip the door frame. My heart throbs in my chest.

Matteo's voice becomes dangerously quiet. "Do not be foolish."

B.J. bites back. "Foolish is running cocaine and heroin from Mexico to the East Coast for you."

Wham!

One step and Tommaso swings his powerful arm, bashing B.J. across the side of his head with his gun, snapping B.J.'s head around.

I gasp as B.J.'s knees buckle and hit the floor.

Tommaso shoves the barrel against B.J.'s temple for a second time today as Matteo steps toward him.

His voice is ice. "I've had enough of this."

I rush to my husband, screaming, "Stop! Stop it!" Gripping B.J.'s arm, I whirl around, facing Matteo, looking him dead in the eyes. "Leave him alone!"

Matteo looks through me as if I don't exist. "Patsy, women don't interfere in business."

His mind isn't on me anymore. It is on making B.J. submit.

Gripping my shoulders, B.J. stands, moving me aside. Blood trickles down the side of his face. "What does it take to end this?"

Matteo cuts his eyes at Al. "The two trips, if he doesn't run up any more debt."

B.J. aims his arm at Al while talking straight to Matteo. "I will never pay another dime for him. He is dead to me."

Al dips his head and stares at the floor as B.J. and Matteo continue to glower at each other, neither man flinching.

Tommaso still holds his pistol in his hand, barrel pointed at the floor.

It feels like forever before the mobster nods. "The two trips and your obligation to us is fulfilled. Unless you decide to continue working for us. We pay well."

"That won't happen."

Matteo snickers. "You never know."

"Fuck off," B.J. says. "You've got me for two trips to Mexico and back. Then we're free of you."

Matteo scoffs. "No one can predict the future, bud."

Chapter Twenty-One
SAFE TRAVELS
Patsy

OUR FATE IS SEALED. B.J. will work for the DeVecchios, at least for a while. With blood trickling down his face, I rush into the bedroom and return with a clean cloth diaper, pressing it against the slash.

B.J.'s eyes are dead. My husband has been betrayed by his closest friend in life.

He had the rug pulled out from under him, learning of whatever it was—some undisclosed connection—between his wife and this slick mobster.

He's been pistol-whipped by the bodyguard and forced to put his freedom at risk by driving illegal drugs across the country for the Mafia.

I'm stunned when Matteo says in a somewhat normal voice, "Come, I will buy a meal for everyone, and you can be on your way."

It sounds like a peace offering, but it is not. It's an order, another one B.J. defies. "We'll pass. We're getting on the road."

Matteo clears his throat. "It appears there is a misunderstanding."

B.J. and I exchange glances and stare at Matteo, who replies, "I said you could be on your way." He tilts his head. "She stays with me."

If B.J. had a gun, Matteo would be dead. I have never seen such hatred in his eyes. My fingers dig into his arms.

The corners of Matteo's mouth turn down. "If I let all three of you leave, what assurance would I have that you won't drive off and never come back? Your reluctance is noted."

B.J. says, "Your assurance is my word. I told you I'd make the trips." *Oh, Lord, B.J. is clenching his fists again.* The thick muscles on his forearms flex. How much further can he challenge this Mafioso?

"I don't know you well enough to take your word for anything." Matteo steps toward B.J. "You just tried to back out on a deal I made with a member of my family." He glares at B.J. "Get this straight. I don't do drugs and I don't gamble. *Your* family stays with me to ensure you fulfill your commitment to *my* family."

"You just want to steal them."

"A lot is riding on this trip. Safe travels, bud."

For whatever reason, Jim Beau picks that moment to tune up. "Mamma!" He calls from the other room, and I hear him tumble from the bed and hit the floor. "Mamma!"

Rushing to the bedroom, I grab my son and return to the living room. Seeing his father, Jim Beau cries, "Daddy!" and stretches his arms for B.J.

I set him on the floor, and Jim Beau runs to his father, who scoops him up and holds him against his chest in one arm.

Matteo's voice is surprisingly soothing. "Your father will be fine, young man. He's just going on a short trip."

"Short trip?" I step out of my shadows. "It's halfway across America and back. Twice."

Holding Jim Beau in his arms, standing on the other side of the living room, B.J.'s gaze zeroes in on me as I approach Matteo. "Matteo, for that kind of trip, he needs new tires. I worried about the tires for this trip."

Matteo nods, addressing B.J., "We'll have your van serviced this afternoon. Whatever it needs. A breakdown would be unfortunate for everyone."

"I'm supposed to be at work on Monday," B.J. says.

Matteo's lips purse into his Mona Lisa pout. "That you can deal with yourself."

B.J. replies, "I want to talk to my wife. Alone."

Matteo sweeps his arm toward me with his condescending bow. "She's your wife. Go right ahead."

We walk into the bedroom, and B.J. closes the door behind us. I reach up to touch his bruised face, but he jerks his head away with angry eyes. "What the hell is going on?"

"Nothing, baby. Nothing."

Fury rages in those golden-brown eyes, but what I see most is hurt. Betrayal. He tilts his head toward the living room. "All of that's not nothing."

I don't answer. I don't know how to. I'm too—I don't know what I am. I'm mortified, confused, afraid, and ashamed.

He demands, "You kissed him?"

Oh, God, what a look of revulsion. I want to crawl into a hole.

"Patsy," he demands.

"Yes, I did."

"Fuck." He tromps to the bedroom window, his back to me. "Goddammit, Patsy." Seconds later, another, "Fuck."

"B.J., nothing happened." He won't look at me. "I thought I lost you to Linda. I saw you go into the bedroom with her, B.J. I was sick. I thought—"

He whirls around. "What? You thought what?"

Oh, Lord, he's so mad. And I'm getting there, yelling quietly because I don't want them to hear us. "You *know* what I thought!"

"You think I'm that shallow?"

"She was all over you, B.J. You took her by the hand into a bedroom."

"I took her in the bedroom for privacy. You know that."

"But I didn't then. We hadn't been together for a month. When I saw you two go into that bedroom, I went outside and cried. I didn't even know he was there. We started talking and he ended up putting his arms around me..."

He shakes his head and turns his back on me again, staring out the window.

I grab his arm to make him look at me—but B.J. stands rigid, holding Jim Beau, his back to me. Unmovable.

Tears sting my eyes. "I'm sorry. Nothing happened. I ran to you when you called me, you know that."

He turns to me, his face cold. "What happened yesterday?"

"He came up to me in the park, and he just kept staring at me like, I don't know, like I was—I don't know. Honestly, it made me uncomfortable. But with everything going on, the party—it wasn't the time or place for me to tell you about that."

B.J. closes his eyes and takes a deep breath. "You're fuckin' taken with him, aren't you?"

He inhales deeply and exhales slowly, his gaze fierce. "I don't like the way he looks at you. But you know what's worse, Patsy? I don't like the way you look at him." His upper lip curls in disgust. "I see it." He aims his arm at the living room, getting louder. "And so does he. I want nothing but the truth, even if it hurts. Do you want him?"

"No, B.J. I Do Not." That's the truth.

It feels like we spend an agonizingly long time staring at each other. Maybe he's waiting for me to say more. I don't.

B.J. holds Jim Beau against his shoulder, one big hand across the baby's back, studying me hard. I have never seen distrust in my husband's eyes until now. "Why didn't you tell me about him?" he demands.

I lift a shoulder and finally reply, "There was nothing to tell."

That's a lie.

I cannot explain what exists between me and Matteo De-Vecchio, but I'll be damned if I'll hurt B.J. even more with some stupid confession when I know—I never wanted Matteo to replace B.J. Not for one second. "Now you give me the truth, B.J., even if it hurts. Did you do something with Linda in the bedroom that night?"

"Damn, Patsy, no. He just wants to drive a wedge between us."

Just like that. As if B.J. snapped his fingers, the fog lifts, and I understand the meaning of the term handsome devil.

Matteo DeVecchio can be kind and charming at will, but he is a cunning devil determined to have what he wants, no matter the cost. And right now, what he wants is me.

My eyes plead with my husband. "B.J., you know how much I love you."

He stares at me for a long minute and finally yanks me to him, and we cling to each other, my cheek on his chest. *This* is the chest I love. I love the arms he wraps around Jim Beau and me. For the first time today, it's just us three—and my guilt. "I'm so sorry, B.J. It's all my fault."

He takes an enormous breath and blows it out. "No, Babydoll, this cluster fuck isn't on you. I never should have agreed to drive the dope." Now, his eyes are pleading. "I'm sorry. But for God's sake, don't fall for his bullshit. He is Satan in a slick suit."

I pull away to peer up at him. "I know he is." Again, I try to tell him I love him with my eyes, but his gaze has left me.

Taking his face in my hands, forcing him to see me, I whisper, "B.J., I'm yours. You know that. You heard me tell him that." I see so much uncertainty in his eyes. "Baby, stop worrying about me. I'll handle him. I don't think he'd try to do anything anyway."

B.J. tilts his head back, gazing at the ceiling. "Patsy, that man intends to have you, and the only way that can happen is if I'm out of the picture, either in the ground or behind bars. Do you not see that?"

No, I guess I didn't. Not like that.

Tears fill my eyes. "What are we going to do?"

"I don't see that I have any choice. I've got to make these runs."

"Can you?"

B.J. snickers. "Can I do what? Drive to Brownsville and back? Well, hell, yeah. That's not the question. The question is—is he willing to give up a load of dope to have you? Maybe he wants me to get caught so he can swoop in and be your hero."

Oh, Lord. That never crossed my mind. My heart misses a beat or three. "Don't say that."

"Once those drugs are loaded into our van, he can put me away for life with one phone call. Small price to pay for the woman he thinks he loves. For a guy like him."

I know the difference now.

What I felt yesterday, driving the van full of pot—that was fear.

This—what I'm feeling right now—is paralyzing terror. It's mind-numbing. I'm suffocating. My ears ring again, and I cover my face with my hands. *No. This is not happening.* "I can't live without you, B.J."

"Yeah, you can." This time, he is snarly and bitter. "You might not want to, but if they send me up for life, you've got no choice but to move on with yours. Just don't move on with that son of a bitch. He's slick, Patsy. He'll figure a way to make you believe in him."

A voice in my head says *panic will kill you.* My father's words.

"Stop it." I grab B.J.'s shoulders. I would shake him, but he's not shakable. "We're not going there." I grip his thick arms. "Was the pot in Brownsville? Did you go down there for it?"

"No. It was in a warehouse in Seguin."

"Then why can't they get the next load of whatever it is sent to Seguin, so you don't have to drive all the way to Brownsville?"

His gaze darts around the room. "It would cut a day off of each trip. It would be that much less chance of getting caught."

"And one more thing. Having us with you lessens the chances of you getting stopped. I mean a family traveling together is less suspicious than one guy in a van. Don't you think? I mean, if you do get stopped for some reason, having a wife and child with you looks innocent enough."

"You can't do that, remember? We can't both get caught. We'd lose Jim Beau."

Oh. Yeah.

"We won't. When we go through Austin, I'll leave Jim Beau with Mom. She's been begging to keep him. If we get pulled over, I'll have to say I knew nothing about it. Besides, if you're right, if I'm in the van with you, he won't call the cops. He doesn't want to see me in jail. It would defeat his purpose."

"Which is why he'll never agree to it," B.J. replies.

"I'll at least ask. He might listen to me."

B.J. shakes his head gently with such defeat in his eyes, and I recognize something I'd never seen in my rebellious husband: resignation. His voice is so sad as he says, "You still don't get it, do you? You can't see how ruthless he is."

I gently touch his wounded forehead. It is already turning blue, but I know B.J. will never mention his pain.

"I do see," I whisper.

I see that I caused this. I have to fix it.

I kiss B.J.'s hand and tuck it under my blouse, over my heart. "This belongs to no one but you." My breast and my heart. "You don't ever have to worry about me wanting another man. *That* you don't ever have to worry about, B.J."

He clutches me to him. "If he tries to force himself on you, I'll kill him."

"I won't let him."

He sets Jim Beau on the bed and grips my shoulders, bending his knees, holding me away to see the whole of me. "How do you think you'd stop him?"

I swallow the lump in my throat. The truth is, I don't know. I don't guess I could. But I don't read him that way. "I—just—don't think he'd try. If he did, I'd push him away."

B.J. scoffs. "Babydoll, you are naïve."

"For some reason, I'm not afraid of Matteo DeVecchio for myself. Only for what he can do to you." I'm going to figure out some way to handle him. "Now stop worrying about me." I grab his face with both hands and kiss him. "I love you, B.J. Always."

He grabs Jim Beau and leads me back. We aren't three steps into the living room when Matteo stands from his place on the couch and says, "It's my turn."

B.J. and I exchange glances, and before we can speak, Matteo snaps at B.J., "I know, I know. She's your wife."

His gaze veers to meet mine as he sneers. "And you love him. But I have something to say—to you, Patsy." He peers at B.J. "Relax. I will not touch your wife. But I will speak to her privately."

My eyes beg B.J. to understand. I am not under Matteo's spell anymore. This might give me a chance to talk sense into him. "It's okay," I whisper, squeezing B.J.'s hand.

With that, Matteo DeVecchio puts his hand on my elbow, guides me to the bedroom, and closes the door.

I'm right back where I was seconds ago with B.J.

CHAPTER TWENTY-TWO

HIS DESTINY

PATSY

MATTEO SAYS NOTHING; HE just studies me in silence. Finally, he says, "You've been with him all these years. Why didn't you tell him what happened between us that night?"

"I don't know."

That's the truth. I remember being so relieved—excited—that B.J. *was* looking for me. First, we fussed about what I saw.

He explained that it was the first time Linda had seen him since he broke up with her, and she was livid to see us together and started crying, so he wanted to talk to her without me or anyone else around.

Then he was mad that I disappeared and he had to look for me.

We got everything smoothed out. We kissed and made up. Telling B.J. what happened between me and a stranger in the backyard while he was searching for me... it wasn't happening.

It would have come out of nowhere. *Oh, and now that we've settled the whole Linda-in-the-bedroom thing, by the way, I just kissed a guy outside...*

I couldn't tell him. Wasn't about to tell him. Then I forgot it.

Matteo's voice pulls me back. "He is not enough for you. You deserve a man who will treasure you for what you are."

How can his voice be so soothing... so silky smooth... so gentle when he talks just to me? My eyes search his, wondering how he can be this way with me—and be how he was in the living room with B.J.

"Sweetheart," he says, "You are magnificent. Royalty."

I can't believe my ears. I shake my head with a bewildered smile. "I don't know where you get this stuff."

He folds my hand in his, holding it against his chest. "You belong by my side, and I am royalty in the world I was born into. I will give you a life beyond your imagination and you would never have to worry about me being unfaithful." He points to the living room. "Your husband, the one who loves you so much? Remember, the guy in a bedroom—"

"All they did was talk."

He snickers. "Yes, yes, yes. All they did was talk." He cocks his head. "Did you tell him that's all we did, too?"

I can't answer.

He goes on. "We both know something happened between us. And I know something happened between them."

"Stop it, Matteo. You're not going to make me distrust B.J. over something that happened years ago."

His brows pinch together. "Years ago? What about today?"

I turn my face from him, but Matteo touches my cheek with his fingers, forcing me to look into his eyes, which are as black as ink. "Your husband jeopardized your freedom driving drugs here, and it doesn't matter whether they belong to me or him like he thought. He put you at risk. He took drugs in front of you and your son—"

I jerk away and show him my palm. "How dare you? You're the Mafia. You bring God-knows-how-many pounds of illegal drugs into this country, profit from their sale, and you have the audacity to judge my husband, who works all day every day? He does not abuse drugs."

Matteo is unfazed. He grins, and his dimple shows. "Mafia is a made-up word, sweetheart. I run a family business. DeVecchio Imports. I didn't choose it. I was born into it. I've been entrusted with its success, and I succeed. The DeVecchio family name is respected."

"Matteo, I don't love you."

"Do you deny what happened between us?"

Our gazes lock like magnets. "Nothing happened."

Matteo shakes his head softly, biting his bottom lip. "Yes, something happened, Patsy. I saw it in your eyes and I felt it in your kiss—and you knew in your heart, I felt the same for you. It was... magical. *Colpo di fulmine.* When love strikes someone like a thunderbolt. There is no other way to describe it."

I draw a deep breath and close my eyes. I can't deny the attraction that was between us. Yes, it existed on some level. But B.J. had an unshakeable hold on my heart first.

"Matteo, maybe in another world." I wiggle my hand between him and me. "Before B.J. and before I knew you were part of the Mafia—"

He interrupts me, showing me his open palm. "Again, made-up word."

I huff in exasperation. "Let me finish, please."

Matteo tweaks his mouth to one side and nods.

"B.J. already owned my heart before I met you." I aim my arm toward the living room. "He's had me in the palm of his hand since the first time we kissed." Our eyes are latched. "Nothing and no one will make me unfaithful to him. I have loved him since I was eighteen years old. That's not going to change."

He just stares contemplatively. Maybe it's soaking in.

"Please, Matteo, respect that. He is my everything and if you hurt B.J., you hurt me."

Matteo studies me for another long beat, reaches out, and touches my hair, rubbing it between his fingers. "Your hair is like silk," he whispers.

I should slap his hand away, but I don't.

His eyes search mine. "So, you love him?" he asks.

Are you kidding me? "Yes. That's what I've been saying."

"Prove it," he says.

I step away to see the whole of him. "What do you mean?"

Matteo lifts his hands, palms up. "Ensure his safety."

"How?"

"Tell him goodbye."

My jaw sags. I can't have heard that right. "You want me to walk away from B.J.?" I'm frozen in time. "Did you hear what I just said? I can't do that. I won't do that."

He lifts his chin. "Sweetheart, you will lose him one way or another."

I cover my face with my hands. This isn't real. This can't be happening. So much for my bravado about handling Matteo DeVecchio. But I try again. "Do you remember the night at Dr. Mancini's house?"

He nods.

"Do you remember what I told you when you offered to take care of B.J. for me?"

He just stares.

"I told you, if he wants her, he wants her. You can't make someone want you. You can't make me want you, Matteo."

He smiles slowly. He is such a cunning fox. "I think you do want me, but you're too bound by loyalty and duty to your loser husband to admit it. Loyalty is an admirable trait."

Watching him, it hits me like a rush of hot air. I finally get it.

From his first day on the elementary school playground, no female ever rejected Matteo DeVecchio. That's why he can't get it through his handsome head. It's never happened. With his looks, his money, and his name—in Matteo's mind, it is impossible for any woman to resist him.

I bite back at him. "You're wrong. If you hurt B.J. I will hate you more than I do right now."

Sadness overtakes his eyes and spreads across his face. He purses his mouth then whispers, "So, I have nothing to lose. You hate me now. If you hate me in the future, at least he won't be in the picture."

I'm stunned.

Matteo grabs my shoulders. His grip is tight. "I don't believe for a second that you don't feel something for me. Whatever it is, we will build on it."

I pull away from his grip. "You're delusional."

Matteo draws back, puts his hands on his waist, and tilts his head to the side, studying me with his soulful eyes. He cracks a crooked grin. "Maybe so," he says. "Time will tell."

He opens the door, ushering me out as he says quietly, "Time is on my side."

B.J. is standing at the windows holding Jim Beau. Turning, seeing us come back into the living room—I don't know what he reads on either of our faces, but his gaze narrows suspiciously.

It's like B.J. had an awakening.

"Wait a minute," he says. "Wait one fucking minute." His glare moves between Al and Matteo. "This is a setup. This isn't about drugs—it's all because you want Patsy."

"I told you, Allesandro owes a great debt." Matteo's voice is flat.

"You let him run up that debt on purpose because you wanted a way to get to Patsy." Rage radiates off B.J. like heat from a grill. I can feel it across the room.

My protective instincts erupt. "Get this straight right now! Everybody!" I'm so furious I'd charge a bull myself. I yell as I turn in a circle, screaming at Al, Matteo, and Tommaso as I point to B.J. "I am his wife!"

I peer up at Matteo, still aiming my arm at B.J. "If any of you hurt him, I will see you all burn in hell."

A creepy silence fills the room as I move to stand beside my husband and son, glaring at Matteo, who stands stoically. He seems unaffected by my rant. "If your little tantrum is over—"

B.J. cuts him off. "She is married to me."

Rage engulfs Matteo as he swings his arms wide and shouts, "This is all about the fucking drugs!" It's like a lion's roar. It is clear why he strikes fear in people.

My fingers curl into B.J.'s shirt, and he tucks me under his arm.

Matteo seems to struggle to control his fury as he pauses, breathes deeply, and lowers his voice.

He takes a step toward us, his voice controlled, but his face is still contorted by anger as he says, "It's business. Not some fucking game you hippies play."

I am looking into the eyes of a killer.

He aims his finger at B.J. "Now you be clear, mother-fucker." Matteo's ferocious glare eviscerates my husband. "What you owe me has nothing to do with her." He aims his arm at me. "I never dreamed I'd see her again." His face is red. The veins on Matteo's neck bulge as he continues trying to control his fury.

Maybe we have pushed him too far. I can only imagine what a beast Matteo DeVecchio is when his anger is uncontrolled. I am petrified as he points at me, his consuming gaze still trained onto B.J. "Fate brought her to me—out of nowhere—twice. I let her go the first time. I'd be a fool to let her go again. She is my destiny."

I'm afraid to breathe.

Matteo nods at B.J., who stands like a statue. "You owe me two runs. I always collect what is owed me. One way or the other."

Silence.

"Your family remains with me to ensure you return with our product." He aims his arm at me again. "I will not touch her unless she wants to be touched. Rest assured I have never forced myself on a woman. I don't have to." He nods at the bodyguard, the one who is not Tommaso. "Pietro, after we eat, you take care of his van."

Okay. Tommaso and Pietro. Pietro nods. Tommaso is the larger of the pair, but both of Matteo's bodyguards dwarf the other three men in the room. I'm not sure either can speak. So far, neither has uttered a word.

That steely edge still controls Matteo's tone. "Come, Allesandro. You will ride with us."

CHAPTER TWENTY-THREE

THE LONG RIDE

PATSY

I NEVER RODE IN a limousine. I sure didn't want to ride in one under these circumstances.

Pietro drives, and Tommaso rides shotgun. How appropriate.

Matteo and Al ride in the back seat, facing forward, across from B.J. and me. I'm holding Jim Beau, who peers out the tinted windows.

Matteo runs his thumbnail along his lower lip, finally acknowledging the damage to his cousin's face. "Allesandro, did you bump into a door?"

Al turns away from his cousin to stare out the window, answering through clenched teeth. "Yeah."

"See the doctor after lunch. That jaw is cracked." I guess the DeVecchio crime family has their own doctor, and Matteo knows a cracked jaw when he sees one.

Al nods and cuts his eyes at B.J.

I'm not sure if those black orbs are filled with hatred because B.J. hit him or shame over what he's done to his lifelong friend. Am I looking at hate, regret, or simple physical pain? He heard B.J. say he was dead to him. He knows B.J. doesn't say things he doesn't mean.

A lifelong friendship. Murdered. Stabbed in the back.

My husband, sitting at my side, is easy to read. His hands are folded together in front of him, his knuckles locked tightly. He clenches them as he stares a hideous hole through Al.

I speak up. "Matteo?"

This eyes meet mine as I clear my throat. "It occurred to me that a family traveling together in a van is much less suspicious to law enforcement than one man traveling alone. Your shipment might be safer if Jim Beau and I accompany B.J."

It's apparently a habit, running his thumbnail along his lower lip as he ponders. At last, Matteo smiles and nods. He turns to Al saying, "I'm sure you know any number of women who can accompany Mr. Cole and act as his wife, don't you?"

Al makes an odd face and nods.

"Make arrangements for someone to travel with him. Someone who looks like she would be with him. Someone who has a child."

"That's not what I meant."

Matteo flashes his sly grin. "I know exactly what you meant, Patsy. But unlike your husband, I will not risk your freedom having you ride in a van carrying drugs. Besides, you stay with me to ensure he comes back. Still, the family thing is a good idea."

I cut my eyes at B.J. and then back to Matteo. "I don't want some strange woman traveling across the country with my husband."

Matteo tucks his chin, studying me. "What's the matter? You don't trust your husband?" He tilts his head at nods at B.J. "This man you plan to be with forever?" He says forever, almost like it's a joke.

"No. I mean, yes, I trust him." I'm stumbling all over myself. "That's not what I meant. But like B.J. said, I go where he goes."

"Sorry, sweetheart. Not this time. Remember, you two are forever. So, what's a day or two apart?"

Al snorts.

B.J. and Matteo glare at him inquisitively.

Al shrugs and shakes his head. He speaks through his pain. "I don't get it." He nods at me and looks at his cousin. "Why can't you two see, she's nothing but a controlling little—"

Quick as a striking snake, B.J. snatches for Al, but Matteo is equally fast. He catches B.J.'s wrist and barks. "Allesandro, that's enough." He releases B.J.'s arm, and his gaze falls on both of us. "I hope you'll enjoy a little free time away from each other. I'm sure we can supply B.J. with a woman who will keep him entertained on his trips."

I am so angry. How did I ever think for an instant that he was a good guy? He's going to have Al hook B.J. up with the sexiest floozy he can find. She'll be all over him and maybe feed him bullshit about me hooking up with Matteo to push B.J. over the edge.

I see his plan.

I despise him now.

For spite, I tug on my husband, pulling him to me, and I kiss him long and deeply.

None of them expect it, not even B.J.

I break the kiss and glare at Matteo.

His eyes flash as he leans forward, saying, "Sweetheart, I thought you said you loved him."

"That's what I'm trying to show you!" My voice is even more shrill than I intended.

Matteo turns his head away from me to stare out the window.

"You are so stupid." Al leans in close, glowering at me. "You're going to get B.J. killed. Do you want him to suffer? Because if you keep goading Matteo DeVecchio the way you are, your husband's death is going to be slow and painful."

I have no comeback.

We travel across town in silence. I'm too numb to speak, and I'm sure B.J. feels the same. My head hangs low, my focus on my wedding ring. When he put it on my finger, I never intended to take it off. But what Al said—I can't let that happen.

I know, in the end, I'll do whatever I have to do to save B.J.'s life.

I know B.J. The only way he would ever let me go is if I convince him that I lied to him and that I truly have feelings for Matteo.

I try to prepare myself. We do what we have to do. I will not let Matteo kill him. Him. The man I love. The father of my son. I will not let that happen.

Only Jim Beau is oblivious to the distress permeating the air, excitedly pointing out the window and jumping on the seat. "Look, Daddy, look! Choo-choo train!"

B.J. takes him into his arms and holds him close. "Yeah, buddy. Choo-choo."

Chapter Twenty-Four

CLIFFHANGER

Patsy

THE LIMO PULLS UP to the entrance of a restaurant, Venecia's, built high on a cliff, hanging over a swift-flowing stream. The restaurant has a red brick front exterior. The rest of the building is glass, designed and situated to offer guests a breathtaking view of lush Virginia hills and the valley it overhangs.

It is a chic place frequented by lawyers, doctors, businessmen, and country club wives.

None of us dressed appropriately except for Matteo and his goons. B.J. and Al look like they just climbed out of a boxing ring. No one seems to notice or care.

Had we not been with Matteo DeVecchio, who probably owns the place or part of it, the maître d' would have sent us packing. Instead, he says with apologetic surprise, "Mr. DeVecchio, we weren't expecting you today. Please give us a moment. We will prepare a table." He hastens away.

Yes, Matteo is treated like royalty, even with his ragtag guests.

As we wait to be seated, B.J. whispers. "I'm not driving off and leaving you two with him. You be ready. When I leave, I'm coming back."

"Do you think it's possible for us to get out of this?"

"I'm damned sure going to try." He reads my mind. He knows me too well. "Patsy, I'm not going to let you give yourself to that son of a bitch to save me."

"I will not let him kill you."

Fearless, positive B.J. lifts my hand and kisses it. "It won't come to that. I'll figure a way out."

We are finally seated at a round table not far from one of the floor-to-ceiling glass walls. The restaurant offers outside dining on a wrap-around deck with steel rails. Lots of people are sitting out there, and I'm not sure why. It must be miserably noisy with all the construction going on. Dust is churning from all kinds of big machines moving around.

Another cliffhanger is being erected on the adjoining property, just uphill from the restaurant. It appears the new building will have at least three floors, maybe more, all hanging out over the valley.

"What are they building?" I wonder out loud.

B.J. mumbles. "An office building. Or maybe apartments."

"Condos," Matteo answers with a glance outside. "It will have shopping on the ground floor, even a gourmet grocery, so residents never have to leave." He nudges his head toward the construction. "That is high-dollar property. It's all about the view from the balconies. I hear ten floors."

Neither B.J. nor I respond.

My eyes are still frozen on all the commotion out there. I've never spent much time around construction sites like B.J. I'm a little unnerved by so many huge machines moving around in such a tight space.

Boom lifts, big cranes, little cranes, bulldozers, and loaders are all operating between the restaurant and the skeleton of the new high-rise. I mean, the back end of a big crane is right there in front of us.

No people are sitting on that side of the wrap-around balcony. The restaurant must have cordoned it off.

"That's all too close for my comfort," I say, peering up at B.J.

He is not concerned, answering, "They do it every day. They know what they're doing."

The cab of the nearby crane is uphill, situated higher than the roof of the restaurant. It is just huge. Its boom extends well above the third floor of the new building, which is being assembled before our eyes.

All these years, I have never gone to see B.J. work. It scares me too much.

It is fascinating to watch. The boom lowers its hook to the ground, workers attach a long I-beam, and the crane operator hoists it up and swings it over to the connectors waiting up high. The connectors grab it, fit it in place, and install enough bolts to secure it safely.

"Are those all the bolts that hold a building together?" I ask.

B.J. snorts. "No. Bolt-up hands come behind and complete the skeleton."

Bolt-up hands. Yes, he's told me before the bolt-up hands are tied off by ropes. Connectors are not.

If a connector makes a wrong move up there, he will fall to his death.

But with heavy steel beams constantly swinging up to them, connectors must be able to move around untethered. It's even more dangerous for a connector to be tied off, B.J. says. They have to be able to maneuver freely.

They are the guys everyone else looks up to—literally and figuratively. Agile, strong, fearless, and focused.

That's what B.J. does five, sometimes six days a week: connect steel. What will happen to his job if he can't show up for a week or more? Oh, well.

Connectors are not only held in high esteem, they are always in demand because not many men are willing or capable of doing what they do. He can work for another company.

As we wait for our order, Matteo has the staff bring bread sticks and Alfredo sauce for the table, which Jim Beau and the goons are enjoying.

A waiter sets a bowl in front of Al, and Matteo says, "Allesandro, warm soup is soothing for a cracked jaw. I took the liberty." He nods at the bowl. "The nutrition is good for healing."

I guess he does care. I guess he speaks from experience.

The rest of us sip sweet, iced tea—except for B.J. He's not eating or drinking. Al sips through a straw.

The conversation wanes. I'm sure it is painful for Al to speak, and it's not like we want to carry on small talk with a man who betrayed B.J. and another who plans to kill him.

Matteo honestly thinks he can make me love him. He believes deep down inside that I do love him. It's the most bizarre circumstance. One I could never have imagined. I hear his words again. "You will lose him one way or another." Then Al said, "You're going to get B.J. killed. Do you want him to suffer?"

How did this happen? How are we going to get out of this?

My love for B.J. is limitless. Since our first meeting, we have never been apart. I cannot let him be murdered. It's not that I don't trust him or his ability to find a way—I just don't see one.

Matteo is crazy obsessed. He has it in his head that I am his destiny, and having seen his rage, I have no doubt about what he would be capable of if B.J. and I were to run away.

What he might do to B.J. I shudder at the thought. With each dragging minute, it becomes excruciatingly clear: I have no choice.

"Matteo?"

His eyes meet mine. I keep saying it, but seriously, his stare is the most piercing I've ever experienced. His eyes are like polished onyx. They glisten and cut right into you. He talks with his eyes.

Maybe I do, too. Tears fill them. I can't hold them back.

I don't have to say anything. He does. "I told you how you can save him, sweetheart. I'm willing to build on what exists."

I close my eyes. Tears drizzle out. I open my mouth to speak, but before I can, B.J. stands and exclaims, "Oh, fuck!"

We all gawk at him.

His eyes are riveted on the activity outside. I don't think he heard what Matteo and I said. He's been too focused on whatever is going on with the construction.

B.J. points, and his gaze meets mine. "A dozer just rammed the shit out of that outrigger."

My skin tingles as I watch my husband. All this time that he's been battling Matteo, I have not seen fear in him.

Now I see fear—or terror—or horror in his eyes. Does he think we're in danger?

I follow his gaze to see men in hard hats scurrying around the construction site, hovering near the loader and the outrigger he pointed to.

Matteo's brows pinch together. "If it loses an outrigger it will fall."

B.J. glares at him. "No fucking shit." He slams his napkin on his plate and strides to the wall of windows, watching the construction crew.

Matteo follows, but before he reaches B.J.'s side, B.J. turns and hollers, "Run!"

Men are fleeing from the crane.

As I push back in my chair, B.J.'s eyes meet mine, and he bellows, "Dammit, Patsy, run!"

It has the effect of a pistol shot starting a race.

Everyone bolts for the entrance. I'm clutching Jim Beau, wedged in a herd of other terrified people, dodging, making my way over fallen chairs.

Reaching the lobby, I hear a loud, high-pitched *Creak!*

Looking back, I don't see B.J.

Where is he? Is he coming?

As I get through the front door, there's an ear-splitting *Pop!*

The gigantic crane, with its boom extended and dangling that long, heavy I-beam, begins to topple over backward like an uprooted tree.

I flinch at the deafening roar as the upside-down crane crashes through the roof, belly up. It makes me think of a turtle on its back.

People fall to the ground around me as the long I-beam swings overhead before it follows the plummeting crane.

Some scream as the upended crane rips the building from the cliffside—a sledgehammer smashing a dollhouse.

Everything and everyone inside disappears.

Metal screeches, squeals, booms, and bangs—it is deafening—as the gigantic machine hits, scrapes, and bounces on the rocky cliff until the building and everything inside finally lands with a thunderous *Thud!*

The earth shakes.

In a matter of seconds, it is over.

A thick cloud boils over us like a West Texas dust storm.

Silt settles like flour over biscuit dough—on my hair, my skin, in my eyes. I blink through it.

Al is at my side, his face powdered, his mouth hanging open. His eyes are frozen wide. I think he's in shock.

I am.

So is everyone else in the throng of people gathered in the parking lot. They are safe because my husband warned them. My husband. As it registers with me, it registers with my son—B.J. isn't here.

Jim Beau wails, stretching out his arms. "Daddy! My Daddy!"

I do a three-sixty turn, my mouth near my son's ear, whispering. "It's okay, baby boy. It's okay." I pet his head as I desperately look for B.J., the powdery dust still settling around us.

All that remains of the restaurant is the lower edge of the front brick exterior wall, entranceway, and lobby.

I move toward the precipice and peer, in horror, through the dust at the mangled metal deep in the gorge.

Steel columns that supported the building still stand like long arms reaching for heaven, with cross beams back and forth, anchored into the cliff wall. Battered and warped, that skeleton of structural steel somehow survived.

"B.J.!" I scream, twirling in a panicked circle. He's nowhere.

I run among the crowd, searching faces, clutching our crying son, desperately yelling, "B.J.!"

Al grips my shoulder.

I pull away from him, clinging to Jim Beau as I continue running and calling for, "B.J.!"

Everyone around me is doing the same, scrambling frantically, calling out the names of their missing loved ones as fire engines, police cars, paramedics, and ambulances converge on us. Everything is crazy, with first responders rushing everywhere.

That fast. B.J. is gone.

I've lost him, after all.

CHAPTER TWENTY-FIVE

OH, HELL, NO!

B.J.

WHAT IS HE DOING? That dozer operator is driving crazy—he's all over the place. And he's moving way too fast around the site. Damn, is he drunk?

Watch out!

"Oh, fuck!" I can't believe what I just saw.

Patsy looks up at me with her wide, innocent eyes, and I'm sure mine are wider as I stand and point. "A bulldozer just rammed the shit out of that outrigger."

If he was trying to sabotage the damned thing, he couldn't have found a better way. He's drunk or high, or he had a heart attack—something—because nobody hits an outrigger like that.

And it's the outrigger on our side. My hackles rise. If the outrigger gives or slips off its pad, that crane will flip over on top of us.

It weighs at least fifty tons and carries as much in cast iron counterweights, and on top of that, if the crane gives, it'll bring the dozer with it right fucking on top of this restaurant.

DeVecchio twists in his seat. "If it loses an outrigger, it will fall."

I slam down my napkin and head for the windows. "No fucking shit." The cocksucker follows me like stink on shit. Does he think I'm going to run away? Leave my family?

The construction crew is running.

"Run!" I shout as I turn to the dining room, waving my arms over my head. The hushed conversations cease as people freeze in motion, their drinking glasses and forks to their mouths, staring at me with deer-in-the-headlights eyes.

No one moves.

Patsy and I lock eyes. She's pushing back from the table as I yell at the top of my lungs, "Dammit, Patsy! Run!" They've got seconds to get out alive. "RUN!"

Everybody moves.

She's wedged in a panicked mob, clinging to Jim Beau.

Oh, fuck, Babydoll—"RUN!"

Patsy glances over her shoulder as she rounds the corner into the lobby. For that fleeting second, I see those beautiful eyes looking back, terrified, searching for me. She can't see me over that mob, all of them a head or two taller than she is.

But I see her. They are safe.

Pop!

That fucking outrigger snapped.

Boom!

I dive for the front of the building as the crane cab rips through the roof, sending a bomb blast of razor-like shards from the disintegrated glass wall.

Everything rains down on top of me with a deafening roar. The floor gives way.

Everything plunges—including me.

I curl into a ball, covering my head with my arms—I'm free-falling amid debris.

Metal smashes on metal, screeching and banging. It is ear-piercing.

Wham!

I hit the ground. Momentum keeps me rolling.

Bam! Bouncing over something, I've got nothing to grab ahold of—nothing to keep me from tumbling over the ledge until—*Thud!*

My back slams into one of the steel columns embedded into the cliff's edge.

Oh, shit. That hurts.

Fuck.

Damn.

I lay still, dazed, trying to breathe through a cloud of dust.

The sudden silence is eerie. After that mind-numbing, clamoring roar, nothing—not even the chirping of a bird.

I must be the last thing down.

Through the settling silt, I make out the crane with its battered boom at the bottom of the gorge.

I don't see the dozer.

Everything from the building—lumber, tables, chairs, tablecloths, shingles, two-by-fours, lighting fixtures—everything that was in the restaurant—lies in the creek bed or on the cliffside.

A briefcase is a few feet away. A purse. Plates. Shattered glass.

Staring at the column, I can't believe it. If I had rolled a foot either way, I'd have toppled off the cliff onto that twisted wreckage below. I'd be dead.

Damn, that still hurts. Shit.

Taking a deep breath, I try to get my head around what just happened, rolling onto my back.

It doesn't hurt to breathe, so my ribs aren't broken. My lungs aren't punctured. I lift my head. I see my boots. I roll my ankles. My neck, back, and legs aren't broken.

How did I just fall that far and have nothing broken? I've got no skin left on my arms, I'm banged to hell, everything aches, and my shirt is shredded, but I'm good. I think. I pick a couple of glass splinters out of my forearm and feel my face. I don't feel splinters.

Patsy. I see her in my head, looking back for me. Seeing her frightened blue eyes, I vapor-lock. Where is she? Are she and Jim Beau safe? My mind locks on that image of her looking over her shoulder for me.

Giant hands grip my throat. I'm choking. I can't breathe. I can't even swallow. I've got to find them. They couldn't survive what I just went through. Patsy doesn't weigh much more than a hundred pounds, and her shoulders and bones are tiny.

She wouldn't know how to curl into a ball and roll, and even if she did, if she hit the ground as hard as I did, it would break every bone in her body. She's so little. She doesn't have enough meat on her bones to absorb the blows.

And she was carrying Jim Beau. Oh, my God, no! My son—my wife—they would never survive that fall.

I gag and choke on bile.

I cough it up and spit as I peer at what is left of that crane below. I can see it clearer now that the dust is settling. Oh, hell. How many people are crushed beneath it?

Could they—?

No! "Patsy!" I cup my hands around my mouth and yell again, my gaze scouring the cliffside. "Jim Beau!"

Nothing.

Sitting upright, I peer along the bluff and call again.

Silence answers me.

Get ahold of yourself. You don't do what-ifs. I close my eyes and talk to myself out loud. "You saw her go into the lobby. The lobby is on solid ground. They're safe." *They have to be.* Get your shit together and get up there.

Sirens. I gaze up at the sound of sirens. Lots of them. Help is on the way.

Queasiness washes through me. I feel numb. We would all be safe at home in Texas if I hadn't agreed to make that run with Al.

What... A... Motherfucking... Moron.

All I saw were dollar signs while my best friend was fucking me. Hard.

How could I have been that stupid?

Al knew damned good and well, neither of us would make as much money as he let on. He lied. He never even mentioned DeVecchio. I was supposed to be just him and me.

"Fucker!" I yell and press my fingers to my eyes, feeling the grit in them. "Son of a bitch!"

If I lose Patsy and Jim Beau, I will kill him. And DeVecchio. I will kill both of them with my bare fucking hands.

If, if, if. Stop it!

I hear a voice inside my head say, "Pull yourself together."

Wiping dust from my eyes, I squint at the restaurant. Nothing is left but the framework that supported it. Some of the beams are warped, but it is all climbable. I've got to get back up there and find them.

What's that?

Tilting my head, I listen, my gaze roaming the area. There it is again. That's a human sound, like a person groaning. Someone nearby is hurt worse than I am. I twist, following the sound. "Patsy?"

Over there. Movement. Maybe twenty feet away, someone is on their back, maybe a foot from the edge. That person had no column to stop them from falling off. I'm not sure what did.

It's not Patsy. That body is too big to be hers. *Sorry, bud, but I don't have time to help you.* With all those sirens, paramedics are up there. I'll send them down.

As I grip the column to start my climb, I hear that groan, the quiet sound of agony. *"Uuuhhh..."*

Dammit. I can't turn my back on someone hurt like that.

I crane my neck to peer over the edge. That's another fifty or sixty-foot fall. A wrong roll, and whoever is over there will be dead.

If I slip, I will be, too.

But I walk six-inch steel every day. I can do this. "Hey! Call out!"

Nothing, just that low moaning.

Slow and easy, I walk toward the body. It's a man lying on his back, covered in fine silt.

Oh, man. That hurts just looking at it. The bone below his knee ripped through his slacks—it's protruding. *Damn.*

Above that same knee, another bone bulges against blood-soaked slacks. God, no wonder he's moaning. That guy is in mind-boggling pain.

I'm amazed to see him slip his hands underneath his back, put his weight on them, and rise to a seated position. He pulls himself up, leaning against a shallow rock rise.

The blood in my veins turns to ice. DeVecchio. Son of a bitching, motherfucking Matteo DeVecchio.

We both freeze as our eyes meet.

"Fuck you." I turn around, walking back to the column that saved my life. I'm going to find my family. He can lay there and bleed to death.

As I near the column, something inside me says, 'You can't do this. You've got to be the bigger man.'

Bigger man, my ass. DeVecchio needs to die. I don't have time to fuck with his sorry ass.

The voice again. 'If you leave him like this, you'll regret it the rest of your life. It's cold-blooded murder.'

I stop. Okay, if he asks me to help him, I will.

I wait. Nothing. Not a peep from him.

Good. Let him die.

Reaching the column, that damned voice comes back again. 'If you do this, you are no better than him.'

Screw it. Yeah, I make my way back to the sorry son of a bitch. "How much do you weigh?"

He eyes me suspiciously. "A buck-eighty, give or take."

Up close, I see his wounds clearly. "Man, you are busted to hell."

"Yeah."

Oh, shit. I didn't notice before. His right foot is pointed perpendicular to his body. His left leg pulses blood like a drinking fountain. No telling what internal injuries he suffered—broken ribs, punctured lungs, spleen, kidneys, or liver.

"Does it hurt to breathe?" I ask.

"It hurts all over."

It was the bad luck of how he fell, hitting and bouncing off rocks on the way down. Maybe a section of the crane swiped him, or glass slashed him. There is no way we will ever know how or why I am standing and Matteo DeVecchio is so badly hurt.

I am certain: "I can climb out, but not with a hundred eighty pounds on my back."

DeVecchio leans against the cliff wall, his head back, eyes closed, resting against the shaded stone. "Why would you help me?"

"Truth is, I'd just as soon see you die."

Through the pain, he sneers. "The feeling is mutual."

"Yeah, but you're not in much of a position to do anything about it right now, are you?"

"Just go." DeVecchio draws a ragged breath, wiping his eyes on his shoulder.

I shake my head. "I can't."

He sighs. "The crane took Tommaso and Pietro. I saw it fall on them. You have Patsy. Go." He rasps, "Just... fucking... go."

"You've got a broken leg, man. It'll mend unless you bleed to death. I've got to stop the bleeding."

He roars at me, "I said leave me alone!" His face flushes red. At least that much blood isn't pulsing out of his leg. He might live a little longer.

"No. I can't do it. I can't leave anyone like this. Not even you."

"Are Patsy and the boy safe?"

Fucker.

"I wouldn't be here if I didn't think they were. She made it into the lobby, holding Jim Beau."

"If they made it to the lobby, they should be safe."

"That's what I just said." I unbuckle my belt and pull it free. "I've got to make a tourniquet."

Squatting beside him, leaning over, I slip my belt beneath his left leg.

He doesn't protest anymore.

He turns his head, looking away from me while I work. The right leg may be broken, but his left leg is spewing blood like a water fountain. DeVecchio won't last any time if he keeps bleeding like this.

I thread the belt through the buckle and measure. I need to punch a new hole to get it tight enough to stop this blood flow. His pants and my hands are soaked. In his blood.

I talk, trying to distract him from the pain. "Damn, man. Your thigh is as hard as mine, and I climb steel every day." I dig in my pocket and find my knife as DeVecchio bites his lower lip, saying, "I've been boxing since I was old enough to make a fist."

"Listen, this is going to hurt like hell, but it's better than bleeding out." Our gazes meet and hold.

As DeVecchio nods, I jerk that belt with everything in me and buckle it quickly in the new hole. He winces and groans, but he doesn't holler or cry out. Instead, he closes his eyes.

Is he dying?

"Hey!" I shout at him. "Are you with me?"

He nods—barely.

I'm afraid he's fading, so I speak loudly. "Can you take off your belt? If you can't, I'll do it for you, but I've got to cinch the other leg."

Slowly, DeVecchio feels and unbuckles his leather belt.

I waste no time pulling it free.

I slip it under his right leg—the mangled one with the bones protruding. "I hate to tell you this, man, but this is going to hurt worse than the other one did, with all the broken bones."

He nods as I pierce a new hole and slip the belt high around his right thigh, above that broken femur. "Catch your breath. This will hurt like hell," but I jerk that belt with all I've got before he has a chance to tense up.

I buckle and secure it. Again, DeVecchio eats the pain.

I'll give him this: he is one tough son of a bitch.

The profuse bleeding has stopped. Those tourniquets are tight—but now he's got no blood flow. That could cost him both legs. "I've got to get up top if you have a prayer of living and keeping your legs. And I've got to find Patsy and Jim Beau."

DeVecchio grips my forearm. It's a surprisingly firm grip for a man in his shape. "You know she should be with me."

He's starting that shit again?

I hear his words and see myself shoving his sorry ass off this cliff. He is lying there helpless. It wouldn't take much. I battle that urge with everything in me until I have to look away. *You cannot end him that way. That would be murder.*

We lock eyes. "She's exactly where she belongs."

"No." He winces in pain. "She is not."

"You're just like Al. You saw a shiny object you couldn't have, and spoiled brat that you are, you let it turn into an obsession." I can't believe this guy. "You don't love her. You want her. There's a difference."

I lean back, taking him in. It hasn't been but a couple of hours since he strutted into Al's apartment, looking down his nose at all of us, showing off his muscle with his bodyguards and his stretch limousine. Look at him now.

He is battered to hell. His designer clothes are in shreds. One shirt sleeve is gone, and the other is hanging on by the gold cufflinks at his wrist. His legs are ruined—and he is still obsessed with Patsy.

"DeVecchio, if you were half as smart as you think you are, you'd know a man isn't stupid because he works with his hands. Because he wears jeans instead of slacks. I know what went on in that bedroom between you and my wife. There's only one reason you would have taken her in there, outside my earshot. You told her to leave me on my own or you'd kill me. You don't think I know that?"

I jab my finger at him, clenching my teeth. "And she loves me enough, she'll do it. If she thinks it will save my life,

Patsy will give herself to you." It's all I can do not to strangle him. I hear myself getting loud. "I'd rather die than see her do that. Get this, you motherfucker: The only way you get my wife, and my son is over my dead body. And if you kill me, she will despise you until hell turns to ice."

He glances away.

"You call that love? Making her choose like that? Why would you want a woman who comes to you that way?"

It takes a while, but his gaze comes back to meet mine. DeVecchio stares at me with those ungodly black eyes—it's a staring contest—until he finally squints and nods. "I envy you." The malice in DeVecchio's eyes morphs to melancholy. "Do you have any idea what it feels like to have everything you want except the one thing you want the most? The one thing you can't have?"

"I can't say I do. I don't have anything I want except what I want the most. Them."

DeVecchio's fingers dig into the dirt, and I can't tell whether it's from grief or pain. Maybe both, as he says, "I wish it were me. I wish she brought my son into this world. You're right. I realize she doesn't... want... me." His eyes meet mine. "But you're wrong about something else. I do love her. It was the thunderbolt. I didn't know it only hit one. I thought she felt it, too." He closes his eyes. "I guess her thunderbolt struck when she saw you. You're all she sees."

His dark complexion is ashen. He's lost too much blood. He whispers, "Go... to her." He is fading fast.

"If I don't go now, you're going to die. I'll send you help."

As I turn, DeVecchio grips my wrist. "I wouldn't have had you arrested."

"You thought about it, just like you thought about killing me."

He cracks a weak grin out of one side of his mouth. "I thought about a lot of things."

As I make my way to the column, I call to him over my shoulder, "You're just going to have to trust me."

DeVecchio winces and nods.

I'd feel sorry for him; only I know if our roles were reversed, Matteo DeVecchio would have already shoved me off that cliff.

I glance back. His eyes are closed. I'm not even sure he's alive.

I begin my climb—like I've done every day for the past four and a half years. Walking the crossbeam, I swing around the next column and walk that crossbeam to the cliff wall. Gripping the jutting rocks with my fingers and finding toeholds—I finally reach the top.

Chapter Twenty-Six

THE MOMENT WE HAVE

Patsy

HE ISN'T HERE. My mind and body are numb as my gaze darts frantically.

Dazed people covered in dust mill all around, and I want to scream at them he saved your lives! He warned the whole room.

Maybe I just don't see him. That's what it is—I just don't see him. He's here. "B.J.!" I yell, turning in a circle.

Oh my God, no. He didn't make it out. He warned them and he didn't make it out.

I can't breathe.

"B.J.," I scream hysterically. "B.J.!"

He has to be here. He has to be here. He has to be here.

Oh, God, no. No. No. No.

My knees buckle, and I sink to the ground, clinging to our son, who is wailing in my arms, reaching for his father.

I close my eyes, weeping into my son.

"Can I get your name?"

I peer up at a man who touches my shoulder. He squats beside me. He's a firefighter holding a clipboard, an older man with gray hair who repeats, "Can I get your name, ma'am?"

I wipe my face with one hand, the other pressed against Jim Beau's back, his face buried in my shoulder. "Patsy. Patsy Cole."

"You were inside?" he asks, pen in hand.

"Yes."

The man's eyes roam over us. He seems to be inspecting Jim Beau and me. "Are you injured? Either of you?"

"No. But my husband—my husband." I choke, saying, "He didn't make it out."

The man squinches his face and shakes his head. "I'm so sorry, ma'am." He rests his pen on the clipboard. "What is his name?"

"B.J. Cole. Beaureguard—"

"Daddy!" Jim Beau squeals. "Daddy!"

Stunned, my eyes follow Jim Beau's outstretched arms as he reaches out, still wailing, "Daddy! My daddy!"

Through a blur of tears, I see him. His hair, his face, and his clothes are covered in silt, muddied by blood. His T-shirt is in shreds. Both arms are raw, bleeding, and bruised.

But he's alive, and he's walking to me.

The firefighter pulls me to my feet.

As our eyes meet, B.J. and I run to each other. He grabs us, lifts Jim Beau and me off the ground, and sinks to his knees, holding us. We sob, clinging to each other, our little boy wedged between us.

B.J.'s chest and shoulders heave as tears stream down his face. He can't speak. He just buries his head in us, sobbing, his shoulders shaking as he clutches us to him tightly. It is a long minute before he mutters, "I didn't know..." He chokes on his words, weeping openly.

I have never seen B.J. cry.

He holds us so tightly that I can barely breathe as I lift my eyes to heaven and whisper, "Thank you, Lord."

B.J. loosens his grip, giving me a chance to study his battered face. His temple is purple from where Tommaso hit him with the gun. Every inch that I can see is bruised or scraped or both. Hardly any skin is left on his cheeks and arms. He is pretty much raw meat above the waist.

He doesn't mention his pain. He presses our foreheads together and repeats, "I was so afraid I lost you."

"How, baby? How did you survive?"

He shakes his head but doesn't answer. I guess he doesn't know how he survived.

"I thought I lost you, too." And I realize, all morning, we both thought we lost each other. Matteo, Al, Tommaso, and that Pietro. What wicked men.

B.J. wipes his face on his naked shoulder, then wipes tears from my face with his dirty, bloodied hand, and I catch my breath, seeing it caked in mud and blood. "How bad are you hurt?"

Surprised, he examines his hand. "It's DeVecchio's."

Matteo DeVecchio. A part of me hoped he was dead.

"B.J., you have glass all in your arm." That hurts to look at.

He peers at it. "Yeah."

"You need a doctor."

"Not yet." Jim Beau crawls into his father's big, bloody arms, and B.J. lifts him high, studying him. "You okay, buddy?"

He pulls the baby close, and Jim Beau sinks his head into B.J.'s neck whimpering, "Daddy."

B.J. strokes his son's back. "It's okay, buddy. Daddy's okay. Daddy's here." B.J.'s voice is so soothing.

"Matty?" Al stands over us.

I forgot about Al.

B.J. answers, "He's hurt. Bad." Seeing Al, B.J. stands, holding onto Jim Beau as he helps me up. "His legs are ruined. I got a tourniquet on them, but he's got to have help, or he'll bleed out. An artery or something major is punctured. I told him I'd send paramedics."

Maybe he reads my face or my mind. "I don't care what he is. I had to help him. I couldn't leave him to bleed to death."

Of course, he couldn't. I nod.

B.J. hands Jim Beau back to me. "I'll be back." He turns to leave, stops, turns back around, kisses Jim Beau and me, and says again, "I'll be back."

"Wait!" Grabbing his wrist, I stop him long enough to pull a shard of glass from his shoulder. "When you get back, you're seeing a doctor."

He grins and nods. "Yes ma'am."

About time he listened to me.

B.J. jogs to the nearest fire truck, huddles with several men, and leads them to the cliff's edge. He's guiding them to Matteo. The firemen and EMTs rappel down the cliff with a rescue basket.

Somehow, B.J. gets down, I guess the same way he came up—like he does every day.

Half an hour or so later, the EMTs lift that basket to the top. By then, TV cameras are rolling. They get the mobster onto a gurney and roll him into one of several emergency vehicles waiting to transfer victims to area hospitals.

We stand there as the EMTs slide Matteo into the ambulance. The man who terrorized us—battered and bruised, his lower body soaked in blood—offers his bloodied hand to B.J.

B.J. clasps the offered hand and nods. Their gazes hold.

Matteo pulls him in close, one hand on B.J.'s shoulder as he whispers something.

His eyes leave B.J. to meet mine. Those onyx eyes, dulled by pain, become misty as he stares into me for a long moment and whispers, "Addio, amore mio." A faint smile crosses his lips as he closes his eyes, and the paramedics close the doors to the ambulance.

B.J. glares at Al. "Now, what the hell did that mean?"

Al cuts his eyes at me, rolls them, and sneers. "It means goodbye, my love."

I ignore his hateful ass, asking B.J., "What did he say to you?"

Oh, that's the biggest smile I've seen in a long time. "He says, I owe him nothing. We're headed home."

Again, I lift my eyes to heaven and whisper, "Thank you, Lord."

Watching the ambulance drive away, a part of me can't help but feel sorry for him. I think Matteo truly believes he loves me—maybe he does—but I cannot return those feelings. That hurts no matter who you are.

Without warning, I am back in Al's apartment, standing beside Matteo as he whispers smugly, "Time is on my side." I am struck by the irony. He hadn't a clue how little time he had.

Life will fool you. You think you're on top of the world, and when you least expect it—*Whack!* Life blindsides you. Knocks you to your knees.

The little part left in me that had, at first, liked him hopes Matteo will find a woman he can love, a woman who will love him back. I'm not sure why my heart would feel anything for him. He doesn't deserve it. But then, nobody deserves it.

I have enough compassion to wish for him the kind of love he wanted and could not have from me.

"Al!" B.J.'s bark yanks me from my thoughts.

He's moving toward his lifelong friend, who stands frozen, watching.

B.J.'s right fist is clenched. His gaze is cemented onto Al, whose jaw was ruined by that same fist earlier in the day. That side of Al's face is swollen purple. He's in pain, too.

B.J. stops a few feet from Al and glares hard for a long moment, their eyes dead even. At last, he tilts his head toward Jim Beau and me. "Be glad they're alive." He turns his back on Al, walks to Jim Beau and me, and, with a beaming smile, he stretches out his hand and says, "Come on, Babydoll. Let's go home."

PART

TWO

CHAPTER TWENTY-SEVEN

SOMETHING UNHEARD OF

PATSY

January 2020

WELL, THAT'S SCARY. THE World Health Organization just issued a warning about an outbreak of a never-before-seen virus in the Chinese city of Wuhan. The death rate from the new virus is alarming. Experts fear that, given the volume of world travel, this will become a global pandemic.

A global pandemic. There hasn't been one of those since the Spanish flu in the early 1900s. It infected 500 million people and killed 50 million.

Fifty million people. Imagine. The prospect is terrifying.

I've been glued to television news for the past week. Each day, the normally unflappable anchors have become increasingly animated about this virus, which is similar to pneumonia but so far is untreatable. And it has made its way to the United States.

Some of the news channels' so-called experts say it originated in an open-air market and spread from animals to humans. Others say it has been biologically engineered—weaponized—whatever that means.

Why would anyone use a virus as a weapon?

I surf the morning news as I sip coffee and cook breakfast, clicking from one news network to another. "A 35-year-old man who checked into an urgent care center in Seattle, Washington on January 21st has been diagnosed as the first American infected with the SARS virus."

I've heard that. Click.

"So far, fourteen cases of the respiratory virus have been reported in the United States, all related to travel to China."

Heard that, too. Click.

"Medical experts are sounding the alarm on this new virus, which is claiming lives at an alarming rate—"

"Turn that crap off." B.J. kisses my head and pours himself a cup of coffee. "It's a virus, Patsy."

Flipping a fried egg in the skillet, I give him a fleeting glance. "Good morning." My attention is divided between the eggs and the morning news.

The broadcaster drones on. "Residents are being warned to stay indoors and avoid crowds."

Click! "Today's forecast..."

"Dammit, B.J., I was listening to that." I set his plate of bacon and eggs on the bar in front of him and plant my hands on my hips. "You knew I was listening to that."

He peers at me over his coffee mug. Finishing his swallow, he grins. He loves needling me. "I need to check the weather." He cuts his eyes at me as he cuts up his eggs.

I aim the spatula at him and wag it, scolding. "You need to take this seriously."

"There's no reason for all this panic." My husband refuses to be afraid of anything. He peppers his eggs. "The news people are hysterical. They're feeding everybody's fear so they can get people like you to watch more TV. It's all about their ratings." He waves his hands in the air. "They cry, the sky is falling, the sky is falling, and everyone watches more news."

He's animated and silly, and I giggle at him. We laugh together. It's been almost fifty years, and we can still laugh together.

That man can still eat faster than anyone I've ever known. He's downed his two eggs before I get mine cut up. "They're talking about closing schools."

He chomps his bacon and talks with his mouth full. "Bullshit." He always eats one thing at a time. Eggs, then bacon, then toast.

"No, I'm serious." Watching B.J. slather strawberry jelly on his toast, I take my opportunity to give him a piece of my mind. "Jim Beau said they'll probably end up closing schools. The kids will have to learn remotely, from home, on the internet, I think."

"That's about the stupidest thing I've ever heard of. Viruses have been around since the dawn of time. They didn't shut down schools over the plague or the Spanish flu. Life happens. Deal with it."

"Honey, I don't think they had public schools during the bubonic plague."

He glowers back. "You know what I mean. Don't instill fear into children. Don't teach them to sit in the house and bite their fingernails, afraid to go outside. It is just... plain... stupid."

I sling him a sneer. "What's stupid is sticking your head in the sand like an ostrich. Pay attention. This is real."

He slowly lifts his brows with a mischievous gaze. "Are you calling me stupid? Or an ostrich? I don't know which is worse."

"I'm calling you a hardhead."

He snickers. "Are you ever going to stop gnawing my ass?" He chomps into that jelly-slathered toast with an air of defiance.

I flash him my most practiced, smart-ass smile. "It's a little late for that, dear."

Talking with his mouth full, he aims his toast at me. "How about that's my fiftieth wedding anniversary present? You quit ragging my ass. If you don't, I'm not going to have enough ass left for you to put in a coffin."

He chuckles at his joke as he finishes his last bite of toast and washes it down with a swill of coffee. His eyes are on me. He flicks those brows. "You look good, Babydoll. I could go in late, you know."

"Behave yourself. You're not getting lucky this morning."

He stands, taking his plate in hand. "You're the one not getting lucky."

Hum. There is that.

But I'm not as chipper as he is, I guess from listening to the news.

He chunks his plate into the kitchen sink and runs water over it. I rebuffed him. He never takes that well. Pulling the curtain aside, he peers out the window into the backyard, rolling his shoulder and rubbing it.

"Is your shoulder hurting you again?"

"Yeah. It's getting cold."

"Getting?" The sky is laden with snow, and the tops of big trees are swaying. "We haven't seen the sun all week." I watch him over my cup of coffee as he dons his heavy work jacket. B.J. never grayed—not like I did.

My dark hair was salt and pepper by the time I turned fifty. Now, it is white.

B.J.'s only gray is in his sideburns, around his ears, and along the nape of his neck—the hair that used to be curly and black. He keeps it all cut short now.

"They're advising people to work from home, B.J. You're the boss. You can do that, you know, on a Zoom call."

"Babydoll, you can't put up a building on a Zoom call," he grumbles. "What's the world coming to? Video meetings all the time. People wearing masks and staying inside, afraid." He shakes his head as he pulls up his collar. "And you ought to know by now, I'm not going to send my men to work in this weather while I cower behind a computer."

Even as general manager, B.J. goes to job sites every day, checking in, eyeing their setup, and talking to his men.

"Yes, I know that. I'm just trying to make you understand. This virus is deadly."

"So is pneumonia. So is the flu."

I want to twist his ear. I stand with my hands on my hips, elbows out, hoping he might listen to me for once in his life. "They do not know how to treat this virus. It is not like the flu or pneumonia. It doesn't respond to antibiotics, B.J. Most of the people dying from it are older, and we're not getting any younger. Maybe it's time for you to retire."

He could have retired five years ago.

He kisses the top of my head. "I'll see you tonight."

I grab his coat sleeve with my most pleading stare. "Dammit, I wish you'd listen to me for once. What if—"

You'd think I'd learn.

He shows me that big, wide palm. "What if what? What if a meteor falls on the house? What if the sun falls out of the sky?"

"What if you get this virus and I lose you?"

He smiles and pulls me to him, enfolding me in those arms I still love. "You're not going to lose me."

But what if I did? My mother lived to be almost ninety. I don't want to live twenty-plus years without him. I don't want to live one year without him.

"In case you haven't figured it out, you're stuck with me." He lets go of me and opens the garage door to leave.

"B.J.?" My hand is on his arm. He turns with surprise in his eyes, hearing my most seductive voice. "Just how late can you be?" I run my hands across his chest.

"You missed your window, Babydoll. It's too late."

"It's not too late for me."

His gaze narrows as he stares long and hard, closes the door, and grins. "Just what did you have in mind, Mrs. Cole?"

What I have in mind is enticing the man I love into staying safely at home with me, and I'm willing to do whatever is necessary to accomplish my goal. Besides, it's not like I'm not going to be equally compensated.

Smiling, I take his hand and lead him to the bedroom. No one can deny the chemistry we have had since the moment our eyes first met.

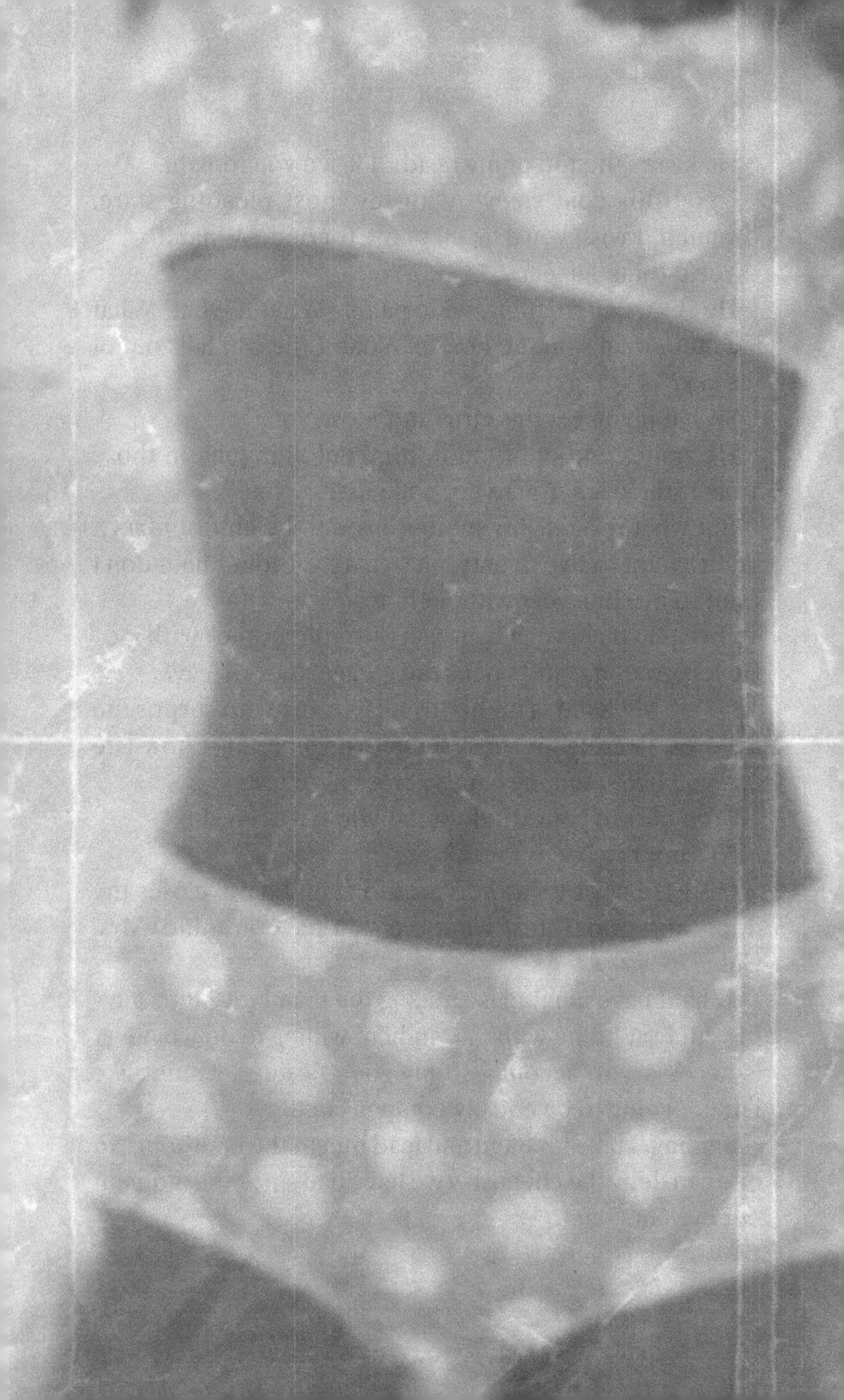

CHAPTER TWENTY-EIGHT
WHAT'S YOUR NAME?
PATSY

June 1969

WE WERE AT BARTON Springs swimming, flirting, sunbathing. A big group from Austin High. It was the summer of 1969, and we'd just graduated.

I was lying on my beach towel, soaking up rays, when a shadow blocked the sun. I peered up at a chiseled silhouette, his hair not quite to his shoulders. Squinting, I shaded my eyes with my hand.

"Don't you go to Austin High?" Whoever he was, he was broad-shouldered, narrow at the hips.

"I just graduated," I answered.

He squatted beside me, and my heart jumped into my throat. B.J. Cole was ogling me in my two-piece bathing suit, which, looking back, wasn't nearly as risqué as I thought it was at the time. "I thought I'd seen you around," he said. "What's your name?"

Geez. Look at those calf muscles. His ripped, tan self was just inches away. I was a little addled. "I'm Patsy... Gentry."

"I'm B.J.—"

"Cole. I know who you are."

He tilted his head cautiously. "Is that good? Or bad?" His reputation preceded him.

I chuckled. "Good." Maybe it was more of a giggle.

"How?"

How? I wanted to say because I used to drool over you—me and every other girl in my class—but instead, I settled for, "You graduated in '67. I was a sophomore. I saw you around then, too. Aren't you at the university now?"

"Yeah, I finished the semester." He paused as he sat down, facing me. "But I'm not going back."

I sat up, leaning on my hands propped behind me, studying him. Our faces were only a few feet apart. He had sun-streaked, sandy-brown hair, golden brown eyes, and a dimple in his chin. His thick, wavy hair wasn't long enough to pull back into a decent ponytail, so it hung loose above his shoulders.

"Why quit school?"

He tucked his knees to his chest, wrapped his arms around them, and peered at the sky. His jaw clenched. "Because I am sick of sitting in class." Those honey-colored eyes came back, studying mine. "You have pretty eyes."

I smiled. "Thank you. So do you."

I cannot believe B.J. Cole is sitting here talking to me. Even up close, I didn't see a flaw.

He stretched his legs straight and reclined on his elbows, taking me in. Not an ounce of fat was on his abdomen. He ran his eyes up and down me. "You're a little-bitty thing."

Before I could figure out how to respond, he said, "My little sister used to have a doll with black hair and blue eyes." He tilted his chin at me. "You're like that babydoll. A living, breathing babydoll."

Embarrassed and blushing, I tilted my head back and laughed at the sky. "And you're big. What are you going to do if you don't go back to school?"

He flicked his brows and grinned. "You want to see?"

"Sure." What I didn't say but meant was, *I'd go anywhere with you.* I couldn't quash the widest smile ever. I was giddy.

He stood and offered his hand, which was covered in sand. "Come on, Babydoll." He had sand on his backside, too. Unlike me, he'd reclined without a towel.

I brushed sand from his back. "Where are we going?"

He lifted his brows and taunted me with a grin. "Are you scared?"

"No, but I'm in a bathing suit, and so are you."

He dusted grit off his butt and legs. "I've got a shirt you can wear." He tilted his head, urging me. "Come on. I want to show you something."

I nudged my best friend Margie, who was soaking up the sun beside me. I'm not sure why B.J. noticed me instead of her. Margie was voted Most Beautiful.

I was just delighted he did.

"Margie, I'll be back." They'd be there all afternoon, tanning and flirting.

She nodded, half asleep. "Um-hum." She didn't see who I was with. If she had, she'd have sat up and taken notice.

He took my hand, led me to a motorcycle in the parking lot, opened the seat, and handed me a T-shirt. It fell almost to my knees. "What will you wear?" I asked.

He glanced down at his chest. "What's wrong with what I've got on?" He was shirtless, wearing cut-off jeans, and looking back, they were short. He wore huarache sandals, too. That was it. That long hair, bare chest, blue jean shorts, and Huarache sandals. And a gorgeous golden tan.

"Nothing," I said as he slipped on sunglasses. "You're perfect." He was.

We jumped on the motorcycle. Neither of us had a helmet, and he took off toward the university. My arms wrapped around his hard, bare middle, and I tucked my face against his bare back to keep his hair and mine from whipping my face. I couldn't believe this was happening. I was riding on the back of a motorcycle wrapped around B.J. Cole. Wait 'til I tell Margie.

He stopped in front of a construction site surrounded by a high chain-link fence and big yellow signs warning, Danger! Keep out! Lots of machines and loud noise.

I slid off first, then he swung his leg to dismount and nodded at the activity. "Houston Towers."

A luxury high-rise apartment complex was being built on Congress Avenue. I'd heard about it. All kinds of big equipment were bustling around it. He nodded and pointed to the highest floor. "See those guys up there?"

My gaze followed his arm, and I pointed, too. "Those guys?" They were like ants in the sky.

He nodded. "That's what I'm going to do."

My jaw sagged. "No! That's so dangerous."

He grinned wide. "Yeah, it is." His gaze was trained on the activity up there.

"Oh, Lord, B.J. Why not be the architect who designs it?"

His gaze met mine. "Because architects sit at desks. I'm not sitting at a desk for the rest of my life. Besides, I can't think of anything I'd rather do than walk in the clouds, building something that will still be standing a hundred years from now."

I shuddered, watching them again. "What keeps them from falling?"

"Nothing," he peered at me. "But I won't fall." He rubbed strands of my hair between his thumb and index finger as he raked his eyes from my head to my feet, climbing back to meet my eyes. I may have been young and naïve, but I noticed his eyes liked what they took in.

He said, "I like my shirt on you. It's yours."

I wasn't sure his mother would appreciate that, but I tingled with delight. This is too good to be true. Even if I never see him again, B.J. Cole gave me his shirt. "Are you sure?"

"Yeah. Go out with me tonight, Patsy."

"Where?" I was still trying to wrap my mind around this. It was happening so fast. I mean, this is B.J. Cole.

"Does it matter? Anywhere. I'll take you anywhere."

Pinch me. One of the most lusted-after guys in town gave me a shirt and asked me out. He said he'd take me anywhere.

B.J. hooked his thumb toward the motorcycle. "Hop on. Let's cruise the drag and get something to drink."

"I need to get back before my friends have to leave. They're my ride."

"I'm your ride. I'll take you home." B.J. never suffered from a lack of confidence. He saw the same thing in my eyes that I saw in his. He knew he had me.

"But they need to know, or they'll worry about me."

A smile took over his face. "So, let's go tell them."

"But you don't know where I live."

"You'll show me." My smile couldn't have been any bigger as I nodded up at him.

Without warning, he swept me off my feet—literally. B.J. scooped me up and set me on his motorcycle, and he said, "Damn, I like you."

He got on, and we took off. And one more time, my arms were wrapped around that hard body, my face to his back as the engine roared and our hair whipped all around.

At Barton Springs, he took my hand. I let him, and we walked back to Margie and my stuff. In my absence, she'd become surrounded by a crowd. Trust me. Margie drew guys like honeysuckle drew bees.

She didn't notice us until some guy I never saw before yelled, "B.J.! Where the hell is Al? I've been trying to find him."

"Baltimore."

"When is he back? He's supposed to have something for me."

"Pretty sure that's what he's taking care of."

Margie's blue eyes widened, and her mouth opened slightly as she recognized me walking up with B.J., hand in hand.

I couldn't suppress my proud smile. Every girl watching was envious. Like I said, he was to die for. Her perfect brows were high as she asked, "Where did you go?"

I glanced up at B.J., who answered before I could. "I took her downtown to see the new high rise going up on Congress."

"Why?" Several asked at once.

My eyes were on him, still admiring. Adoring. Lovestruck.

"Isn't it, like, Houston Tower or something?" a tall guy with curly blonde hair asked. I didn't know him either.

Some of these guys must have been people from UT because I didn't recognize them from Austin High.

"Yeah," B.J. answered.

"What's going on there?"

He nudged his head toward me. "I showed her where I start work on Monday."

"For the summer?" That question came from yet another guy I didn't know. His dark hair was much longer than B.J.'s.

"No. I'm going to help build it, Dan."

There was a collective gasp.

"You're dropping out of school?" That was Paula Hauser. Her, I knew. An auburn-haired girl who graduated between me and B.J. I think they dated for a while. The shock in Paula's voice was palpable.

"That's exactly what I'm doing." B.J.'s tone was biting. Watching his expression, I realized this was a battle he had already fought.

The dark-headed Dan sat up straight. "Oh, man, B.J. You better think."

B.J.'s eyes flashed. "A classroom isn't the only place you can learn."

Paula pleaded her case. "But B.J. People who drop out never earn as much as—"

B.J. showed them all his palm. "I don't need this," he peered at me. "Are you willing to go out with a dropout?"

I smiled, nodded, and peered at Margie, who, by the look on her face, was still in shock seeing B.J. Cole and me holding hands like a couple. "Will you take my beach towel and bag home with you? We're on his motorcycle. We'll talk tomorrow."

She nodded with an expression of intrigue and made the phone sign with her fingers. "Call me."

———

B.J. walked me to my front door. As it turned out, we didn't live far from each other. "You want to come in?" I offered.

He shook his head gently. "I'll clean up and come back."

"What time?"

"Seven. That gives us time to get to Mount Bonnell and climb it."

My eyes got big. "Climb it?"

What a beautiful grin! And there was something about that dimple in his chin.

He chuckled. "Yeah, you have to climb to the top of Mount Bonnell to see the sunset."

My brows raised high, and my heart thumped. I was no mountain climber. "You mean like, climb-climb?"

Tilting his head back, he laughed heartily. "No, but it's a steep hike."

"Oh... Okay. I can do that."

"Wear comfortable shoes. Nothing fancy. No sandals and nothing with heels. Tennis shoes are best."

I nodded.

He rubbed strands of my hair between his thumb and forefinger again. "How have I never noticed you before?" To my dismay, he kissed me right there at my front door. A sweet peck on the lips. "I'll be back, Babydoll."

CHAPTER TWENTY-NINE
GETTING TO KNOW YOU
PATSY

I CAN'T COUNT HOW many times I watched the sunset atop Mount Bonnell with B.J., but that was our first.

Texas sunsets are nature's kaleidoscopes. One of God's greatest gifts to man.

A few high-wispy clouds in a cerulean sky? We'd watch swirls of pink lemonade slowly deepen to purple before turning the color of Manischewitz wine.

When a cloud layer settled over the Hill Country, the sunset might be striated in glowing bands of yellow, orange, and red.

When the clouds were billowy puffs, the setting sun shone through them in swatches of lemon, melon, and fuchsia that morphed like a lava lamp.

And, when a storm threatened from the west with dark clouds climbing to the heavens, we'd watch lightning flash inside as they roiled, turning bluey-purple, sometimes with a tinge of blood orange.

Oh, those quiet moments watching those big Texas skies, with his strong arms wrapped around me, my back resting against B.J.'s chest, both mesmerized by the slow-changing sky. Now that's heaven.

We had a lot of firsts on top of Mount Bonnell.

He smoked pot that first night, which didn't surprise me. Even in high school, most people I knew smoked marijuana, but I'd already learned that I couldn't handle it. He didn't try to coax me.

We were sitting side by side. Instead of taking my hand, he tilted his head and summoned me, spread his legs wide, and rested his back on a boulder. "Sit here and lean against me."

I did.

He wrapped his arms around my middle, and I felt his warmth surround me. As I rested my head on his shoulder and we watched the sunset in silence, I felt something move through me that I had never experienced before—physical desire—an aching deep down inside.

I tilted my face to his.

His eyes searched mine as mine did his.

B.J. leaned down, kissing my lips softly. His lips parted, and I followed his lead. His tongue exploring my mouth ignited a firestorm of feelings I never knew existed. An ache surged inside my body and I wanted to feel more of that.

He did, too. "Oh, Patsy," he sighed. "Damn." I felt his strength as B.J. lifted me into his lap, once again mastering my mouth, his kiss overpowering yet gentle. His tongue sliding against mine did something to me I never imagined. He knew what he was doing—I didn't—and his unending kiss sucked all the common sense right out of my head. I was lost in a myriad of new sensations. My heart fluttered like a little rabbit's in his arms.

It was an awakening. A coming-of-age kiss.

B.J. was a gentleman. Had he not been, I'm not sure when I would have had the wherewithal to stop. He had given me something I would crave for the rest of my life. He was so good at that.

He pressed my cheek against his chest, and I felt the drumming of his heart. "We need to get down before dark." It was a steep climb up and a sketchy descent in the dark. B.J. held my hand, guiding our path.

"That was awesome," I said as he opened the passenger door for me. *Not just the sunset but the kiss.* "Thank you."

He smiled. "I'm glad you liked it." He stood at the door, leaned in, and kissed me again, holding his gentle kiss for a long moment. When the kiss ended, his eyes danced across my face as I reached up. With the tips of my fingers, I softly traced the curve of his lips, memorizing the outline of his jaw in the dim glow of the parking lot lights. Looking at him, taking him in, it was something else. Best. Date. Ever.

He almost whispered, "Patsy, you're the cutest girl I've ever seen."

My heart sank. *Cute.*

It was like he read my thoughts because he cocked his head to the side and asked, "That's a bad thing?"

I tried to sluff it off. "No." I flashed a weak smile. "Thank you. It's just, everybody says I'm cute. I guess, I hoped you would think I was pretty."

He tilted his head back and laughed. "God, Patsy, you are pretty. Very pretty. I guess I didn't say it right. To me, cute is better than pretty."

Again, he read my expression, this time of surprise. He said, "Cute is pretty plus."

"Plus, what?"

He snickered as if I should know. "Personality. I watched you before I ever came up to you."

"This afternoon?" I had no idea.

"Y'all were in the water playing horse when I pulled up. I thought then, that's the cutest girl I've ever seen."

We stared at each other for a moment. I was speechless. He wasn't. "I don't know, there's just..." He paused and shrugged. "Something about you, Patsy. Your face, your eyes, your hair, your figure, your laugh, your spunk—hell, Babydoll, you've got it all." He twisted his neck. "You are the whole package."

He took my breath.

All I could say was, "Thank you. And you know how handsome you are, right?"

"I guess. Whatever." B.J. Cole had heard that many times, I was sure. Coming around the truck, sliding behind the steering wheel, he asked, "Where to now?"

I hadn't thought that far. "Are you hungry?" I asked.

"Starving."

"Mexican? Pizza? Barbeque? Burgers?" I began tossing out options. "Honestly. I'm not a picky eater. You chose."

He started the truck engine, cutting his eyes at me. "Do you like Greek food?"

"I've never eaten it."

He had a cagey grin. "Want to try it? Something new?" He patted the bench seat, indicating he wanted me to sit beside him.

I scooted over. "How do you know Greek food?" I asked.

He watched over his shoulder as he backed out, his arm spread across the seat back. "My Mom. She's made sure we try every cuisine in the city: Japanese, Chinese, Italian, Mexican, Greek, Korean. You name it."

"What is your favorite?"

He cut his eyes over and down at me. "After chicken fried steak, mashed potatoes, and gravy? Greek."

"Greek it is then. And someday Chinese?"

"You bet." He rested his hand on my shoulder and pulled me tightly against him.

And that was it.

I was in the arms of a guy I was already crazy about, and he just said I was cute—he said cute was better than pretty, which I never dreamed of, and he said I was the whole package. And the way B.J. made me feel when he kissed me—Oh. My. Lord. I was on top of the world.

I had my first ever baba ghanoush and moussaka, both made with eggplant, in a little Greek family restaurant on South Congress. I don't remember the name of it. It was like an old gas station turned into a café with plate glass windows all around, not far from the river.

The place didn't have many customers at that hour.

We sat outside at a table for two, eating and learning about each other. He was one of five kids, the youngest son. He had a much younger sister. "She was a surprise," he said.

"So, you're getting grief about quitting school?" I asked a while into the meal.

B.J. never drank with a straw. His eyes met mine over his soda glass, which he clomped onto the table. "You could say that."

I chewed my food and my thoughts, watching him. "I'm sorry."

His gaze intensified, gripping mine. "You don't think it's a mistake?"

I crossed my forearms on the table and leaned in close. "I know how I felt having to sit through Algebra knowing I will never use Algebra in real life. Total, total drudgery. If that's how you feel about school, it is pure punishment."

He closed his eyes for a moment and shook his head softly. "Nobody else seems to get that. I hate it."

My eyes searched his, soft and brown, finding those few flecks of green in them. "I just worry about you getting hurt. You know if you fall from those heights..."

He joined me, leaning in close, his expression dead serious. "Patsy, if you can walk a six-inch shadow on the ground, you can walk a six-inch beam in the air. And besides, they won't send me up if I don't prove myself. No one starts as a connector. It's the highest-paid position in construction."

"It should be."

He drew back, sitting straight in his chair, his head back, his gaze darting about the sky, silent for a long moment before his eyes met mine again. "When I was a kid, I had an erector set. Lincoln logs. As long as I can remember, I've liked to build things. Now, I want to build real things. Big things that will last a hundred years. Build them, not design them."

I was a little shellshocked. B.J. Cole, a boy I had literally dreamed of, was opening up, revealing who he was beneath that cocky, handsome exterior.

"I have a dream I haven't told anyone." He leaned his forearms on the table, our faces close again, as he looked me directly in the eyes. "I want to be the guy who runs it all. The guy who turns a bunch of steel and concrete into a landmark. You can't learn that sitting in a classroom."

He finished his soda, watching me, and set his empty glass down. "I want to look at a big building like the one I showed you today and remember when we laid the foundation and set the first column—and the last. I want to drive by it when I'm an old man, show my grandkids, and say, "Grandpa helped build that." He held up his hands, fingers spread wide. "These hands were meant to build things."

Just look at him. I was totally hooked on B.J. Cole. Already.

He wasn't dropping out of school—he was going to his own school, forging his own way. What courage he had to face criticism from his family, endure ridicule from his friends, and hold firm to his convictions. He faced the world, saying, "I don't want to be who you want me to be. I want to be who I want to be." I was in awe of his faith in himself.

I surprised him. I was brazen. He watched me curiously as I got up, walked around the table, and ran my fingers through his thick, long hair, combing it back, taking his handsome face in my hands, and I kissed him the way he'd kissed me at the truck—slowly, softly, gently.

Somehow, the way he had complimented me, the way he'd made me feel so desired, B.J. gave me the guts to do that.

Looking into his eyes, I told him, "B.J. you are the whole package. I believe in you."

REAL
VIRUS

Chapter Thirty

His Defiance

B.J.

Late March 2020

"Mornin' boss." My secretary meets me every day with a chirpy little smile. I can see it under her pink flowered face mask. I hate those things. Patsy will not get off my ass about wearing one. She gnawed on me last night and through breakfast. If I wanted to wear a damned mask, I would.

"What's good about it?" I snap at her.

"Spring. If you haven't noticed, it's beautiful outside. Why are you so sour?" Jill places a cup of coffee on my desk. I can see it behind the mask. She is Pollyanna in the flesh.

I take the cup and nod. "Thanks. And I say this with affection—what's wrong with me is—"

She shows me her palm. "Got it."

I taste the bitter brew and wince. "Is this Starbucks?"

"No."

Shoving the cup aside, I tell her, "Whatever it is, it tastes like crap." My wife makes the best coffee. "Get me something else."

"It's all we have. Corporate is buying the coffee."

Are you kidding me? "Since when?"

"Yesterday."

Corporate. I should have known. They can't leave well enough alone.

"I'll get Patsy to start buying coffee for our office."

I've run this company, answering only to the owner, since 1995—until two years ago—when these fucks bought us, asking me to stay on as General Manager, answering to them while the former owner is playing golf somewhere in the Bahamas. Or Tahiti.

It wouldn't be a bad gig if the people I answer to knew the difference between an I-beam and an H-beam—besides the shapes. I have to explain everything to corporate like I'm talking to a brand-new hire. They may be in the construction business, but they don't have a single person in upper management who ever walked an I-beam.

They're finance guys, salespeople, human resource Nazis, and marketers. They don't have a fucking clue what it's like to work in the field.

Jill gives me a smug smile and tilts her head, her arms folded across her chest. "How long have we been working together?"

I know her. I know where she's going. "I'm warning you, Jill. I'm not in the mood today."

Jill never backs off. She's always happy to jerk my chain. "I'm just saying, B.J., I've known you for a long time, and when you hit the door as grouchy as you are first thing in the morning—invariably, Patsy pissed you off."

I peer at her over my coffee mug, giving the chicory-tasting crap a second chance. "You'd think after fifty years, she'd stop trying to change me."

"What did she do?"

"She wants me to wear a damned face mask all the time. This virus has her scared to death."

Jill snickers. "That's not trying to change you. She's trying to save your life. Dummy."

"Take a hike." I wave her off.

She flashes a Patsy-like smirk. "B.J., first of all, the government says you have to wear a mask, and two, it's not just Patsy. Everybody in the world is afraid of this virus." She turns to leave my office, calling over her shoulder, "Everybody with a lick of sense, anyway."

Bunch of cowards. "We're all born with an expiration date," I call to her as she leaves my office.

I had more scrapes with death while I was connecting than most people can imagine. One time, we were working maybe thirty feet up when my foot slipped, and I landed flat on my back on a six-inch beam. Didn't fall. Another time, an I-beam caught the hem of my jeans. Almost flipped me off that crossbeam. To this day, I don't know how I lived through any of that. But I did.

I never carried all that shit home to Patsy.

I turn on the computer and sign in. When I started, we didn't have computers. I didn't have to remember all these passwords. I begin scrolling through e-mails. I'm pounding out a reply to H.R. when Jill returns with something that looks like a cloth wrapped in plastic, tossing it on my desk. "Here."

I look from the monitor—to the package—to her. "What is it?"

"I think they call it a neck gaiter," Jill says. "Corporate sent them this morning, along with a mandate for everyone to wear them. Everyone." She stresses the last word and points at the computer monitor. "Read your e-mail. It's like a scarf that goes around your neck. You pull it up over your mouth and nose in place of a mask that hangs over your ears. It's supposed to be more comfortable."

"Jill, everybody's already wearing a hard hat. If they wear this, too, how's anybody supposed to know who the hell they're talking to?"

She raises her hands and hikes her shoulders. "What do you always say? Deal with it."

Give me a break.

She turns to leave, then turns back around. "Don't forget the conference call at nine. Oh, and your number came up. You have to get drug tested."

"Today?"

"Yeah."

"Damn." I haven't had to be drug tested since—hell, I can't remember the last time my name came up. I'm not in the field anymore. But I do call the shots. The buck stops in this office. The government wants to make sure we're clean and sober from top to bottom. C.Y.A.

"Okay."

CHAPTER THIRTY-ONE

PLEASE. NO.

PATSY

April 2020

"B.J. BREAKFAST IS READY." What's going on? He never oversleeps. I shake his shoulder. "B.J.? Honey, wake up." He's usually out of the shower before I finish cooking breakfast.

He draws up on his elbow. "What time is it?"

I glance at the bedside clock. "Six-fifteen." He's been at work before 7 a.m. every day for fifty years without setting the alarm.

B.J. sinks back onto his pillows. "I don't feel good."

My skin tingles. "What's wrong?"

"I'm... tired." He closes his eyes as if his eyelids are too heavy to hold open. "I ache." A few seconds later. "My head hurts."

I place the back of my hand on his neck. "Oh, God. You're burning up. I need to get you to the doctor."

He shakes his head softly. "It's just the flu. Some guys are out with it."

"I'll call the doctor's office and see if they will call in some medicine."

"Just let me sleep." As I turn to leave, he sits up in the bed. "Wait. I need to call work. Will you bring me my cell phone?"

B.J. never—I mean never—asks me to bring him anything.

I go to the den, where his phone is on the charger, and return to the bedroom. He's propped on pillows.

Offering him the cell phone, I ask, "Do you want a cup of coffee?"

He nods.

When I return, he's giving directives to whoever is on the phone. "Yeah, I know. Pain in the ass DOT. I got mine a week ago. Keep me updated. I don't need to expose you guys to whatever I have. I'll be available on the phone."

Holding out his coffee, I ask, "You got what a week ago?"

"My drug test."

"Why? You haven't been drug tested in years."

"It's random, Patsy. When your name is drawn, you've got a couple of hours to get your test. My name came up."

My throat tightens. "Where did you get this drug test?"

He shrugs. "That drug screening place on MoPac."

MoPac runs through the middle of Austin. My throat closes, and I squeak out. "Was it crowded?"

"Well, hell, yeah. I wasted my morning waiting."

I groan. "And you didn't wear a mask, did you?"

He glowers at me over his coffee. "Yeah, I did. They made me." He hands the cup back. "This coffee doesn't taste right."

It tasted fine to me. I lift my eyes to heaven. *Please don't let this be that virus.* "I'm going to take your temperature." I head to the bathroom for the thermometer.

"Why?" he asks.

"Because if it's too high you're going to the hospital. The doc in the boxes and crowded places like that damned drug screening place are where most people are catching coronavirus. I can't believe the Department of Transportation made you go there."

"If I have it, I'm not going to the hospital. I watch the news. They're putting people in isolation."

He may be the most stubborn man ever born. "Dammit, B.J."

And here comes that palm. "Pat, just let me sleep. And in case it is that virus, I guess you better sleep in one of the spare bedrooms."

I hold out a cocktail for him to swallow. No, not alcohol, although a good, stiff drink might make him feel better. He does like his whiskey. This cocktail is two acetaminophen and two ibuprofen, a combination our doctor prescribed a few years earlier when we both came down with the flu at the same time. It reduces fever fast.

"We've slept together every night since you got tested. If I'm going to get it, I've already got it."

"We don't both need to be sick. I don't want to give it to you." He sounds so tired. He takes the pills and lays down.

I kiss his forehead. It's hot. "Sleep, baby. I'll be here."

B.J. trudges into the kitchen. I don't think he realizes I see him grip the edge of the kitchen counter as he moves across the room. To steady himself? To support his weight?

He says, "I want to sit up." It's not his strong voice. Whatever this bug is, it has kept him down for a week. He says, "I'm sick of lying in bed. I think I'm getting bed sores."

If he's feeling well enough not to want to lie in bed, maybe he's getting better. He still thinks he has the flu. I've never seen the flu hit him this hard. He constantly struggles for air as if he has asthma or bronchitis. His body aches, like with the flu, but his fever has never gone away and stayed away. It breaks sometimes, and he sweats all over. Then it comes back.

But he refuses to go to the doctor. He shows me the hand every time I bring it up.

I've been controlling a creeping terror as this lingers. He leans on the counter as he moves across the kitchen. Not once before have I seen him do this.

From the bar, he makes it without support into the den, clutches the back of his recliner, moves around it, and sits down.

Had I tried to help him, he would have protested. He has to do it on his own.

"Do you want a lap quilt?" I ask.

"I'm good." He turns on the TV.

If he's diagnosed with coronavirus, they will put him in isolation. It's all over the news: families protesting about not being able to see loved ones in nursing homes and hospitals. The thought of being isolated from his family keeps him from seeking help. He won't budge. And I don't want him somewhere I can't be with him. If I could stay with him in the hospital, I'd make him go.

Damn, those people who make the rules. Damn them, and damn this virus. "Can you eat something?"

He shakes his head. "I guess I'll try coffee again."

"Toast?"

"I guess. I don't know. I've lost my taste buds." He leans back in the recliner, clicking through channels. I'm pouring his coffee when he calls out. "Pat! Look!" He points to the TV.

I turn to see Matteo DeVecchio and Al Mancini enter a courthouse surrounded by news cameras. The mobster's once-black hair is gray. The news anchor says, "Drug king-pin Matteo DeVecchio surrenders to authorities in Washington, D.C. after being indicted by the Department of Justice on charges of—"

Click!

"B.J.! You just told me to look. I was watching that."

He grumbles, "I don't want to look at your old boyfriend."

He never got that out of his craw.

"Stop it. You know that's not true." I offer him his cup of coffee with a kiss on his head.

He glances up. "What if you ended up with that fucker?" There's more than a tinge of bitterness. "Your husband would be in prison."

"First of all, I wouldn't have married him and secondly, he's not going to prison, and he knows it."

B.J. glares at me. "You know something I don't know?"

I reply over my shoulder as I return to the kitchen to butter his toast. "No, but a man like him? He and Al have bought off every judge on the East Coast by now. He's not going to prison. Now turn it back on."

"Fat chance, Babydoll."

Rawhide comes on.

"Really?"

He tilts his head to see me and raises his brows with a hint of mischievousness. "Are you gonna give me a hard time while I'm sick?"

I can't help but chuckle to myself. I don't blame him for not wanting to see Al and DeVecchio.

I'm looking in the fridge for his favorite strawberry jam when B.J. says over his shoulder, "You know, as much as I hate that motherfucker, he singlehandedly changed who I am."

Did he say what I thought he said? "What?"

B.J. shrugs. "What he said about what kind of man would do drugs in front of his wife and child." He struggles, inhaling a long breath, and closes his eyes. "I never should've done that." I stand beside him with his saucer of toast slathered in jam, which he takes, his eyes on mine. "I never told you I was sorry... I'm sorry."

He takes a bite of his toast and says, with his mouth full, "Funny. Sometimes, the people you hate the most end up having the greatest effect on you."

I sit in my recliner beside his, a lamp table between us. "Those were different times, baby. We were so young. I didn't think less of you for it."

"Well... I did." We sit in silence for a good while. He's deep inside his head. "I guess I wasted my youth trying to see how far I could push the boundaries." He shakes his head slowly, regretfully. "Just for the hell of pushing, I guess. Giving the finger to the system."

I want to laugh, but mostly I want to cry. He is still the same. I want to shout at him, "Why do you think you're where you are today?" The system told you to wear a mask. *Here's the finger, buddy. Nobody's going to make B.J. Cole wear a damned mask.*

Age mellowed him, but he is still B.J. Cole.

"One toe over the line, huh?" It is the best I can muster.

"Yeah, I guess." He leans his head back. "You know, I always thought Al and I were brothers. Two peas in a pod. I didn't have a single happy childhood memory that didn't have Al in it." He cuts his eyes at me, and they are filled with a sadness I had never seen. "I thought we were best buds for life." His voice quietens. "He's never apologized. Not once in all these years."

He has never spoken of it.

He reaches across the table, palm open, and I put my hand in his. His weary eyes search mine. "If it hadn't been for that crane falling, DeVecchio getting hurt so bad—me or him one would have died. For you, Patsy. Do you realize what a desirable woman you are?"

No words can make it through the clog in my throat. I shake my head, biting my cheek to fight the tears. I can't count how many years it's been since I thought of what happened in Richmond. Has it haunted him all these years?

"Patsy," he says later, his head leaning against the recliner, his eyes closed. "I've never asked. Did you regret your risk?"

"What risk?"

His gaze finds mine, and if I didn't know B.J., I'd swear I saw tears. "Babydoll, I know loving me was the only risk you ever took in your life. Did you regret it? Do you regret it?"

The question hits like a blast of icy wind that stings your eyes and takes your breath.

I get up, move to his chair, and go to my knees, peering up at him with my hand on his, my wedding ring on top of his. "B.J., not one second in fifty years did I regret us."

B.J. wipes his eyes with the back of his hand, lifts my hand to his lips, and kisses it. "You know what I could use?"

"What?"

"A drink."

"A drink? At this hour?"

He snickers. "What's it gonna do, kill me?" He laughs, and that's good to see until he has a coughing fit.

I pour him two fingers of whiskey with a teaspoon of honey and a squeeze of lemon. "Try this." I hold it out for him.

He sips and nods. "Tastes good." He gets his air back, resting his head again on the tall recliner. "Come here." He tilts his head, summoning me, and I obey, sitting on the arm of his recliner. B.J. says, "I'm going to kick this bug, and you and I are going to take a real vacation. Hawaii maybe. What do you say?"

I kiss his forehead. "B.J., I'll go anywhere with you."

———

"Sit down, Pat, and talk to me."

He's weak, struggling for air. The days are dragging, and he's not getting better.

My hackles rise. I don't remember him ever saying that. *Not that way.* He has lost so much weight he is beginning to not look like B.J. anymore. His cheeks are gaunt. His eyes are weak.

I hold up my tea glass. "I'm just going to freshen my tea. You want some?"

"No." B.J. pats the bed weakly. "We need to talk."

I don't want to talk! I know what he's going to say. *No, we're not going there!* My throat clogs, and I can't respond. I walk into the kitchen, gripping the countertop and putting it off. *No. No. No.*

Our master bedroom is right off the kitchen. "Pat! Come in here. It's time to face reality."

I feel bad for making him shout. He doesn't need to expend that energy.

My heart pounds as I return and sit beside him on the edge of the bed, feeling his neck with the back of my hand. *Fucking fever.*

He enfolds my hand tightly, but his voice is soft. "Lay beside me, Patsy." He closes his eyes. My robust husband is so weak. "I want to feel you. One last time."

"NO!" I stand, and my voice is loud. "Don't say that to me, B.J.!"

Our eyes meet. "Please, Pat. I don't want to fight."

"Then don't say one last time. You're going to beat this."

"I don't think so. Not this time."

Tears fill my eyes.

He pats the bed again. "Rest your head on my shoulder with your hand on my chest. Let me feel you and look into your eyes and remember. I need that, Pat."

I think he's going to cry.

Tears slide down my face.

His eyes follow me as I walk to my side of the bed and remove my gown, standing still and naked so he can take me in. I should be embarrassed, an old woman standing naked, but it's what he wants.

He smiles. "You're a beautiful woman." He pats the bed again.

"Thank you, baby." I know I'm not beautiful, but he loves me, he wants to feel me, and I will give him anything he wants. Anything.

B.J. opens his left arm wide, and I snuggle my naked body against him, resting my head on his shoulder, my hand on his chest—the way we went to sleep every night when we were young. I stroke his chest and abdomen. "You're naked."

"Yeah."

"Are you feeling frisky?"

B.J. snickers and tucks his chin to see me. "I'm afraid those days are gone. I just want us to feel each other." He runs his right hand along my collarbone and shoulder, and it comes to rest, cupping my breast. That hand, which can ball into a fist and break a man's jaw, delivers the tenderest touch. He never lost that.

We are both as naked as when we came from the womb, but sex isn't on either of our minds. This is naked love. Touching. Feeling. Remembering. People underestimate the importance of touch.

My eyes close as I savor this moment, just feeling him—his still-powerful chest and still-hard abdomen—as he runs his thumb softly across my breast. I recall admiring his muscular body when he leaned back on his elbows that first day at Barton Springs.

I'm remembering. He must be, too. Looking up at him, I see his eyes are closed, but I know he's not asleep. He's fondling my breast. "B.J.?"

"Uh-hum?"

"What are you thinking about?" I ask.

A smile forms on his face. "Valentine's Day, 1970."

Chapter Thirty-Two

Best. Valentine.
Ever

Patsy

February 1970

Using pliers, B.J. held a silver spoon over the open flame of a propane stove burner. It was beginning to glow orange. "What are you making?"

He glanced at me. "Spoon rings."

I peeked over his shoulder at his labor. Between the pliers and the spoon, he had a cloth. "What's the rag for?"

"It keeps the pliers from scarring the spoon. Silver is soft, especially when it gets hot." He focused on his work, twisting his wrist and bending the metal. His hair was long enough that he pulled it into a short ponytail at the nape of his neck.

We were at his parents' weekend cabin on the Colorado River outside Bastrop, and no, they didn't know we were there.

"How'd you learn to do that?"

He gave a quick shrug, bent over his work. "I figured it out. It's kind of like making horseshoes. Heat the metal and bend it."

"Who are the spoon rings for? Are you going to sell them?"

He drew back and peered at me, bewildered. "It's Valentine's Day, Patsy. Who do you think I'm making them for? Us."

It took me a moment. "Like steady rings?" I asked.

He snickered, focused on his task, not me. "We are going steady."

True. We'd seen each other every day since we met, but nothing had ever been committed.

"B.J.?"

"What, Babydoll?" He was perturbed by my interruptions, intent on shaping the ring. Flowers vined across the flat, wide silver spoon handle, which would form the top of the ring.

"Where'd you get the silver spoons?"

"They were my grandmother's."

I giggled. "Oh, B.J.!" My fingers covered my mouth. "Your mom will be furious."

"She won't miss them. They've got more of these things than they can count."

The threat of getting in trouble never deterred B.J. from doing whatever he wanted.

"They're old, aren't they?"

"Yeah." He paused his toiling with the ring to answer. "I think, like, maybe from the Civil War or just after."

And he's turning them into rings for us?

I watched in awe as the first spoon handle was transformed into a ring. Using the pliers, he held it up with a big smile. "What do you think?"

I stared at it in amazement. It was as pretty and unique as any ring I'd ever seen in a store. "It's beautiful, but I don't understand. What do matching rings mean for us? Exactly?"

His gaze moved from his new ring to me. "What do you want them to mean?"

"You're making them. You tell me."

We made out, but we'd never made love. Oh, don't misunderstand. B.J. tried. To his frustration, we'd gotten—well, let's just say, almost there, but I always put him off. I was old-fashioned. I wanted to be married first.

"I don't know, Patsy. I wanted to make us matching spoon rings. Not a real deep thing going on here."

My heart dropped with a thud, along with my gaze. "Oh," I said quietly.

He plunked the pliers and ring on the wooden cutting board and glared at me. "Now, what does that mean? You sound disappointed."

I picked at the tablecloth. "I don't know. You've never said I love you. Never made a promise or commitment. And now you're making rings? For us?"

He held up his palm. "I thought that was understood."

I lifted my gaze to meet his. "What? What was understood?"

"That I love you. We've been together every day for six months. I've never looked at another girl. I don't want to."

My jaw sagged. "No. That wasn't understood."

His eyes grew wide. "Well, I understood that you love me." He tucked his chin. "Don't you?"

He was so cocky.

I chortled. "Yes, B.J. I love you. Very much."

He extended his arm toward me with a smirk. "Well, you never said it, either."

Because I thought the man had to say it first.

He said, "I guess I thought you knew it." He came to me and squatted beside my chair, his hand on top of the chair back, peering into my eyes. "So just to be clear, for the record: I love you, Patsy Gentry. Will you wear the matching ring that I'm making for you and me?"

"What do the rings mean? Do they mean we're engaged?" Yes, I wanted to marry him. It had become my dream to be Mrs. B.J. Cole. If he wouldn't ask, I guess I just did.

His head tilted back, and he snickered. "As far as I'm concerned, we're married right now." He scowled. "Without the benefits."

Now my jaw dropped. He was going to get a piece of my mind.

He saw it coming and sighed. "Patsy, do you want to get married? Like officially? With a preacher and all? You know, we don't have to have a piece of paper issued by the state to be man and wife."

Marriage was out of fashion in Austin, Texas, in 1970. People just lived together.

I knew him. He wanted to do it his way, not yield to society's dictates. Just give me a ring, move in together, say we're married, and finally, have his benefits.

I wasn't quite the rebel he was. I was way more afraid of my parents than he was of his.

Our gazes were locked, and I was about half mad. "My father says we do."

He chewed his lower lip and squinted as his eyes devoured me.

My gaze held steady. "I love you B.J. But I won't just live together and not be married. You have to tell my parents and your parents. It was to be real."

Ooh, that made him mad. Those brown eyes flashed. "It is real!" He stood, and I watched anger overtake him. "I don't need a damned piece of paper from the State of Texas to know it's real." He paced. Outside the big kitchen windows, the muddy Colorado River overflowed its banks behind him. The winter sky was gray.

He was on a rant. "Hell, people get those pieces of paper every day and two years later they rip 'em apart. Get divorced. Make a mockery of marriage. What makes a fucking piece of paper so important?" He tapped his chest. "It's what's in here, Pat. I love you. I've loved you since I laid eyes on you."

My heart caught. B.J. had never said those words.

I was afraid to ask, but I had to know. My voice was timid. "Are these our wedding rings, B.J.?"

His gaze fell to the floor. I held my breath. He cleared his throat, his eyes and voice apologetic. "I can't afford diamonds, Patsy. I guess that's what I was thinking."

I beamed. "So, you knew you were making wedding rings. Why didn't you just say so?"

He was cornered, and he knew it. "I don't know. Maybe I wasn't sure you'd say yes to a spoon ring."

"Why? A ring that you made for me? I can't imagine any ring I would love more than this one."

Oh, his beautiful eyes glowed like warm honey. "God, I love you." He had never said it before that day, and now he had said it three times.

I met his gaze and answered through tears. "I love you so much. Yes, I want to be your wife."

He picked up the ring from the cutting board where he'd left it and slipped it on my finger. It was beautiful but way too big.

I held it out to him. "So, this is yours?"

"I can make it fit."

"Say it, B.J. What do these rings mean to you?"

He took the ring, got down on one knee, and held it out to me. "Will you marry me?" He closed his eyes and sighed. "If you want an official ceremony in a church, okay. But with or without a church and a ceremony, Patsy, I know, I never want anyone but you."

Of course, I cried and nodded. "Yes."

As the wind howled and bare trees swayed, as the Colorado River was pelted by a freezing February rain, B.J. finished our rings. He put mine on my finger and whispered, "Forever." He kissed me softly. "And a day."

I slipped his ring on his finger and promised, "Until the end of time."

That was our wedding ceremony.

Chapter Thirty-Three

Mine. All mine.

B.J.

I PUT HER RING on her tiny finger and promised, "Forever. And a day."

She slipped my ring on my finger and whispered, "Until the end of time."

I was higher than I'd ever been in my life. Higher than any drug ever took me. She was Patsy Ann Cole now. Mrs. B.J. Cole. We didn't need a piece of paper from the state. She believed in me.

I picked her up. She wrapped her arms around my neck, and I carried her to the bedroom. For the first time, Patsy didn't say, "Stop."

She unbuttoned my shirt, her blue eyes latched onto mine.

I pulled her sweater over her head, reached behind, and unhooked her bra. It slipped to the floor. She didn't try to cover herself.

God, she was so beautiful. Her breasts were perfect.

I dropped to my knees, flicking my tongue over her nipples as her fingers locked on the back of my head, holding me to her. She whimpered as I sucked one breast into my mouth. While I devoured it, I unbuttoned her jeans and yanked them down.

She stepped out of them, and I carried her to bed with nothing on but her little lace panties. Which I quickly removed. The graceful arc from her tiny waist to her hips was what men fantasized about—but I knew that from the day I first saw her at Barton Springs.

Now, she was mine. I was going to taste all of her.

Patsy watched me stand over her as I removed my jeans and climbed out of the briefs. Her eyes opened wide. I think, for a second, she was afraid, and I realized Patsy had never seen me naked. She had never seen any grown male naked. She had never put her hands down my pants to feel me. She'd felt me hard against her—but this was her first look at... all of me.

"Don't worry, Babydoll. We'll take our time."

I laid beside her on the bed, pulled her against me, and kissed her hungrily... but that was all. I kept it at that. We just wallowed in that bed, tasting each other, feeling each other the way we had for months... only this time, we were naked. Skin on skin. Legs wound around legs. Her breasts pressed against my chest.

Even before I felt her instinctively hunch against me, I knew she felt what I felt. Patsy took my hand and guided it between her legs, and I caught my breath. She was so wet. We both moaned as I slid my finger inside of her and began to rub her silky clit with my thumb. She was so... perfectly... wet... It made me throb.

She whispered. "B.J., make love to me."

"Not yet. I want to make sure you're ready." My cock ached to get inside, but I held back.

She shuddered as I kissed her breasts, tugging at her nipples, working inside of her now with two fingers—all the while rubbing her gently—until she buried her head in my neck, arching her back. "Oh, B.J., please. Make love to me. I want to feel you inside of me."

"Are you sure?"

"Yes."

I put her on her back, holding my weight off of her—and she guided my shaft to her entrance, her gaze hungry.

I slid in slowly... she gasped. She was tighter than I imagined.

I was giving her something she never experienced. "B.J." It was something between a whimper and a moan. I loved hearing her say my name like that.

My wife was the only virgin I'd ever been with. I'd never taken my time. It had always been about me. This was different.

"Just... feel... it...." With my weight on my hands on either of her, my thrusts were slow, controlled, not deep in the beginning. She had no idea—how... damned... tight... she was. How wet. How difficult it was not to release. But no. I had to please her first.

She had finally given herself to me. I claimed her. She... felt... like... heaven. This was heaven.

"B.J.!" Her nails dug into my back, and I took that as a signal. Slipping my hand beneath her hips, I lifted. "Wrap your legs around me."

She did—and cried out again as my cock buried as deep inside of her as she could take me. I pulled out, and we moved together, our gazes locked, both of us thrusting once... twice... and on the third time, my wife's walls pulsed... quivering around my shaft as I held her hips tight against me.

"*Oh—B.J.,*" Patsy trembled in my arms.

Her fingernails dug into my shoulders, and she held onto me like I was a lifesaver until her arms fell limp over her head—as if she was totally exhausted.

My God—that beautiful smile.

She arched up and kissed me hard and deep, her tongue mastering mine. When she finally broke away, her eyes adored me. "I never felt anything like that." She sighed deeply. "I had no idea."

It was my turn to smile. That was worth the seven—no eight—months of blue balls. "Welcome to the rest of your life, Babydoll."

I rolled onto my back, bringing her with me. I didn't want all my weight on her, but I needed to move.

She sat up there, straddling me, as I gripped her waist, pressing her hips down, as I drove into her over and over and over again—until my cock erupted with a pulsing, hot rush. I surprised myself, hearing my low groan as I... kept... coming... until I was spent, like her.

It was February, and I was sweating like it was mid-July.

I never felt anything like it, either. I'd had sex. But I never made love. This—she was the best drug ever. I would never get enough. "Oh, Patsy—fuck."

She giggled. "We just did." Then, her face turned to panic.

Her expression frightened me. "What, Babydoll?"

"We didn't use protection."

I chuckled and held up my left hand, showing the silver ring she had placed on it. "We're married."

"What if I get pregnant?"

"I guess we'll have a baby."

Her eyes grew even bigger. "You're okay with that?"

"Yeah, I hope we have lots of kids. Are you okay with that? Having a baby—now?"

"I never thought about it."

I had to laugh, this time a good one. "Well, it's a little late now."

She smiled and lifted a tiny shoulder. "I guess if we get pregnant, we get pregnant. I'm good if you're good."

I smiled and stroked her beautiful cheek, using my fingertips to brush the hair stuck to her face and neck, all the while admiring her perfect body. I couldn't get enough of looking at her. Naked.

"I'll take off work tomorrow. We'll get a marriage license for your parents."

She kissed me with an enormous smile.

"We'll find an apartment. And we'll go together to Planned Parenthood. Get you on birth control, if that's what you want. If you don't—we will definitely have a baby. I mean, lots of babies. Because I am your sex slave for the rest of your life."

Chapter Thirty-Four
No, God, no
Patsy

"Pat." He clutches me tightly. "God kept me alive to take care of you. I'm sorry I won't be able to finish the job."

It's more than I can bear. "Please, B.J., stop saying that. Please."

He says nothing.

Craning my neck to see his face, I assure him, "Baby, we're going to get through this just like we've gotten through everything else. Yes, it's harder than you thought it would be. It's harder than I imagined. But we will get through this together, one day at a time."

He shakes his head softly. His hand still cups my breast, rubbing his thumb gently over it, remembering, maybe, the passion he poured into them over the years. My body was and still is his playground. "Not this time." He sighs deeply. "God knew the number of my days before I was born. If it wasn't the virus, it would have been something else."

I swallow the lump in my throat, fighting to be positive. "You're going to beat this."

He doesn't say yes, and he doesn't say no. Instead, he whispers, "Pat, bury me with my wedding ring."

I lose my battle against the tears, begging, *No, God, no.*

Without warning, I'm angry. I want to rage at the world. At the fucking virus. At the people who make the rules. I'm just fucking mad. I want to scream. I cannot bear to think of him giving up. It's in my voice. "B.J., you're the strongest person I've ever known. If anyone can beat this, you can. You will."

"I'm trying, Babydoll."

I wrap my arms around him, kissing the side of his face. He has a short beard now. He hasn't tried to shave, being so sick. "You will. You will. I'll be right here to help."

I know him. He's tuned me out. He'd give me the open palm, but he doesn't have the energy. He says, "Do you remember when the crane collapsed? How we lost each other for a little while?"

"Yes." *Where's he going?*

"We're going to lose each other again." Our gazes hold. He searches my eyes intently as I search his. "Just because my body dies, it doesn't mean my love dies. We will be together again." He rests his head back on the pillow, closing his eyes. "We will find each other the same way we did that day."

He strokes his fingers through my hair as tears begin to roll down my face, onto his chest, and slide down his side. He presses me to him. "You and me, Babydoll. We're forever." He pauses long enough to drag in another breath. "I'm not an educated man, but I know that. I've always known that."

I sit up in the bed and kiss his lips. His skin is so warm, but it's too soon for more fever reducer. "Do you have any idea how much I love you?"

He smiles. His voice is slow and low and weak. "I do." He closes his eyes again. Maybe my gentle petting is lulling him to sleep. He mumbles, "You loved me enough to rag my ass all these years... always trying to save me from myself... knowing how much it pissed me off." He chuckles as best he can. "I still wouldn't have hidden in the house from a fucking bug."

"Do you think they say fuck in heaven?"

He doesn't answer. *Is he asleep?*

Just as I decide he has nodded off, he murmurs, "I don't know... I hope I get a chance to find out."

A Few Days Later

I'm losing him. I feel it. B.J. is slipping away from me. He sleeps almost all of the time. It's been three weeks, and he still can't shake whatever this is. He still refuses to go to the hospital.

All night, I wafted between desperation and numbness as I watched B.J. and listened to his breathing become more and more ragged. Shallow. He just cannot get air into his lungs. I called Jim Beau, who is a pharmacist, at three in the morning, and he came right over, wearing a mask and gloves, of course, like the rest of the world. He brought a portable oxygen machine, which he hooked up.

B.J. didn't wake up, even when Jim Beau put it on him.

We stand at the foot of the bed. Tears threaten Jim Beau's eyes, locked on his father. It's the first time he's seen B.J. since he got sick. "Oh, God, Mom. It's so hard to see him this way. He's lost so much weight. He looks so weak."

"I know. Do you think oxygen will help him beat this?"

Jim Beau shifts his shoulders as the corners of his mouth pull down. "I don't know. It can't hurt. But there have been people in hospitals on oxygen machines for weeks and weeks who never came out of it. Healthy, young athletes are dying from this. They say it is the most baffling virus mankind has come across."

"Should I have him transferred to a hospital despite his protests?" I've second-guessed myself every single day. I realize B.J. was right: Loving him *was* my only risk and my greatest reward. I can't fathom my life without him.

Jim Beau clenches his jaw, just like his father, his voice forceful. "No. Absolutely not." His gaze shifts from his father to me. "First of all, I'm telling you, they don't know what they're dealing with. They're rushing around, trying to make vaccines because they don't have a fucking clue how to treat it effectively."

His gaze shifts to his father and back to me. "But more importantly—and you know this, Mom—you have to respect his wishes. Dad's right. They will put him in isolation, and you won't see him again until he's in the morgue."

His big hands grip my shoulders, and he bends his knees so his eyes align with mine. "Mom, listen to me. Look at him. Dad's body is shutting down." He points at B.J., asleep or unconscious in the bed, whatever you want to call it at this stage. "I know my father. If he dies, when he dies—he doesn't want to die alone in a hospital. He wants to die in your arms."

Jim Beau studies me, his gaze narrow. "You don't feel sick at all? You've never gotten sick?"

I shake my head. "I'm beginning to wonder if I didn't have it before anyone else. I had a horrible flu right after New Year's—the worst I can remember. I wonder now if it wasn't this virus and I just got a lighter dose and maybe developed an immunity, because no. I've been with him every day, slept with him every night, and I haven't gotten sick."

"If you had coronavirus in January, why wouldn't Dad have had it then?" This is the first time Jim Beau has seen his father like this. His eyes are moist.

"He was in Denver. They had a corporate retreat that lasted ten days. By the time your father got home, I was well. I had washed bed sheets and Cloroxed everything in the house. Like I said, I thought it was the flu. For all I know, it was."

We watch him wearing that oxygen mask. He is breathing better already. With more oxygen in his lungs, I have renewed hope. He is so strong. He will fight his way back. *Why didn't I do this earlier?* Easy answer. Because he wouldn't have worn it. He will rip it off when he wakes up.

Watching our first born watch his father, my mind drifts back the day he came into this world.

CHAPTER THIRTY-FIVE

BABY BLUE EYES

PATSY

May 1973

OH, NO. BLOOD WAS on my panties when I went to tinkle.

My hands trembled as I dialed the telephone. "Mom. I'm bleeding."

The baby was more than three weeks past due. My belly looked like an enormous beach ball. I'd exploded these past two weeks. I couldn't remember the last time I saw my toes.

"Oh, my God. I'm on my way!" Mom sounded as nervous as I felt. What happened? *Would I lose our baby?*

I called B.J.'s work. I knew they could get a message to him on his break, and he was expecting a call. "This is Patsy Cole. B.J.'s wife. Can you get him a message when he takes a break? Tell him I'll be at St. David's. Hurry."

"Is this an emergency?" the woman asked.

"Yes."

"Oh, my. Yes, dear. We will deliver the message."

———

As terrified as I was—everybody at the hospital was certain we had all the time in the world. They dragged their heels. I tried to explain. "I'm spotting. I have blood—"

"You said your water hasn't broken," an old admitting clerk cut me off. "There's no rush."

I disagreed. My belly was hard, and again— and again, *I was bleeding.* That couldn't be good.

My mother attacked like a pecking hen. "We need to get her admitted. This baby is two weeks past due and she's bleeding."

The clerk snapped back laconically. "It's her doctor's day off."

Mom's temper flared. "Well, find someone who can deliver a baby!"

It wasn't long before I was in the maternity ward. Back then, all you got was a metal bed surrounded on three sides by curtains and a monitor that let you hear the baby's heartbeat. *Whop-whop, whop-whop...*

A few curtains down, a woman shrieked at the top of her lungs, "Oh, mamma! Oh, mamma! It hurts so bad!"

Geez. I wanted to knock her in the head. So far, I wasn't hurting worse than the Braxton Hicks contractions I'd been experiencing. It was the bleeding that concerned me. What was happening to my baby?

The nurses came and checked me. "You're only dilated to four. This is going take forever."

To our surprise, they returned maybe thirty minutes later, announcing an about-face. "We're going to break your water."

My heart caught. "Is that safe? Doesn't your water break on its own when the time is right?" I still wasn't hurting badly. I had experienced nothing like women described as labor pains.

"Yeah," the nurse said. "But we talked to Dr. Thomas. This is what we're going to do."

Mom and I exchanged glances. "Is the baby in danger?" I asked.

"No. But you're spotting and past your due date, so Dr. Thomas says it's time for you to deliver. Some women—their water just doesn't break unless we break it."

Another nurse assured us, "Dr. Thomas is on the way. He'll be here in time."

The curtain swished open. B.J. stepped in. I smiled, so relieved to see him.

His eyes were huge. His gaze focused on my enormous, hard belly. "Are you okay?" Anyone could see he had just gotten off work. He'd been promoted to a connector within months of hiring. He still wore his red bandana wrapped around his head, which he used as a sweatband under his hard hat.

B.J. was covered in oil, rust, and dust that settled mainly in the rivers and pools of his sweat. The bolts he handled were greasy. Grease got on his gloves and then wiped onto his jeans and shirt. Yes, I spent plenty of time and money at the laundromat.

His muscles were pronounced under the short-sleeved, once-white T-shirt stretched tight across his chest and biceps. After B.J. started connecting, that naturally thick chest burgeoned. I reached for him. "I'm so glad you're here."

A nurse rushed in, barking at B.J., who already had his hand resting on my stomach. "You can't be here," she barked.

He glared at her. "What do you mean? This is my wife." He nodded at my belly. "And this is my baby."

"Only one visitor."

We both looked at Mom.

She smiled. "I was just holding your spot." She kissed him on the cheek. Everyone loved B.J. "I'll be in the waiting room." She turned to me. "And I'll call your father." She peered at B.J. "Do your parents know?"

He shook his head. "Will you?"

"Of course."

The grumpy old nurse barged further in. "Both of you need to leave for a minute." She shooed Mom and B.J. with her hands. "We're going to break her water now." She glowered at B.J., raking her hawkish eyes over him. "And you need to clean up if you think you're going to stay in here."

B.J. peered at Mom pleadingly. "I'm sorry, Audra. Can you swing by the apartment and bring me clean clothes?"

Mom nodded, but another nurse interrupted, tossing B.J. a set of blue doctor's scrubs. "Here. Go to the men's room. Clean up and change into these." The young blonde glanced over her shoulder, scowling at the older nurse. "And don't listen to Mildred. She's just a grouch. She was here before Saint David."

Mildred glowered, Mom chuckled, and B.J. squeezed my hand, grabbed the clean clothes, and darted. "I'll be right back."

The young nurse called after him. "The men's room is off the maternity waiting room!"

With B.J. gone, Mildred broke my water. Big mistake. Whatever had been progressing slowly inside my body went into hyperdrive. Before B.J. could get back, my belly contracted. Hard. I mean hard, hard, hard. I felt like a lemon must feel in B.J.'s fist.

Excruciating, squeezing pain. I'd never imagined cramps like that. Nature's vice grip contracting to push the baby out. *This was labor.* And I understood why it's called labor. "Oh, B.J.," I whispered. "It hurts."

I would not be like that wailing woman a few beds down. Her incessant hollering had given me resolve. One screamer was all the ward could handle. I closed my eyes and doubled up on my side, eating the pain.

He stroked my head with one hand and offered the other. "Here, give me your pain. Squeeze it into me, Babydoll. Squeeze my hand as hard as you need to."

I did.

With a damp cloth, he sopped my sweating head as I squeezed his free hand with all the force I wanted to use to scream. I understood why she cried out. But knowing how her loud wailing affected other people, I just would not do it. Still, in her defense, she didn't have B.J. to take her pain, and hers had gone on for much longer than mine.

"Scream if you need to," B.J. said. He'd heard her.

The pain of childbirth is inconceivable to anyone who has not endured it. Sweat poured from my head, face, and neck, but I told myself I could stand anything as long as I knew it would be over. "I'll be alright."

And I was. It wasn't thirty minutes until I was certain. "B.J. The baby is coming."

He ran to the curtains, yelling, "We need help in here!"

No response.

He hollered louder. "We need help!" I was pretty sure they heard him in the waiting room.

Finally, Mildred plodded toward him with an irritated sigh. "I'm telling you, kids, these things take time."

"Get in here and check my wife!"

Out of spite, Mildred took her time. She was a big old gal with a square face, kinky, short, permed gray hair, and black-rimmed glasses. She grumbled and checked me. Her eyes flared wide, and she hollered over her shoulder. "This baby is crowning! Where's Dr. Thomas?"

The room burst to life.

I don't know how many nurses rushed in. They rolled me onto my back, my knees bent, spread eagle, and covered me with a sheet.

"Push!" a nurse commanded.

I did.

B.J. cradled me, holding me up. "Push, Babydoll. Push as hard as you can."

I clenched his hand, closed my eyes, and pushed with all my might—emitting an un-ladylike roar—and the pain stopped. Immediately.

My heart caught. Nothing. No sound. I couldn't see what they were doing. But my baby wasn't crying.

Tears flooded my eyes. "B.J.!" He was down with the nurses at the foot of the bed.

A second later, a baby cried. "It's a boy!" Mildred yelled.

I leaned back in relief, unable to contain my smile.

B.J. was at her side, beaming, peering down at the wailing baby in her arms. He came to me with the expression of a child at Christmas. "We have a son, Patsy. We have a son! Oh, Babydoll, you did so good."

The doctor came in barking orders. "Everyone out. I need to check her."

B.J.'s shoulders bowed defiantly. "You weren't even here when she delivered. I'm not leaving her."

Dr. Thomas, who'd been our family physician as long as I could remember, eyed him with dismay and shrugged. "Suit yourself." He took a stool at the foot of the bed, inspecting me. "What a mess." He peered at B.J. over my sheet-covered raised knees. "We make an incision so there's no tearing, but your son came so fast they didn't get to do that. He literally ripped out of your wife's body." He stood. "I've got to get her into the delivery room and do the best I can to fix this." He nodded at the nurses.

Someone gave me a shot, and I heard fear in B.J.'s voice. "Is she in danger?"

"No," Dr. Thomas said. "But it's going to take her a lot longer to get back on her feet than if she'd had an episiotomy. She is torn up."

B.J. stroked my face. "You did so good, Babydoll. He's got one hell of a set of lungs, ten fingers, and ten toes." He flicked his brows and smiled so wide. "I counted." He kissed my forehead. "He's perfect."

I sighed with relief. Groggy now. "Can I hold him?"

"After they fix you up."

"I want to hold our baby." My eyes were heavy.

I heard him say, "I'll be here when you come back."

That was it. All I remembered. B.J. held our son before I did.

He burst into my hospital room hours later as I was waking from the anesthesia. "Oh, damn, Patsy! He has your eyes! The baby has your big blue eyes!" I had never seen such a beautiful smile on anyone.

B.J. is the father of my children and the first and only man I ever loved. What I know of love and life, I learned at his side.

CHAPTER THIRTY-SIX

EMPTINESS

PATSY

I WATCHED MY UNCLE break a high-spirited horse once. A big bay that did not want a man astride his back. But once that rope slipped around his neck and tightened, my uncle simply wore him down.

No matter how many times the horse reared on his back legs, whinnied, and snorted—no matter how many times he bucked, tossing my uncle to the ground, the man dusted himself off and climbed back on. Again, and again and again—the horse thought he won.

Each time, my uncle climbed back in the saddle—until, at last, the horse stilled. Broken.

Even as a child, seeing it saddened me.

That memory haunted me as I watched my husband struggle. For his life.

I want to incinerate the earth around anything and everything having to do with that virus.

May 2020

I'm hiding in our bedroom. More than wanting solitude, I need it. I've embraced silence. The house is full of people. I know they are well intended. They want to show me support. But I don't want to socialize. I wish everyone would go home.

Jim Beau opens my bedroom door. "Mom, it's time." His voice is always gentle.

Despite having my eyes, I peer up to see his young father's face—the same strong brow and pecan-colored hair, the same dimple in his chin.

I hesitate, glancing around the bedroom. I don't want to leave. This is my sanctuary. This is where I slept with B.J. for twenty years. This is where he died.

He built our home. Oh, not with his own hands. We had the money by then to pay builders, but he oversaw the contractor. He did much of the work himself, not just to save money but because he loved working with his hands and wanted to help build his family home, just like he made our wedding rings. As he once told me, his hands were meant to build things.

I run my fingertips over my ring. No one else in the world has a wedding ring like mine. "Give me a minute." I hold up my index finger, stalling him. "I need to freshen up."

Not really. I'm just biding time.

In our bathroom, I close the door and fight to gain my composure, preparing for what I must do. It was one thing to lose him. Another to put his body in the ground.

I weep. I cannot stop. When I finally do, I stare at his picture framed on my dressing table. I keep it there because when I doll up, I still do it for B.J.

Rubbing my fingertips across his face, I whisper to his picture, "How am I supposed to carry on?" He thought he was impervious. I think I believed it, too.

Sometimes, I think life is like a road trip. When you stare out the windshield, the highway seems to stretch to infinity. It feels like you'll never get where you're going, but when you turn your head to the side, you realize the landscape is rushing by.

That's life. Fifty years gone in a blur.

I close my eyes to see him smiling at me that first day, scooping me up, placing me on his motorcycle, saying, "Damn, I like you." I'm resting my back against his chest, sitting atop Mount Bonnell, feeling his arms around me as we watch the sun say goodnight. I'm sleeping in the crook of his arm. *Thank you, God, for letting him love me.*

"Mom?" Jim Beau taps on the bathroom door. "We've got to go."

I pull tissues from the box, pat them against my eyes, and dry my face. "I'm coming."

Staring in the mirror, I search for a shred of the girl he fell in love with so many years ago—the face that looked back at me in the gas station in 1974. Whatever beauty once existed is gone, replaced by crow's feet, sagging skin, and gray hair.

My only solace is knowing that all of today's beautiful young women, should they be fortunate enough to live so long, will someday look in the mirror with the same disappointment.

Time assails all who outlive youth.

As we get into the car, Caroline says, "There'll be a lot of people, Mama." Our daughter is two years younger than Jim Beau. She has her father's soft brown eyes and pecan-colored hair, but she's small, like me.

Our youngest, Luke, works on an offshore oil rig in the Gulf of Mexico. Like his father, Luke didn't care about college. He wanted to work with his hands. He's the only one who got my dark hair with B.J.'s eyes. Genetics. Go figure.

"Is Luke meeting us?" I ask.

Jim Beau responds. "His flight just got in, Mom. He's catching an Uber."

"Daddy has a lot of friends." Caroline chokes and wipes her eyes. "Had."

"Yes, he did," I reply.

She and Jim Beau exchange glances in the front seat. They understand I'm not in a talkative mood.

As Jim Beau drives us across town in silence, my mind rolls back to that long drive across Tennessee in 1974. Odd. I can somehow smell the pines and feel the cool mountain air. We were so young.

"You're going to give me the silent treatment for the rest of the trip?"

"I don't know. Are you going to rag my ass the rest of the trip?"

"I'm going to rag your ass for the rest of your fucking life if you don't straighten up!"

I chuckle out loud and wipe tears with my fingertips. I can see B.J.—how mad he was at me in that grocery store parking lot when I told him to put Jim Beau and me on a bus and send us home, seeing him turning in a circle like his hair was on fire.

Both kids look back at me, and I shake my head.

I remember us fussing and making up at the bus station. He held me off the ground, kissing me with such passion in front of the whole world. He didn't care who was watching. I can't contain the smile that comes with that memory.

Jim Beau studies me in his rearview mirror. "Are you okay, Mom?"

"Just remembering your father."

B.J. and I always fussed like that, almost always because, as he would say, I was ragging his ass. I guess I was. But we always made up—and almost always the same way.

Just because you wear a tie doesn't mean I have to. I don't want to wear a tie.

You say real men wear their hair short? I'll show you. I won't cut mine again.

You say I can't smoke pot? Hide and watch.

Tell me I can't climb steel or that I can't be a success without sitting in a classroom. By God, watch me.

B.J. knew his mind, and he would not bow to society's expectations—and my mind does not accept that he is gone. Tears begin to flow down my cheeks, and I bury my face in my hands. Oh, God, he's gone. He's really gone. I have never known this emptiness.

I never knew until he got sick how deeply Matteo's remarks cut him. After B.J. said it, I realized he never took drugs after we got back from Richmond. He just smoked his pot. I never connected it to what Matteo said to him.

He gave up marijuana when the Department of Transportation started randomly drug-testing construction workers. He cut off his ponytail when he got tired of messing with it. The older he got, the shorter he wore his hair.

B.J. quit connecting and went to work for a steel erection company a year or so after we returned from Virginia. He ran the crews that sent all that material up to the connectors. He understood what it was like to be up high and what the connectors needed from the ground crews.

The dream B.J. shared with me in that little Greek restaurant on our first date—he made it come true. Yes, he was defiant, but he was equally determined.

I glance out the car window. May is beautiful in Texas. The highway median brims with bluebonnets, Indian paintbrushes, coreopsis, and primrose—and the tears come rolling back. I dab my eyes. Everything makes me cry.

Why would beautiful flowers prompt tears? I lean my head back and close my eyes. Because they are living proof that life goes on. Life will go on without him. Nothing changes. And yet, everything has changed for me.

Matteo is coming. Maybe that stirred up the memories. Al sent word he was bringing Matteo DeVecchio to B.J.'s funeral. The mobster wants to pay his last respects.

I don't know all that happened between them on the cliff's edge that day, but I know B.J. would just as soon Matteo not be there. Al didn't have the guts to tell me. He knew I'd tell him not to bother. So, he left a message with Jim Beau.

Just the mention of their names puts me back in Al's living room that day, and I see, I hear B.J. yelling at Matteo, 'Keep your fucking eyes off my wife!'

That makes me smile, too.

Jim Beau is watching in the rearview mirror. I guess he thinks his mother has finally lost her mind as I morph from laughing to crying to smiling.

Caroline jolts me from my thoughts. "Momma, we're here." She smiles at me. "The parking lot is full."

Luke grabs me at the door. He's been waiting, and we cry into each other. "Oh, Mama, I'm sorry I wasn't here."

I search his face. He's the largest of our three children, taller and bulkier than his dad. We named him John Luke, an Americanized version of Jean-Luc.

"Honey, if you had been here, you couldn't have seen him. If you were exposed, you couldn't have gone back to work. It's just too dangerous. Caroline didn't see him, either and she lives here. She couldn't risk exposing her family."

I pull away, addressing all three of our children. "Your father didn't want you to see him so sick. We both want you to remember him the way you knew him."

CHAPTER THIRTY-SEVEN

DeVecchio's Surprise

Patsy

THEY SEAT US IN the front row and begin playing a music video montage. Pictures of B.J. through the years dissolve one into another on a large-screen monitor. My heart tightens and aches as I watch him age before my eyes, always the handsome man I married.

I watch a lifetime of memories listening to a mix of songs B.J. loved. Jim Beau and Caroline did that. They show our wedding picture. *Oh, Lord, look at us*. I was nineteen. He was twenty-one.

Another photo... B.J. is drop-dead gorgeous, standing on an I-beam eighty feet in the air, wearing a hard hat, his arm high, waving at me with a broad smile. He's holding Jim Beau... Jim Beau and Caroline... baby Luke in his father's arms. All five of us on vacation.

Don't tell me not to cry when you do that to me.

His closed casket is right up there, in front of me. B.J. lost so much weight fighting that virus, he didn't want the children or grandchildren to remember him that way. Neither do I. Only Jim Beau and I saw what the virus did to him. Keep it that way.

I can barely stand to look at it, knowing his emaciated vessel is inside. But he's not there. I held B.J. as he left this world. He did die in my arms. I'm back beside him in our bed, stroking his face. In a moment of lucidity, his eyes caught mine and he whispered, "Thank you for sharing your life with me."

"Oh, baby." I clutched him and wept.

He struggled for breath as our gazes held. "All the buildings. The only thing I built that mattered, I built with you." His eyes filled with tears. "Our love built this family. Our children are all we leave behind that matter." He lifted his forearm and cupped my face in his hand, his eyes adoring me—mine adoring him—as he wiped my tears with his thumb. "Stay with them as long as you can, Babydoll. I'll be waiting for you."

I kissed his hand, dampening it with my tears. "Promise me," I begged.

"I... promise." B.J. closed his beautiful eyes, and as I softly kissed his lips, his soul slipped free of its earthly vessel. As I clung to him and sobbed, I couldn't help but think of a butterfly escaping its cocoon, taking flight to God.

Caroline squeezes my hand hard, bringing me back. She leans close and whispers, "I'm not supposed to let you fall apart."

I wipe my face with both hands, unable to respond.

She hands me a tissue. "Go ahead."

Jim Beau wraps his arm around me. Our eyes meet, and I see his are full of tears, too. My oldest son kisses my forehead, and I lean against his shoulder, recalling him asleep beside his father, both with their arms at their heads like goalposts. Tell me, where do the years go?

The lights dim as the music fades, and the video freezes on a photograph of B.J. in the prime of his life. I'm glad they did that. Remember him when he was at his best.

A man walks to the podium, and a spotlight shines on him. He's not our preacher. Rebel that B.J. was, he was never a churchgoer. He found God in the setting sun.

Who the man at the podium is isn't important to me. Either the kids chose him, or the funeral home did. "Thank you for being here," he says.

He is a tall man, maybe Jim Beau's age, who leans into the microphone and speaks directly at us—B.J.'s family. "We gather today to celebrate the life of Beauregard Jean-Luc Cole." The grandchildren sit with their siblings and other parents behind Luke, Caroline, me, and Jim Beau. Luke is the only one still single. B.J.'s brothers and sisters and their families, as well as all the cousins and their families, are there, as are mine.

The man says, "We have a special guest who asked to speak here." He extends his hand to the other side of the room, and out walks Matteo DeVecchio, using a cane.

I suck in my breath—audibly—and my hand covers my mouth. I feel my children's eyes zoom in on me.

He's going to speak? I knew he was coming, but I had no idea Matteo intended to speak. *Oh, Lord, B.J. is rolling over with his fists clenched.*

Matteo is dressed in a black suit and tie. His once jet-black hair is shiny silver. For his age and legal problems, that old gangster is still frighteningly handsome. He exudes power and authority.

Al is at his side, thin as a willow. He's lost most of his hair, but his fringe is still black.

Matteo takes the podium and leans into the microphone. "Ladies and gentlemen, some of you guys know who I am. Some of you don't." His mobster's voice is gravellier than I remember. "For those of you who do know who I am, just let me say, don't believe everything you hear. For those who don't know me, my name is Matteo DeVecchio."

He turns to Al, extending his arm. "And this is my cousin and attorney, Allesandro Lorenzo Mancini, a life-long friend of B.J. Cole."

My hackles rise as people look at each other.

They are well-known names, even if their faces are not. DeVecchio and Mancini have been all over newspapers and cable news networks since the FBI charged Matteo with orchestrating the murders of three competing mob bosses—ala Michael Corleone.

Al speaks for Matteo whenever the TV cameras get in the mobster's face. With that name and those dark Sicilian looks, who would ever guess Al was born and raised right here in Austin, Texas? He left Texas in his rearview mirror five decades ago.

The room is silent as Matteo begins to speak. "Mrs. Cole. Where are you?" He peers into the darkness, and once more, I tense. I have no idea what he might say.

All eyes in the room search for me.

Matteo spots me and steps around the podium. "Stand up if you will. Please." His palm facing up, he waves his fingers, coaxing me.

I comply.

Matteo stares at me for what feels like a long moment and stretches his arm toward me. "Still a beautiful woman. He was a lucky man." He bows, as he did that day in the park. "And you, sweetheart, are a lucky woman. And your son? The boy I met? Will he stand, please?"

I nudge Jim Beau to stand with me, and he does. Matteo studies him for a long moment, nods, and smiles. "I see your father with your mother's eyes. Thank you."

Matteo's words weaken me. Jim Beau holds my arm, steadying me as we sit.

Matteo turns to address the funeral attendees. "It's a sad day that brings us together. I made this trip so I can be sure you all remember the real B.J. Cole."

I bristle again, recalling how he belittled B.J. that day. Surely, he hasn't come here to mar my husband's image. My gaze darts to Al, who stands behind Matteo, his hands folded reverently in front of him. Poker-faced.

Although I hadn't seen him since 1974, he and B.J. kept in touch through mutual friends. B.J. heard Al married several times. None of them took. He has no children.

Matteo briefly turns to take in B.J.'s portrait on the big monitor. He moves back to the podium microphone and tilts his head at B.J.'s image with a grin. "I bet you didn't know he saved my life."

Murmurs fill the audience.

Matteo glances over his shoulder at the flower-draped casket, then faces his audience and says again, "Yes, B.J. Cole saved my life when he had every reason not to." He snickers and raises both hands, showing the audience his broad palms. "And I won't explain why."

My heart catches as people exchange glances, laughing nervously. I don't think they know what to expect from this infamous mobster. I certainly don't.

Matteo tells the story of the crane crashing through the restaurant, stressing how many lives B.J. saved that day by having the acuity to recognize a disaster unfolding. He tells how B.J. saw what was about to happen and warned the room, yelling for everyone to run.

A dozen people died in that crane collapse between the construction site and the restaurant. Matteo's two body-guards, Tommaso and Pietro, were among those who per-ished in the fall or were crushed beneath the heavy debris and construction equipment.

Dozens, like Matteo, were severely injured. But imagine how many more would have perished had B.J. not been there.

Matteo tells how he and B.J. went down with the crane, each landing on the cliff's edge close together. He explains how one of his legs was shattered, the other badly gashed, and how B.J. used their belts to make tourniquets to keep him from bleeding to death.

When he tells them that B.J. said he could climb out, but not with a hundred eighty pounds on his back, the audience laughs, knowing B.J. They are becoming more comfortable with the infamous Matteo DeVecchio.

"Then he tells me I'd just have to trust him." Matteo pulls away from the podium to stand straight and spreads his arms wide. He makes big air quotes. "Trust me." He gives his neck a slow, deliberate twist, chortles, and leans into the microphone. "Now, ladies and gentlemen, that's not something you want to hear in my business."

He gets a hearty laugh.

"But I did... trust him." He lifts his still-broad shoulders. "I had no choice. I couldn't move." He takes a deep breath, and as he continues speaking, he no longer gazes at the audience but into some abyss above them.

It feels like he's back on that cliff, reliving that moment, recognizing how long ago that was, knowing, in his old age, that he isn't going to live forever, either.

He talks with his hands. "I laid there, helpless, and I'm watching him shimmy up that long, steel column like a monkey. He walks across that narrow piece of steel, way up in the air—like it was no big deal."

Matteo chuckles again, telling the audience. "My jaw dropped, sitting there watching him. It looked like he was on a damned tightrope to me." He glances over his shoulder. "Excuse the language, Father."

People laugh again—this time, even louder, friendlier—as Matteo holds his audience captive, telling his tale. "Then I watch him scale that cliff wall. I expect him to fall to his death any second." He jabs his finger at the audience. "And, believe me, I had a lot riding on that climb. If B.J. fell, I would die right along with him. But he doesn't fall. He makes it to the top—and I watch him disappear."

He pauses for a long moment, takes another deep breath, and speaks again. "Now, that's where the trust comes in." Matteo is silent, his gaze darting around in the darkness over the audience, as if choosing his words carefully. "I'm telling you—all of you—B.J. Cole could've gotten to that ridgetop, looked down, and told me to where to stick it. I would've bled to death down there and nobody—I mean nobody—would have ever known the difference."

He shifts on his feet and jabs his finger at the audience. "And let me tell you, under those circumstances, that particular day," he turns and speaks directly to me, "a lot of men—no, most men—would have done just that."

Matteo grips the podium with both hands, leaning in. His knuckles bulge as his gaze slowly moves from me back to his audience. "But B.J. came back with medics." He clears his throat and peers back into that well of memories. I swear, now, he's speaking through tears.

I glance up at Jim Beau. Tears are streaming down his face. I check the other two. Luke and Caroline are weeping, too.

Matteo goes on. "I wouldn't have a wife, children, and grandchildren." He raps the podium with his knuckles. "I would not be here today—if it weren't for B.J. Cole."

I glance around. Everyone is spellbound, especially our grandchildren. Very few people have heard that story. It wasn't like we came back from Virginia and talked about it. Jim Beau had been too young to remember.

Matteo continues. "B.J. told me that day that he was a common man." The corners of his mouth turn down, then he bites his lower lip and finally makes his big air quotes again. "Common." Matteo's brows lift high, and you hear his incredulity as he repeats, "B.J. said he was a common man."

Matteo shakes his head slowly. "Not hardly." The gangster leans into the microphone, rapping the podium again with his knuckles as his voice gets loud. "I owe him this: I am here today to make sure everyone remembers, B.J. Cole was anything but a common man."

The dam breaks.

Matteo DeVecchio is the only person I ever saw get a standing ovation at a funeral.

CHAPTER THIRTY-EIGHT

EXPIRATION DATE

PATSY

August 2023

AUGUST IS ALWAYS AN awful month in Texas, but this one has been particularly punishing. It seems God set a glass dome over the state and turned on a heat lamp. The dome denies us rain and traps in the heat.

Texas will not; cannot cool off. We've endured triple-digit temperatures for two months without a drop of rain: 105 degrees, 107 degrees, 109 degrees, day after long day. And still, nutgrass grows in my flowerbeds—little bastards.

Nutgrass has become the bane of my existence. It spreads from nodes underground, and it is impossible to eradicate. Someday, I intend to ask the good Lord why He made it. What good does it do? What purpose does it serve?

Sweat slides down my face. I wipe it with the back of my hand because my palms and fingers are too dirty. I've been pulling weeds.

Unlike my sister and girlfriends, I'm not a quilter, artist, or craftsperson. I cannot draw a stick figure. That's not modesty speaking. I am mortified every time I try to make a craft. It looks like something a first-grader would be embarrassed to turn in.

So, the yard is my passion. It's rewarding work. Last year, it was named Yard of the Year. Sometimes, people stop on the sidewalk to admire my mass of Black-Eyed Susans and purple verbena, which makes me proud.

Yes, my pups and my flowers are what I have taken care of since losing my husband.

My husband. I draw a deep breath and close my eyes. I miss B.J. every single day. There is not a day I don't wake up and look at his side of the bed and remember. He's been gone for more than three years now.

Oh, I made myself get busy. I stay active. We do what we have to do. I garden, shop, and play Spades with my girlfriends.

I go to the grandkids' ball games and school plays. I go to church and eat Sunday lunch with Jim Beau and his family or Caroline and hers. But they're all busy. Mostly, it's just me and the pups like today.

It's noon. I give up on the nutgrass battle and push up off my knees, which is getting harder to do every year. Standing so suddenly makes me feel a bit woozy-headed. I steady myself, leaning against the hoe.

My mind hasn't been focused on the flowerbed, anyway. I've been preoccupied with the morning news. They said the famous Mafia Don Matteo DeVecchio died in the night. I'm not sure why that makes me a little sad.

But then, I never understood the effect that man had on me. He was oh-my-God handsome and oh-my-God scary at the same time.

The news took my mind back to that party at the Mancini house fifty years ago. Sitting alone in the moonlight, Matteo took my breath. I remember seeing him again in that little park in the summer of '74 and how stunned he was to see me.

Then I remember how cruel he was to B.J.

Had that crane not collapsed, had B.J. not saved his life, Matteo would have forced me to make that choice. I would have had to leave the man I loved or see him be killed.

Matteo DeVecchio was, indeed, a handsome devil, but I know, buried deep inside, there was kindness in him to be so gentle and consoling with me that night when my heart was breaking and for him to have traveled across the country to eulogize B.J. He didn't have to do that.

His words come to mind, saying B.J. was anything but a common man—which I'm glad he recognized—and those damned tears come back. My husband was one of a kind.

I glance around. My black and white border heeler is chasing a grasshopper. He pounces like a cat, trying to catch it. I call to him, "Let's take a break! Buddy! Junie Bea!"

The old bloodhound slowly gets up from her nap at the base of a big shade tree, shakes her long ears, and plods to me. *Da-doop-ta-doop, da-doop-ta-doop.* She's older than me, in doggie years. "We'll both join them soon, girl."

Yes, I talk to my pups.

I hold the kitchen door open for them. "Let's get inside, where it's cool."

The pups race past me for their water bowl. It's the only time Junie Bea moves fast anymore, heading for food, water, or a cool spot.

Well, crap.

Holding the door open, a fly darts in. I hate flies, and Buddy does, too. He jumps and snaps at it, but the fly eludes the jaws of death. I'll get him later.

After washing my hands, I go to the refrigerator, pour sweet tea into a big glass of ice cubes, and take a long drink. I need to cool off. I let myself get too hot.

Jim Beau fusses at me about working outside in the summer heat, but I'd rather be outside than alone in the house. Loneliness lets go of me when I'm outside.

Jim Beau wants me to sell the house and move in with them. Sweet boy. But I can't. B.J. built this house, and he died in it. I'll die in it if I have my say.

I wet a washcloth with cold tap water, press it to my face and neck, and let cool water run over my wrists, resting against the sink. I'm nauseous. Maybe I am getting too old for this.

I could hire a gardener, but then what would I do with myself? I can't imagine sitting in this house all day, every day. No. I need my yard work.

Turning on the ceiling fan, I carry my iced tea to my recliner beside B.J.'s, slip off my shoes, and sit down. Even my feet are hot.

Grabbing the TV remote, I tell the pups, who have each taken their place on a nearby pillow, "Let's see what's on TV." Maybe they'll say how Matteo died. I'm just nosey. Did he die naturally? Or did another mobster kill him? I know he killed a rival or two in his lifetime.

As the news anchors' voices drone on, I dig through a box of family photographs on the side table beneath the lamplight, looking at my kids and grandkids and remembering.

I push back in the recliner and smile, pressing this one against my heart. It's an old black-and-white photograph of B.J. when he was maybe seven years old, holding a bow and arrow and grinning wide. What was that? Mid-fifties, maybe?

That fly lands on my tea glass!

I wave it away, tromp to the kitchen, grab the fly swatter, and carry it back to my recliner. It lands again on the side table. Slowly, I raise the swatter—but the wicked little fly darts off. He's safe for a while longer, but I'll get him.

It occurs to me, with the fleeing fly, that it's not just human instinct. Every creature that lives wants to keep living. Even a fly darts away when it senses death looming nearby.

Why?

I think instinctively, everything knows; the moment we have is all we are guaranteed. We learned that in Richmond.

And no one knows for sure what happens after we draw our last breath. We can have faith until the cows come home, but there are no guarantees. Thus, all living creatures cling to life.

It seems counterintuitive, then, that sometimes I wish my time would come. But I know why I do it. The three years since B.J. died have felt like a lifetime.

Sometimes, when I dream of him—of us—I don't want to wake up in the morning. Just let me dream. And yet, inevitably, I open my eyes to another day, and I cling to the belief that I will be with him again—somehow, somewhere, someday.

I hear his voice in my head, "Just because my body dies, it doesn't mean my love does." I've given it a lot of thought since he said it, and it makes sense to me. Body and soul—they are two different things.

The body is merely the vessel of the soul, which is where love resides. If the soul survives, why wouldn't the love within it survive, too? Makes sense to me.

I peer at my wedding ring, the one he made, and run my fingertips over it. B.J. and I never said, 'Until death do us part." We always said, 'Forever.'

Yes, I choose to believe my husband's dying words. He promised he would make a place for me and be waiting when I got there. He always kept his promises. I choose to believe.

The news comes on. A banner scrolls across the bottom of the screen. Mafia Don Matteo DeVecchio murdered outside his home early today... gunned down. A violent death. I'm not surprised.

I take a long drink of tea, savoring the sweet taste as it sinks in: all the men are gone. B.J. went first, then Al. Now Matteo. Like me, all of my girlfriends have outlived their husbands.

Why did God make it so that women outlive men?

I guess for the same reason He made us bear children. Maybe, someday, I'll understand.

It was such a blessing to bring life into this world, to hold our children to my breasts and watch them grow, but it is a curse, you know, to be the last one standing—holding onto sweet, faded memories—just waiting... to go. Waiting for my time.

Our generation doesn't have much time left on this Earth. Like each generation before us, we Baby Boomers will soon be nothing more than names on tombstones. Who will know we lived?

And why should that matter? *We* know we lived.

I know I loved B.J. He loved me, and our love made three wonderful children. Though our bodies die, the genetic material that made us who we are lives on in our children... and theirs... and theirs.

B.J. was right about that, too. Our children are our only lasting legacy—not a headstone, not a monument, not a building.

I turn up the TV. They're talking on the news about a new strain of coronavirus. That damned virus. I get mad every time I think about it.

I take another long sip of my iced tea—see the fly—grab for the swatter—and the tea goes down the wrong pipe. *Dammit.*

I choke. I can't clear my throat. I'm coughing, hacking, trying to clear that liquid from my windpipe. Like every living creature, I instinctively fight for life. I wish B.J. was here to hit me in the back.

Oh, that's a stabbing pain.

Finally, it's clear.

I inhale deeply and press the cold glass against my hot cheek. But that pain. I... feel so... light-headed. Perspiration beads on my forehead and upper lip, and my mind drifts back to when I fainted in Richmond.

Buddy rests his chin on my lap. Those big brown eyes are trying to talk to me. He whimpers and jumps, putting his front paws in my lap. His nose is in my face. For some reason, he seems worried about me.

I reach to pet him to assuage his fear—and the tea glass slips from my hand.

It clangs against the table. Ice and liquid pour into my lap.

I exhale deeply and feel it: It is like a butterfly breaking out of its cocoon, the soul being freed from its earthly vessel, taking flight to heaven.

God knows the number of our days. We don't.

Oh! There's Jim Beau. Where did he come from? He's kneeling over me. "Mother! Mother!"

My sweet son. A flash of light. I see his birth.

My poor son cradles my body to him and rocks me in his arms, weeping, "Momma. Oh, Momma."

I reach for him, but he doesn't see me.

"My sweet son. Momma isn't there."

Death is a rite of passage, as is birth. It is not to be feared.

The agony of death is endured by the living.

Chapter Thirty-Nine

EPILOGUE

Patsy

I CAN'T WAKE UP from the most surreal dream. I dreamt I died. I saw Jim Beau holding me, crying. I want to wake up, but I can't.

"Patsy." It sounds like B.J. But still, I cannot open my eyes.

Why can't I open my eyes? It's a dream. Open your eyes.

No. If I wake up, he won't be there. I want to enjoy him, even if it is a dream.

There's a sharp little slap to my cheek. It stings. "Pat?" My body shakes. "Patsy, wake up."

My eyes open to the blinding light of a clear mid-summer afternoon, forcing me to shade them with my hand.

Where am I? What is happening? Did I faint again?

"Babydoll." Still shading my eyes with my hands, a silhouette appears, like on that summer day at Barton Springs—and just as it did fifty years ago—my heart catches seeing B.J. squatting at my side.

Just look at him. He takes my breath.

"Hey." He strokes my face.

I am frozen, staring. I feel my eyes grow wide. I've never had such a vivid dream. "B.J.?"

He grins wide. "Yes, Babydoll. I'm here."

Overwhelmed at the sight of him, I stutter. "Is this real? Are you real? How are you real?"

This is a dream. Just another dream. He is young again, wearing that long ponytail.

B.J. scoops me off the ground and stands, cradling me in his arms. "It's real, Babydoll. I've been waiting." He clutches me to his chest like a rag doll.

It's his chest. I know his chest. I love his chest. I bury my face in it, feeling the moisture of my tears.

"It's natural at first," B.J. says. "They're tears of joy." He sets my feet on the ground, but I cling to him. I'm still not sure. This has to be a dream. I've had so many.

B.J. kisses me. I know his kiss. Yes, I feel his lips. I feel his skin. *I feel him!*

Pulling away, I grip his biceps, taking him in. I stroke his cheek. Yes, I feel his stubble. I reach and touch his hair, the curly sideburns. I want to shout, "Oh, Lord, thank you!" But still, I'm not convinced. How can I be sure this isn't a dream?

I blink, peering around. "B.J., how do I know this is real?"

A smile spreads across his face. "I promised you I would be here. Waiting." Those big, strong arms hoist me back up, dangling my feet in the air as I'm pressed to his chest with his arms wrapped around me. "Patsy, it wasn't a dream. Your time on Earth is over. Now you're here with me."

"Are we in Heaven?" I ask.

His smile fades along with the glimmer in his honey-brown eyes. "No, Babydoll, we didn't make the cut. I'm thinking we said fuck way too many times while we were on Earth."

Alarmed, I clutch his arm. "So where are we? Is this?" I'm afraid to say it. "Hell?"

"No, we weren't that bad."

"Then where are we, B.J.? What is this?"

He lifts a shoulder. "I can't say where we are, physically. I think the Catholics call it Purgatory, but I always picture Purgatory to be almost Hell. This place is more like almost-Heaven. The Jews who are here call it Gehenna, the Muslims call it al-A'raf and the Hindus call it Naraka. Everybody has a different name for it, but we're all here until we overcome the things that held us back. It's a place to redeem ourselves. As it turns out, they really don't say fuck in Heaven."

"How do we redeem ourselves?"

Another gorgeous smile. "Congratulations, Mrs. Cole. You are now what is called a Guardian Angel. We are each assigned to look after those we love who are still on Earth—and plenty we don't love. We're all working on earning our Angel wings."

"And you've been here all this time, looking after us?"

He strokes my cheek softly. "Do you remember seeing Jim Beau holding your body when you left?"

I nod, watching B.J. with wide eyes, intrigued.

He's a little smug. "I sent him."

"How?"

"I put nagging thoughts in his head. I kept telling him, 'You better go check on your mother... look at the tem perature... you know she's outside, working in her yard.' I hoped he'd get to you sooner because I knew you were letting yourself get way too hot, but traffic lights got in his way." B.J. lifts his hands. "I'm still learning to control some things."

He rakes his fingers through my hair, combing it away from my face, his eyes adoring me. "But at least you're here with me now. Finally." B.J. draws me back against him, pressing my cheek to his still-perfect chest.

"You sent Jim Beau?" I blink in dismay. "It broke my heart to see my son holding me, crying. B.J., I saw his birth—I saw you holding him as a baby—"

B.J. blows a sad sigh. "I know, Babydoll. Seeing you crying over me broke my heart, too. The sad truth is death is harder on the living than the dying." His brows shift high. "From here you see that life is a test. When we're living it, we think the test is about survival of the fittest, who can earn the most, out-think or out-perform everyone else. Here, we learn the test of our lives had nothing to do with any of that. The test was about our souls. Here we have a second chance to get the test right."

I close my eyes and squeeze his hand. "This time we won't fail." But my mind immediately returns to Jim Beau holding my body and B.J. sending him there. "So, when we hear things in our head, it's our Guardian Angel talking to us? Like when I heard my father's voice saying panic will kill you—that was Daddy? Whispering advice?"

"It couldn't have been your dad. He was still alive."

"Papaw?"

He shrugs. "No way to know. But yes, I'd bet that was your Guardian Angel, the same way when I was walking away from DeVecchio to let him die—I heard a voice in my head saying be the bigger man... that would be cold-blooded murder. I think listening to that voice that day, listening to my Guardian Angel, turning around, and going back to save DeVecchio, is the only reason I made it here."

"No, B.J. You were such a good man, good husband, good father."

He offers a sad smile. "Thanks, Babydoll, but I've seen how many mistakes I made."

"We all made mistakes, B.J. It's called being human."

He pauses for a minute, glancing left and right, and whispers, "Speaking of DeVecchio, at my funeral, I saw that—"

I clamp my hand over his mouth. I know him. I know what he was about to call Matteo. "Don't say it. You just said we can't say that word and get into Heaven. And if you were watching, you heard him say very nice things about you."

He growls. "Yeah, he did. That was nice, I have to give him that." He flexes his jaw. "But I didn't like the way he looked at you again." He sneers. "And Al acting all pious, best friend." He rolls his eyes. "I let out enough f-words, I was afraid they might throw me out, but they didn't. They're both gone now, and I don't think they made it here. I haven't seen either one of them."

I let my head fall back as I chuckle. "I can't imagine they would." But my mind is back on Guardian Angels. "So, Guardian Angels are real?"

"Yeah. And we have work to do. Luke is about to make some bad choices, and he won't listen to Jim Beau. I've been talking to him—"

"How?" I'm fascinated. This is amazing. I never knew Guardian Angels were real.

"He was daydreaming about some girl just the other day, and he would've gotten killed if I hadn't given him a hard jolt to look up and dodge. He knows he can't daydream like that on a job like his."

"Oh, B.J." The thought of Luke being hurt makes my heart ache.

He hugs my shoulder. "It'll be alright. Now that you're here, he'll listen to his mother's voice."

"I will make him listen. They're our babies. We have to take good care of them."

"Together, we'll steer him in the right direction." Eyeing me from head to toe, B.J. twists his neck. "I'm so glad we're together again."

"B.J., I can't tell you how much I've missed you."

"I know, Babydoll. I've been watching." He nudges his head. "Come on. I've got so much to show you."

It's like the first day we met—I'm giddy again in his presence—but this time, I don't just think it; I say it. "Baby, I will go anywhere with you." I turn in a circle, taking in the rolling, white rock hills of what looks like Texas, covered in wildflowers. "Bluebonnets in August?" Even I hear the wonder in my voice.

As he smiles—B.J. has been smiling since I got here—it's evident that he doesn't have a care in the world. He swings his arm wide. "All the flowers you love all the time." He bends down, picks a bluebonnet, and tucks the stem in my hair over my ear.

As he does, I see my hair is dark again, like it was when I was young. And it's long. "Am I as young as you?"

He feels my hair, rubbing strands between his thumb and forefinger. "Like the first day we met."

I am in awe, watching a new blossom form to replace the bluebonnet B.J. just picked.

He grins, watching my eyes. "Pretty cool, huh?" B.J. picks me up, holding me off the ground, my feet dangling in the air again with my arms around his neck, and he says, "As the old song goes, Babydoll, you ain't seen nothin' yet."

I let my head fall back as I giggle at his music reference. We're face to face as he turns me in a slow circle, his beautiful eyes studying mine. "You know, we can watch the sunset whenever we want now."

"How is that possible?"

"I don't know." He kisses my lips sweetly with that big smile. "But I climb Mount Bonnell and think of you—of us, Patsy all the time. Now we can watch the sunsets together again."

"Are you sure this isn't Heaven?"

"Yeah, darn it." He flicks his brows and grins. "You notice I didn't say the bad word. We do have to break bad habits if we're going to make it up the stairway to Heaven."

Another music reference. I giggle again.

I'm a silly schoolgirl being back with him. Taking his handsome face into my hands, I kiss his lips softly, holding it a long, tender moment, as I did in that Greek restaurant so many years ago. "I love you so much. We will make it up the stairway to Heaven together. I'm expunging bad words from my mind and my mouth forever." I aim my finger at him. "Now, you do the same."

He tilts his head back and laughs. It's a good one. His eyes twinkle. "So, you're giving me orders already?" He lifts his brows mischievously. "You know, Babydoll, I have wondered, once you finally got here, if you planned on ragging my ass for eternity." He winks. "I've kind of missed it."

We laugh together and I kiss him again. "Baby, I guess time will tell."

B.J. hoists me higher, so we are eye to eye again. Oh, that's the widest smile I've seen since Jim Beau was born, and he says, "Babydoll, time is one thing we have plenty of. Come on, let's go home."

Yes! He knew it instinctively. Souls don't die and neither does the love that dwells inside them.

AFTERWARD

The World Health Organization reported three million people died of COVID-19 in 2020 alone. Each was loved by someone.

To this day, the debate continues over the virus's origins. Did it jump organically from animals to humans, as did Ebola and bird and swine flu? Or was it bio-engineered? We may never know. But it changed everything.

COMING NEXT

BY HARPER DALE

Matteo Dante DeVecchio lives on with a love story of his
own by Harper Dale and Rupert Bossier

DEVECCHIO

AN ISSUE

"MATTY," TOMMY APPROACHES WITH urgency in his pace and voice. "We've got an issue."

Issue is never good. My skin prickles. Judging by the look on my capo's face this is bad.

"Matteo!"

Before he can explain, we're interrupted by a high-pitched squeal, and our gazes arc toward the shriek to see a strawberry blonde race across the room with open arms, her smile like a slice of watermelon. "It's so good to see you!"

The girl plasters a pink lipstick kiss on my cheek, tries to wipe its traces off with her thumb, and threads a well-tanned arm around mine, squeezing it tightly. "I'm so glad you're here."

"Thank you, Miss..."

"Albright." Her watermelon smile melts like ice cream in August. "You don't remember me?" Her hazel eyes flash.

Sweetheart, I don't have a clue. "I'm sorry..."

"Adeline." She answers with a pretty little pout. She's about to stomp her foot. "We went sailing in Charleston, remember?"

My mother, standing nearby, has the eyes and ears of a hawk. She nods with stern brows, and I respond quickly. "Yes, Adeline, I'm so sorry."

Adeline smiles with relief.

Donna DeVecchio, always the consummate hostess, wraps a supple arm around the girl's shoulder, drawing her close. "Thank you for coming, dear. Matteo and his father have spent most of the summer in Europe and I wanted them to be surrounded by friends on their return." She shoots me a strained smile. "Adeline is Dr. Albright's daughter. You two met when we were in Charleston last spring."

Okay, Mother. I get it.

I give Adeline my fondest smile. "Well, of course. How could I forget?"

The tall, shapely girl wears a navy-blue polka-dot sundress that shows off her golden tan. Freckles dot her shoulders, cheeks, and nose.

I stroke her arm, and she beams brightly as Mother redirects this conversation. "Adeline, are you still studying at Columbia?"

"Yes, Mrs. DeVecchio, I'm a senior this year." She turns from Mother back to me, batting big eyes. "I'm at the University, Matteo."

My face must be blank—again, my mind is on Tommy's issue—as Adeline adds, "University of South Carolina. I'm studying interior design."

She may still stomp her foot.

"Oh, interior design!" Mother claps her hands, deter-mined to right this sinking ship. "I love it. Tell me all about it, dear."

"Adeline, would you like something to drink?" I ask.

"Oh, please. A chardonnay?" She is as bubbly as Alka-Seltzer.

"I'll be right back."

Mother deflects. "Now, Adeline, remind me. What sorority are you in?"

I'll thank Mother later.

Their voices trail off as Tommy and I head for the bar. My imagination swirls. "What's the issue?"

Before he can answer—

"Matteo?"

I know that silky voice and it doesn't belong here.

I turn to see Sophia Gabicci wearing a mid-thigh, emerald-colored dress showing off a body that will make any dick stand at attention. A teardrop diamond necklace accentuates her supple cleavage.

At her elbow is a man I despise.

I smile anyway.

"Sophia, sweetheart." I kiss her cheek and inhale her familiar fragrance, whispering in her ear. "You should have let me know you were coming."

Her dark eyes spark. As she uses her finger to wipe the smudge of Adeline's kiss from my cheek, Sophia whispers with a hiss. "Your mother invited me, Matteo, not you."

"I didn't invite anyone, sweetheart. It's not my party. You brought Geno."

Her black eyes smolder behind long lashes. She kisses her fingertips and plants them on my lips. "I didn't want to attend unescorted. You don't mind, do you?"

Geno Gabicci and I exchange our usual go-to-hell glares as I squeeze Sophia's soft hand.

He is a hard son of a bitch to stomach. I smirk every time I see the ugly bastard with his parrot beak of a nose slightly askew. His granite jaw left me no choice but to go for the nose several years back.

We stand eye to eye. "How's the nose, Geno?"

If looks could kill, we'd both be dead.

His gaze narrows. "About like your ribs, I suspect."

Ribs and noses. Cartledge never heals back to its original shape.

Tommy clears his throat, reminding me we don't have time for this pissing contest.

"Sophia," I nod. "Excuse us. I've got something to attend to."

Geno polishes off his red wine and sets the empty goblet on the side table, glaring from Tommy to me. "What's your rush, DeVecchio? Got a problem?"

Our gazes lock as I fight the urge to break his nose a second time. My mother's party in my parent's house isn't the place for Geno and I to go at it again.

My ticker takes it up a notch as I turn my back on the fucker, and Tommy and I thread through the crowded room.

"What are those two doing here?" Tommy asks.

"Beats me. What's the issue, Tommy?"

"The shipment."

Dammit, I was afraid of that.

"Chardonnay," I bark at the bartender. "Allesandro." I summon my cousin, standing at the end of the bar. His mother is my father's sister, so even though Allesandro is a Mancini, he carries the DeVecchio genes, drawing girls to his side like a vacuum cleaner sucks dust.

Alessandro looks up from his cadre of admirers, all versions of Adeline—young and coiffed, showing off their tits, which, even if they're not big, are pushed up and pinched together to make them look big.

"A favor, please. Carry this to Adeline over there with Mother. Tell them something came up that I have to deal with. And make nice with Adeline." Allesandro takes the wine glass with a suspicious gaze, followed by a nod. "Excuse us. Tommaso?"

As we continue toward the office I try again to get answers. "What happened?"

"I'll let Chris explain."

I open the office door and stride to the telephone on the desk, furiously dialing the warehouse.

On the first ring my other capo answers. "Baka."

"What happened?"

Chris clears his throat, forcing me to hold the receiver from my ear. "I gave them thirty minutes leeway, considering traffic. When they were thirty-one minutes late, I sent a crew to backtrack the route. Sal just called."

He clears his throat again, this time louder. "Looks like the highway patrol pulled the truck over—"

Fuck!

"Where?" Covering the mouthpiece with my hand, I whisper to Tommy, "Get Pop."

Breathe.

We pay through the nose to make sure things like this don't happen. Pressing my fingertips to my eyelids, I ask, "Exactly, where is the truck?"

"Just south of the city limits on ninety-five."

Anne Arundel County.

"Is the driver in custody?" My heart throbs from my throat to my fingertips.

"He's in the back of the trooper's patrol unit, in bracelets, as we speak. They must be waiting on a tow truck."

Already handcuffed. It wasn't a random traffic stop. My scalp tingles. *Don't lose your cool.* When you lose your temper, you lose control of the situation.

I'm pouring a drink from the heavy decanter on Pop's credenza as the office door opens, and Pop enters with our consigliere, both faces weighted with concern. I signal for them to sit as Tommy closes the doors behind them.

Pop and Antonio sink into stuffed chairs in front of the desk as I put Chris on the speakerphone asking, "Do you trust this driver?"

Chris replies in a hushed tone, as if he doesn't want to be overheard. "He's a new kid, Matty, but he was vetted, and he took the oath."

Pop and I exchange glances. Omerta. The oath of loyalty.

I don't know. With some young kids, omerta doesn't mean what it used to.

"What's his name?"

"It's Joey. Joey Carbona, Leo's kid."

Pop tweaks his mouth to the side and nods. Leo Carbona is a trusted soldier who has been with the family for decades. This kid was born into the DeVecchio regime.

"The tow truck isn't there?"

"Not yet. Sal's on a payphone down the road. He can see everything. The tow truck isn't there and the troopers aren't searching. They're just standing around bullshitting with some big guy in plainclothes like it's party time."

"A narc."

"Would appear."

"Get on the phone with that public defender you're so fond of. Head her that way. She needs to get Joey released asap. I'll call you back."

I dig in my jacket pocket, find my black book, and dial another number.

A woman answers, "Rhinehart residence."

"Good evening, Mrs. Rhinehart. Is your husband there?"

"He's in the backyard." Her voice is distinctly Southern. There is no 'r' in her *yawd*.

"May I speak with him, please? This is John Smythe. That's Smythe, with a 'Y.' I have an urgent matter."

"He's barbecuing." Again, the *r* is missing.

"Please, if you tell him who's calling, he'll want to take the call. I promise. John Smythe. Be sure to tell him Smythe with a Y."

She clomps the phone receiver onto wood, and we listen to her plod across a hardwood floor. A heavy woman. From a distance, she calls, "Alan!"

I refill my two fingers of Glen Livet neat, the telephone still on speaker as we wait.

I would offer Pop and Antonio a drink, but they each have one in hand, and Tommy, leaning his back against the office door with his arms crossed over his chest, won't drink on duty.

Other than the noises from the Rhinehart house, silence blankets Pop's office. Too much is at stake for small talk.

My hair stands on end. I'm sure theirs' is, too.

"Mr. Smythe." It's Rhinehart's husky voice. "I understand you have a problem."

My eyes are on Pop as I speak. "Troopers pulled over our eighteen-wheeler in your county."

Sheriff Rhinehart is slow to respond. When he does, we can barely hear him, like he's speaking into his cupped hand over the mouthpiece. "I can't control state troopers."

"Then why do we pay you!" My father roars as he stands and joins me at the desk.

Francesco DeVecchio is not known for his patience.

The sheriff clears his throat. "Mr. Smythe—"

Pop doesn't let him finish. "Rhinehart, do you need to be reminded—?"

Silence. Tommy and I exchange glances.

"Do you?" Pop demands.

"No." Rhinehart answers, his voice lifeless.

Pop sits back in his chair, nods at me, and I give Rhinehart instructions. "Hang up and call dispatch right now. Tell them whatever tow truck company they called—call them off. They made a mistake. It's another company's turn in rotation. Then you call Jeremiah's Tow Truck Service. Make sure no one touches that truck but Jeremiah. Understood?"

"Yes."

"You've got the number?"

"Yes."

"Make it happen. Next week, Rhinehart, we'll visit. You, me, and my father."

That'll have him pissing his pants. My father is Capofamiglia. Nobody wants to be summoned to a meeting with Francesco Matteo DeVecchio. Not even me, and I'm his underboss.

Tommy and Chris—Tommaso Ricci and Christos Baka—are my capos. I run the day-to-day business, delegating to them. They answer to me, and I answer to Pop.

Ours is a tricky business.

The pezzo da novanta are all alike—always with their hands out, wanting us to pay them more for doing less. Politicians and bureaucrats are loyal only to money. But we need them. So, we do the dance.

Rhinehart wouldn't be in office were it not for the DeVecchio family.

He knew what he signed up for when he accepted my father's campaign contributions and what was expected of him: a warning if any law enforcement agent in his county was after us.

The problem is that Rhinehart is as lazy as he is greedy.

Hanging up from Rhinehart, I call Chris. Learning Jeremiah's on the way, he knows what to do.

This has never happened, but it's a drill the men have practiced.

Our imports and exports are stamped with the family crest, an ancient Roman warrior emblem—an eagle with its wings spread wide, holding a banner with the family name.

Legal cargo is carried in boxes stamped with the green logo. Our men must remove everything *not* stamped in green before the truck reaches impound.

"Have Sal use the payphone to report a robbery in progress when he sees Jeremiah pull up. Get dispatch to divert those troopers so they won't follow Jeremiah."

"Got it."

If everything goes as planned our driver will be released after the truck is searched and nothing is found.

One slip-up and we are screwed.

In Gratitude

No book comes to fruition simply through the imagination and experiences of its author. As it takes a village to raise a child, it takes a litteraria familia—a literary family—to birth a book. It may begin with the writer, but it takes an editor, copy editors, cover designer, and publisher to get it in the hands of readers.

I am deeply grateful to Rupert Bossier, editors Kassy Paris and Jean Lauzier, cover designer Dana Nicole Joiner, and Georgia Joiner for beta-reading, as well as to my husband for inspiring me.

ABOUT THE AUTHOR

Harper Dale traded a successful career in the news business for the artistic freedom of writing fiction.

NEW & UPCOMING RELEASES:

DEVECCHIO: COLPO DI FULMINE
BY HARPER DALE

SO F*CKING SPECIAL: 1996
BY RAYE MURPHY

SO F*CKING SPECIAL: 1998
BY RAYE MURPHY